First published in October 2013
by Big Finish Productions Ltd
PO Box 1127, Maidenhead, SL6 3LW
www.bigfinish.com

Executive Producers for Big Finish: Nicholas Briggs and Jason Haigh-Ellery
Blake's 7 Producer for Big Finish: Cavan Scott

Executive Editor for B7 Media: Andrew Mark Sewell

Managing Editor: Jason Haigh-Ellery

Production Editor: Xanna Eve Chown
With thanks to Peter Anghelides and Matthew Griffiths

Cover design: Anthony Lamb

Dramatis Personae complied by Peter Anghelides

Copyright © MG Harris, RA Henderson and Gillian F Taylor 2013

The right of MG Harris, RA Henderson and Gillian F Taylor to be identified as the authors of this Work has been asserted by them in accordance with the Copyright, Designs and Patents Act 1988. All rights reserved. The moral right of the authors has been asserted. All characters in this publication are fictitious and any resemblance to any persons, living or dead, is purely coincidental.

No part of this publication may be reproduced or transmitted in any form or by any means, electronic or mechanical, including photocopying, recording or any information retrieval system, without prior permission, in writing, from the publisher. This book is sold subject to the condition that it shall not, by way of trade or otherwise, be lent, resold, hired out, or otherwise circulated without the publisher's prior consent in any form of binding or cover other than that in which it is published and without a similar condition including this condition being imposed on the subsequent purchaser.

Blake's 7 ™ © B7 Enterprises Ltd 2013. All rights reserved.

Blake's 7 wordmark and logo are trademarks of B7 Enterprises Ltd and are used under licence.

Based on the original television series Blake's 7 created by Terry Nation.

Blake's 7 television series pictures © BBC 2013 and used under licence.

Hardback ISBN: 978-1-78178-259-0
eBook ISBN: 978-1-78178-260-6

A CIP catalogue record for this book is available from the British Library

***BLAKE'S 7* BOOKS**
FROM BIG FINISH

AVAILABLE NOW:

1: THE FORGOTTEN
2: ARCHANGEL
3: LUCIFER
4: ANTHOLOGY

COMING SOON:

5: LUCIFER: REVELATION

www.bigfinish.com

ANTHOLOGY

CONTENTS

DRAMATIS PERSONAE..6

TRIGGER POINT...............GILLIAN F TAYLOR.............9

BERSERKER........................RA HENDERSON...............85

COLD REVOLUTION........MG HARRIS......................149

DRAMATIS

THE LIBERATOR AND CREW

***Liberator*:** A powerful spacecraft that far exceeds anything known to Earth technology, it is equipped with neutron blaster weaponry, force wall defences, auto-repair systems, and a teleport. The main computer, Zen, is the speech interface to the ship's systems.

Kerr Avon: A technical expert, particularly with computers, Avon's attempt to embezzle millions from the Federation saw him exiled from Earth. He escaped to the *Liberator*, where his instinct for self-preservation meant that he became the most unwilling member of Blake's team – perceived by the others as a man whose cold calculation is primarily self-serving.

Roj Blake: Once leader of the Freedom Party and a charismatic opponent of the Terran Federation, Blake was captured in a lethal ambush by Travis. When their attempt to brainwash him failed, the Federation trumped up charges and banished him from Earth. Blake escaped and commandeered the derelict *Liberator*. Since then, he has cajoled or bullied his reluctant outlaw crew in a renewed fight against their enemies.

Cally: A telepath from the planet Auron, who can communicate her thoughts to others. Sole survivor of a guerrilla attack on a Federation facility, Cally felt unable to return to her isolationist homeworld. Her mutual distrust of the *Liberator* crew mellowed, and her growing empathy has made her an instinctive medic.

Vila Restal: A petty thief, a conjurer, but most of all an expert lockpick who can breach even the most complex security systems. Vila has been in trouble with the Federation since he was a juvenile. He prefers to be lazy, even if that might look like cowardice, and has a weakness for drink and an eye for pretty women. Vila is smart enough to know that playing the fool is a good way to stay safe.

PERSONAE

Olag Gan: When a security guard murdered his woman, Gan killed the armed man with his bare hands. He was banished from Earth, but not before he was fitted with a limiter implant in his brain. This prevents him killing again, despite his great strength and size. Rescued by Blake from the penal colony Cygnus Alpha, Gan is brave, selfless and trusting.

Jenna Stannis: A smuggler sentenced by the Federation to exile on the penal colony Cygnus Alpha. Jenna assisted Blake's mutiny and commandeered the *Liberator*. The ship's name was taken from her thoughts when she first came aboard. Jenna's expertise has made her the *Liberator*'s principal pilot. Although she has some reservations about their fight against the Federation, Jenna is loyal to Blake.

THE FEDERATION

Servalan: Supreme Commander of the Federation's entire military organisation. Servalan is responsible for the brutal repression of all resistance, and has been charged with destroying Blake and his crew – though she wants to capture the *Liberator* for the Federation. In an organisation governed by men, Servalan is a rare, powerful woman who has exploited her seductive charm and amoral ruthlessness to fight her way to the top.

Travis: A brutal Federation Space Commander appointed by Servalan to lead the capture of Blake and the *Liberator*. Travis previously encountered Blake on Earth, when he ambushed a group of Freedom Party rebels and slaughtered them after they had surrendered. In the attack, Blake severely wounded Travis – who required a cybernetic eye replacement, and a prosthetic limb that incorporated a laseron destroyer.

TRIGGER POINT

GILLIAN F TAYLOR

ONE

'I don't like it,' Jenna said firmly.

Cally turned to face her. 'Is it the idea you don't like, or is it me you don't like?'

Jenna stared evenly back at her. 'The *idea*, I don't like; *you*, I don't trust.'

Blake stepped forward, holding his hands up and drawing the women's attention back towards himself.

'You know Cally isn't to blame for what happened,' he reminded Jenna patiently. 'It was Saymon who was controlling her when she sabotaged the *Liberator*.'

Blake looked around the flight deck of the *Liberator* as he spoke, making sure he caught the eyes of the other three. Vila was closest, sitting in the horseshoe of seats below the ship's control units. The idea of a lounging area on a flight deck still seemed decidedly alien to Blake but he was beginning to see its value. It provided somewhere for the crew to gather and discuss things, while still having easy access to Zen, the controls and the view screen. The padded bench seats were also a lot more comfortable than the narrow, perch seats at the control units.

Vila's expression was somewhere between fascinated and worried as he watched the two women. Gan was standing behind the bench where Vila sat, his bulk looming protectively over the smaller man. His open, honest face was concerned as he listened to the argument. Avon, typically, was apart from the rest. He was at his control unit, ostensibly reading the displays, but Blake had no doubt that his attention was more on the confrontation in the lounge area.

Jenna lifted her chin as she looked at Blake.

'How can we be sure there isn't something influencing her now, making her suggest that we fly to Belzanko?' she asked.

Blake gave a short sigh. 'We can never be one hundred percent sure about anything, Jenna. Sometimes you just have to believe that the odds are in your favour, or that motives are genuine. It's not healthy to be suspicious all the time.'

'Smugglers who aren't suspicious all the time soon get unhealthy,' Jenna retorted tartly.

'The same goes for anyone who lives outside the law.' Avon's precise tones were easily audible across the flight deck. 'Thieves, murderers, fraudsters or terrorists.'

Blake swivelled to face him. 'So that's why we're going to make contact with someone with a history we know about. I didn't pick Allston's name out of a hat; Cally knows about him through the resistance on Saurian Major.'

'Otha was with us on Saurian Major for a year,' Cally said, referring to one of her fellow resistance fighters who had been killed by the plague unleashed by the Federation. 'And he'd been with Anwar Allston for two years before that.'

'So Allston has spent at least three years rebelling against Greerson's presidency and hasn't achieved anything yet,' Avon drawled, his dark eyes contemptuous.

'Revolutions take time,' Gan pointed out.

'How long is it acceptable to have your planet bled dry before you finally organise yourselves enough to actually do something?' Avon said.

'They are organised,' Blake fired back. 'But Greerson has the military to back him. The resistance can't win an all-out fight, so they've been gathering information and finding other ways to bring Greerson down. With the resources we have on the *Liberator* we can help them make a decisive move.'

'Not an all-out fight?' Vila asked, his brown eyes round with anxiety. 'People shooting at me? I don't want people shooting at me.'

'Of course you don't,' Avon answered smoothly. 'You're not a hero, are you?' He spoke to Vila but his mocking gaze was aimed directly at Blake.

Blake forced himself to ignore Avon. 'No, Vila. We're not getting into a straight fight. But Allston's people have been gathering data on some important installations to strike.' He looked at Jenna and Gan as he spoke, his voice becoming firmer. 'If we work with them, we can hit harder and more effectively than either group working alone. With the data from the ground, we can use the teleport to get in and out quickly and attack them before they know what's happening.'

'And then we leave?' Vila asked.

Blake smiled. 'And then we leave,' he said.

'And go looking for another "good cause" to jump into feet first.' Avon's tone was withering. 'And another and another until we jump into a mire that sucks us down and drowns us.' He stepped down from his control panel, turned his back on the others and walked off the flight deck.

'We know what we're getting into here,' Cally said, glaring in the direction Avon was leaving. 'It's a real opportunity to strike back.'

'I agree.' Gan stood up straight, looking at Blake. 'I think we should go to Belzanko and help.'

Vila shrugged and nodded at the same time, seeming uneasy but unwilling to fight stronger personalities. Blake looked expectantly at Jenna. She gave Cally a long, calculating look, then shrugged.

'I didn't have anything else planned,' she remarked, turning away.

Cally fixed her large, eager eyes on Blake's face. 'Otha was lucky to escape from Belzanko before Greerson's security caught up with him. Greerson doesn't just govern the planet, he dominates it. He sets taxes high, he awards government contracts to companies that he owns and his friends get the best jobs so they have a vested interest in making sure he stays in power. If we can get rid of Greerson, there'll be a real opportunity for change on Belzanko, and it'll be a warning to other corrupt officials that they won't be able to get away with it forever.'

Blake smiled at her and nodded, heartened to know that at least one member of his crew truly felt the way he did. 'We'll help Allston bring Greerson down and then, yes, we'll help rebellions on other planets to fight injustice. The *Liberator* will live up to her name.' He turned to face Zen's slowly blinking lights. 'Zen! Set a course for the planet, Belzanko. Standard by five.'

'CONFIRMED.'

Lights flashed on Zen's fascia and the soft hum of the engines increased as the huge ship turned and set itself on its new course through the stars.

Blake settled the belt and holster comfortably over his lightweight jacket, then glanced around the teleport room. It seemed busy, with five people present, but there should have been six. Blake glanced impatiently at his wrist.

'Allston's people are due to start their diversion in four minutes,' he announced. 'Vila should be here by now.'

'Perhaps he's having second thoughts,' Jenna suggested, from her seat behind the console.

'I find it hard to believe that he ever gets as far as first thoughts,' Avon said.

Jenna stifled a snigger and busied herself double-checking the co-ordinates already entered into the teleport controls.

Cally handed a black tube of explosives to Gan, and swung another one onto her own shoulder.

'Maybe I should take those as well?' he suggested. 'You and Avon are going into the admin area to get technical data, not to blow things up.' He smiled affectionately at her.

Cally shook her head briskly. 'We might as well destroy their computer facilities, once we've got the data we want.'

'The quantity of mines you can carry won't do significant damage to the pursuit ship plant,' Avon explained, raising his right hand slightly to point in Gan's direction. 'The more data we remove or destroy – technical specifications, supply details, even personnel records – the longer it will take for smooth production to resume. Therefore we need...'

He was interrupted by the rapid thud of boots approaching along the corridor.

Vila clattered down the steps into the teleport room, a large, red box swinging from one hand.

'You're late,' Blake accused.

'Sorry, sorry.' Vila stood gasping for breath. 'It took me ages to find the stuff I need for my toolkit.'

'Here.' Cally snapped a teleport bracelet around his left wrist.

'We need to be in position,' Blake ordered, pointing Vila towards the transmission area.

Gan followed, and a few moments later, the three men were standing ready for teleport. All three were wearing two-tone, hooded jackets from the *Liberator*'s clothing rooms, with matching trousers, as were Avon and Cally. Each person had chosen a different colour, but the similarity of style gave all five a shared look. Blake felt they looked more like a team than ever before. He smiled across the room at Jenna.

'Set us down, please,' he requested.

The teleport shimmer filled the bay, and the three were gone.

Jenna sighed softly. 'I still haven't got used to that.' She snapped back to full alertness as the communicator chimed. '*Liberator* here.'

Blake's voice was slightly tinny through the speakers. 'Down and safe.'

'I hear you.' Jenna was watching Cally and Avon as they positioned themselves ready for teleport. 'Sending team two down in a moment.'

'Good work, Jenna. Out.'

Jenna switched to the second set of co-ordinates provided by Allston. 'Ready?'

Cally and Avon both drew their handguns, holding them ready for action.

'Put us down,' Cally said.

Jenna slowly drew back the controls, watching fascinated as the two figures flickered and vanished, leaving her alone on the vast ship.

Blake, Gan and Vila materialised in a broad alleyway between two storage units. Vila managed to land off-balance and lurched into Gan. The big man stood firm and caught Vila's shoulder, helping him regain his feet.

'Sorry,' Vila muttered. 'I don't think that machine likes me.'

Blake shushed him as he glanced quickly around, his handgun poised ready for use.

There was no immediate sign of danger, so he reported in to Jenna.

'Is this the right place?' Gan asked softly, standing with his back against the nearest wall. He, too, was holding his gun, even though he was unable to fire it. The plant's security guards wouldn't know about his limiter, so the gun was still useful as a threat.

Blake eased forward a couple of steps and peered cautiously around the corner of the store. The first thing that struck him was the smell. After months aboard ship, and most of a lifetime in a dome city, Blake wasn't used to air that wasn't recycled and chemically cleaned. This air smelt of vehicle emissions, oil and metal. The storage units were made of some dull, grey material, scuffed and old. The section of assembly plant he could see on the far side of the concrete roadway was similarly functional, but at least it was punctuated high up with windows. The only spots of colour seemed to be warning signs dotted here and there around the site.

Blake rejoined the other two between the stores. 'The layout matches the description Allston gave us,' he said reassuringly.

Vila didn't look very reassured. His eyes were anxious as he stood close to Gan's protective bulk. 'If it's a trap, we've arrived in the right place then,' he said.

Blake raised his left arm to show off the teleport bracelet. 'If they try to trap us, we can disappear from under their very noses,' he reminded them, smiling. 'Now, we need to get going. We've got some expensive and important equipment to blow up.'

The *Liberator* had arrived at Belzanko two days earlier. Blake, Cally and Avon had transported down to meet Anwar Allston and discuss the best way of freeing the planet from President Greerson's control. The planet was not part of the Terran Federation but had close political and economic ties. Belzanko Space Industries was one of the most profitable companies established there. Its plants produced a variety of spacecraft, but the most important were the pursuit ship fighters used by the Federation. Even Belspin's shipyards couldn't produce all the fighters that the Federation wanted, but it supplied almost a quarter. Damaging production would not only disrupt the planet's economy enough to make President Greerson vulnerable, it would seriously affect the Federation's ability to defend itself, for a while at least.

The meeting between the local rebel leader and the crew of the *Liberator* had resulted in a plan for attacking the fighter plant. Allston's men supplied crucial data for teleport co-ordinates and the general layout of the plant. One of the regular protests outside the President's Residence would turn into a riot, distracting security forces and filling the airwaves with the babble of newsmedia and security broadcasts while Blake and his crew made the attack on the high-security plant.

Now, Blake waited and watched at the corner of the storage unit, gun ready in his hand, the other two close behind him. It was only a short dash across the open ground to the main assembly building, but a pulsating hum warned him to stay in place.

'Security robot approaching,' Blake hissed. 'Stay quiet.'

Vila promptly froze in place.

'Breathe, Vila,' Gan reminded him in a whisper.

The hum, and a steady beep, grew louder as the robot approached. Blake crouched low and peeped around the corner of the building. The security robot glided along. Scanners mounted around the multi-sided head allowed it 360 degree vision. Information from Allston's people was that the robots had no set routine, making their appearances difficult to predict. Vila and Gan had withdrawn to the shallow cover offered by a doorway in the wall of the storage building. Blake rose and hurried to join them, his soft-soled boots making almost no sound. All three pressed themselves back into the doorway as the humming sound grew louder.

Blake turned his head, but his field of vision was limited. He could see the storage unit on the other side of the alley, but only a little of the roadway the stores faced, and of the main assembly building that was their target. As the sound of the robot got closer, he had to fight down the urge to lean forward and look to see where it was. A sideways glance in the other direction showed Gan, waiting patiently, and Vila with his eyes screwed shut.

As the humming grew louder, Blake found that he, too, was holding his breath. He stared at the section of roadway in front, heart pounding in time with the humming. Then – yes – the noise was moving away again. Blake glanced at Gan, seeing his alert, hopeful expression, and quietly let out a long sigh. All three men stayed exactly as they were until the robotic humming faded away altogether.

Again, Blake crept forward and peered round the corner of the building.

'It's gone,' he hissed. 'Quickly now; we don't know how long we've got till it returns.'

Close together, they sprinted across the open ground to the door of the assembly plant. This wasn't the main entrance, but the security would be just as good. Gan turned to keep guard as Vila set his box on the ground. Removing the lid, Vila withdrew a slender probe and quickly touched it to the corners of the locking mechanism. Blake noticed that Vila's hands were steady as he worked, concentration replacing the earlier fear. The cover of the lock popped.

'Can you get it open?' Blake asked, assessing the circuitry he could see. He'd been an engineer himself, back on Earth, but locks were not his speciality.

Vila swapped tools. 'Of course I can open it,' he replied indignantly.

'Can you open it quickly?' Gan asked, still watching along the concrete road.

'And without setting off an alarm?' Blake added.

Vila stopped and looked at him. 'You don't get to be the best thief in the galaxy by setting off alarms.'

'Stop bragging and start opening,' Blake ordered.

'Stop interrupting.' Vila was unusually sharp.

Blake mentally conceded the point, and turned to keep watch in the other direction to Gan.

He heard faint electronic noises as Vila worked, then a rustle and clatter. Turning for a quick look, Blake saw Vila removing tools from the top of the box and putting them on the ground, out of his way. Vila rummaged further in the compartments below, seeking something else. Blake stifled a sigh and turned his attention back to sentry duty. A few seconds later there was a sound of satisfaction and Vila rose to resume work on the lock. Another minute passed, silent apart from the quiet hum of Vila's probes, and soft, coaxing sounds made by the thief as he communed with the lock and his tools. Then, faintly, Blake heard that pulsating hum again.

Gan also heard it, drawing in a little closer. Blake looked over his shoulder at Vila, who was half-smiling to himself as he worked.

'Vila! The robot's coming back,' he hissed.

The half-smile disappeared. Vila quickly moved the probe to another spot on the exposed circuits and studied the display on a hand-held sensor.

'How long?' Blake demanded.

'It should be a couple of minutes,' Vila replied absently.

The robotic hum, and beeping, were steadily getting louder. Blake glanced across the open road to the spot they'd sheltered in before.

'We don't have a couple of minutes!'

Vila turned and listened for a moment, then went back to the lock, the look of concentration fiercer than before.

Gan shifted his weight uneasily. 'We need to move.'

Blake's lips narrowed. Other people were depending on them to get into this plant, at this time. If they were going to hide, they needed to move now. He was about to give the order, when another idea occurred to him. Raising his left arm, he opened the teleport bracelet's communicator.

'Jenna. Stand by to pick us up at any moment.'

'Copy that,' she answered crisply.

'It'll be quicker than running,' he told Gan.

The big man nodded, and turned his head to listen. The robot was much closer now. Blake gave a brief, impatient snort, and pressed the communicator again. 'Jenna...'

'Got it!' Vila exclaimed.

There was a click and the security door began to hiss open.

'Cancel,' Blake told Jenna, as Vila slammed the lid of his toolbox and snatched it up.

He'd barely got it off the ground before Blake pushed him through the widening doorway. Vila staggered forward as Blake followed him through, stepping aside to make room for Gan. Blake had found and hit the door-close button even before Gan was completely inside. Grey daylight vanished as the door slid shut behind them. The dreadful, pulsating hum of the security robot was gone, silenced by the strong door between them and it. All Blake could hear now was Vila's rapid breathing as he recovered.

Blake looked around the starkly lit, utilitarian corridor, getting his bearings.

'Good work, Vila,' Gan said. 'But a little less drama next time, please?'

Vila looked indignant. 'If I hadn't been able to open it in time, I'd have said so. I'm a professional. And a coward,' he added with disarming honesty.

'A professional coward?' Gan asked, his eyes sparkling with humour.

Vila nodded. 'Better a live coward than a dead hero, I always say.

I'm always very careful about what I do, which is why I'm so good at it.'

'If you're done congratulating yourself, we need to move on.' Blake said, gesturing with his handgun along the corridor. He took the lead as they moved away, Vila behind him and Gan bringing up the rear.

Outside the door, the security robot paused, beeping, as its head swivelled. The scanners recorded unusual tools lying at the foot of the wall under the lock. The robot's brain noted that the probes hadn't been there on its last patrol, and flagged the discrepancy to the security monitoring station. That done, it rolled away again, waiting for any new orders.

TWO

After the bright, artificial light on the *Liberator*, the evening light on Belzanko seemed to Cally even greyer than it really was, as she and Avon materialised on the planet. She looked swiftly around, all six senses alert for danger. They were between a multi-storey vehicle park, and the administration building, just as promised. Cally spotted the door they wanted and sprinted for it, Avon following close behind. A fluid spin put her back against the grey wall, letting her keep watch as Avon holstered his gun and bent to pay attention to the lock.

Cally glanced at him, seeing the intense concentration on his rather severe face. He'd spent part of the previous day in one of the *Liberator*'s workshops with Vila in preparation for this raid. Now he was running some hand-held gadget they'd cobbled together over the lock, and frowning at the readout.

'It would have been much quicker to teleport directly inside,' Cally complained.

Avon didn't look up. 'Allston's men had to estimate co-ordinates from outside the compound. It was risky enough teleporting to open ground on approximate co-ordinates. If we'd tried teleporting directly inside a building without precise co-ordinates, we could have materialised inside a locked room, or even a wall.' His dark eyes flashed as he glanced at her. 'I don't know if it is possible to materialise in the same space as a solid object, but I have no intention of offering myself as a test subject.'

Cally glanced about again. 'How much longer are we going to have to stand out here in plain sight?'

There was a faint click. Avon straightened, drawing his handgun, and gently pushed the door open. He smiled as he gestured with mock grace. 'Ladies first.'

His self-assurance nettled Cally, but she tried not to let it show as she slipped past him and into the admin building, her gun at the ready. Avon followed, closing the door quietly. They found themselves in a minor corridor, with a few, anonymous doors at intervals along it, and a staircase immediately on their right. Safety doors at the far end probably led to the main corridor of the building. The working day had finished an hour earlier, so the building would be mostly empty by now. Avon gestured towards the stairs with his gun. Cally nodded, and led the way up.

On the first floor, they ventured out into the central corridor.

'Which way?' Cally whispered

Avon looked up and down at the numbered doors, frustrated.

'I wasn't issued with a map either,' he hissed.

He moved to the nearest door, stood with his ear close to it and listened. Cally raised an eyebrow in silent inquiry.

Avon shook his head. 'Empty.' He glanced down the corridor at the other doors, then back at Cally. 'Can you... sense the presence of other people?' He studied her with the curiosity of a scientist.

'Not really,' Cally answered, rather reluctantly. She didn't care to discuss her abilities with Earth humans: most were rather afraid, worried that she was reading their thoughts; others looked at her as some kind of specimen, as Avon was doing. 'Humans can receive my thoughts,' she explained, knowing that if she refused any information, he would simply persist with questions. 'But you can't broadcast anything. I can sometimes pick up vague emotion, but rarely from strangers. My abilities are stronger with people I know.'

Avon nodded. Cally could see that he wanted to know more, but the pressure of the mission came first.

'We'll just have to keep trying doors,' he said.

They moved along to the next one. Cally pressed against it, listening, and stretching out with her mind in case she did pick up something. She felt and heard nothing though, and was just relaxing when she got a brief impression of intention from a little further along the corridor. Acting instantly on her feelings, Cally opened the door and slid through, drawing Avon after herself. He hastily and quietly closed the door and they stood in silence as the lights automatically flickered on in the empty office. There was the click of a door being closed, and footsteps, barely audible through cheerful whistling. The slightly off-key melody came level with their door, then faded as the whistler passed and walked away.

When the sound had faded, Avon went to investigate the desks. Cally remained by the door, her gun in her hand, as he studied the computer workstations. At the third desk he looked up, a genuine smile transforming his saturnine face.

'As I hoped, someone didn't shut down their terminal properly when they left for the day.' He holstered his gun and sat down, bringing the workstation online again.

'Can you get the technical data from there?' Cally asked. 'I thought we needed the main computer centre.'

'We do.' Avon's eyes were fixed on the screen. 'But I should be able to find a map or something on here that will tell us where the computer room is.'

He applied himself to the workstation, his fingers agile on the keys. Cally stayed at the door, senses alert, but there seemed to be no danger. A sound drew her attention back to Avon; he appeared to be studying the screen steadily. Cally moved round to join him, peering over his shoulder at the schematic displayed. It wasn't a regular map, but a maintenance diagram, showing the layout of ducts, cabling and pipes throughout the building.

'We're supposed to be finding the computer centre,' Cally reminded him tartly.

Avon flashed an amused look at her. 'Your wish is my command.' He gestured at the screen. 'It's that room.'

'How can you tell?' The space he'd indicated was one of the larger ones, but Cally couldn't see anything to indicate its function.

'Look at the infrastructure that supplies it.' Avon's finger traced different sets of lines. 'A lot of electrical cabling, and a separate, back-up system powered by a local generator. Extra air ducts and fans to keep all that electrical equipment from overheating, and high-capacity data cables, all heavily shielded. Numerous power points and data ports throughout the room.'

'Where is it?' Cally asked practically.

'Up one floor and at the south end of the main corridor.'

'Then let's go.' Cally barely gave Avon time to shut down the terminal and join her, before she opened the office door and led the way out.

Avon's detective work was correct. They very soon found themselves in front of a door with a *Computer Room* sign. Unfortunately, it also sported a bright sign warning *Restricted Area – Authorised Personnel Only*. Once again, Cally stood watch as Avon examined the lock. She waited in tense silence for a minute, before looking to see how he was getting on.

'Vila would have had that open by now,' she remarked lightly.

Avon didn't answer, but his shoulders tensed. Cally hid a grin and turned her attentions back to their surroundings.

It took another minute and a half, but Avon got the lock open without setting off any alarms. They entered the computer centre cautiously. There was no-one still at work. Avon holstered his gun and made straight for the rows of consoles. Cally prowled around the room as he made his selection and sat down. He produced a fabric bundle from his jacket and unrolled it, displaying the tools neatly arrayed in their pockets. There was a look of calm satisfaction on his face as he selected a probe and settled down to work. It was different to how he looked when he was investigating the mysteries of the *Liberator*'s technology. That was a scientific challenge to grasp an alien technology, which kept him fascinated and frustrated in about equal measure from what Cally could tell. This task, involving human computers, was his speciality, and he was supremely confident in his skill.

Cally watched for a moment as he began the puzzle of hacking into the computer. Satisfied that all was well so far, she sent a silent, undetectable message to Blake.

We are safely in the computer centre. Avon is looking for technical data now.

She felt him receive the message, and got a vague impression of satisfaction from him. Cally stifled a sigh; she missed the warm communion of mind-talk on Auron. Life among humans was so *silent*. She swung the tube of explosives from her shoulder and began looking for the best places to plant them.

The demonstration outside President Greerson's residence was an unusually rowdy one, bordering on violence, but it would make no difference. Captain Gratex watched the live newsfeed a few moments longer, then turned her attention back to the screens she was meant to be watching. Gratex liked to imagine that the main office of Security at Belspin Industries was like the flight deck of a space liner, and that she was the captain in control of the ship. She had never been on a space liner, let alone in the cockpit of one, but surely they also had banks of screens and monitoring stations. Pilots wore uniforms too, she was sure, though possibly more flattering ones. Off-duty, Gratex liked to dress up and look stylish. On duty, she sometimes whiled away long, quiet shifts by mentally redesigning her security uniform into something more attractive.

She prided herself on being professional, though, so before she started to daydream, she checked the monitors and status displays arrayed before her. A blinking red light instantly caught her attention, bringing that immediate little jolt of adrenalin that came with an alert. It was a flag from one of the patrolling security robots, indicating a non-specific discrepancy in its surroundings. Gratex quickly brought the flagged image onscreen and studied it. A quick check of the robot's ID code confirmed her guess that she was looking at one of the east side doors to the main assembly building. It took her a moment to spot the tools on the ground by the door. Even at full zoom, she couldn't quite make out what they were – some kind of electronic repair kit, she guessed – but there was no good reason for them to be just there.

A call to maintenance told her that no work had been done just there today. Gratex sat back in her chair and thought. She called up scans from the last robot to patrol that point: there were no tools in sight. Someone had been there in the scant minutes between robot patrols. Gratex made another call, this time to the security checkpoint at the front gate. No-one had left the site in the last few minutes, so it seemed unlikely that the tools had been dropped by an assembly worker leaving late at the end of the day shift.

Puzzled, Gratex gently swung her chair back and forth as she thought. Her eye was caught by the footage from the protests. Some of her security team had been drafted in and she could see them on the screen, moving in formation to press demonstrators away from the Official Residence. It meant that there were few guards left at Belspin, but then the plant was a high-security facility and it was unlikely that any terrorists or protestors would be able to actually get inside in the first place. But those tools suggested that *someone* had been at the assembly plant door.

Suspicion hit Gratex like a jolt of electricity. What if that futile demonstration was nothing more than a diversion? She still couldn't see how an outsider had managed to get into Belspin unnoticed, but with most of her staff attending the protest, the plant was vulnerable to attack. Gratex bit on her lower lip, looking again at the image of those tools lying by the door. They seemed very little to base a theory on, but Gratex decided to go with her gut instinct. After all, better a false alarm than no alarm. With her mind made up, she contacted the security room and ordered a half-squadron to investigate the second east door of the assembly plant.

Gan paused, his attention caught by a panel on the wall of the corridor. It looked as though it might be an access panel to the wiring conduits, maybe an important point like a control box. He studied the panel, trying to see whether he could remove it to check his theory, and maybe to plant a bomb directly against the circuits, rather than on the wall.

As Avon had pointed out, the compact bombs they had were not sufficient to do serious damage to the main pursuit ship production lines. Instead, Blake's team were to attack the subsidiary production areas. Gan had left Blake and Vila planting bombs in a specialised area that assembled the electronic components of the ships' systems. Most of his own bombs had gone in what Gan thought was the control room for the various computerised systems that ran the largely automated plant. The room hadn't been very large, so he'd saved a couple of bombs to plant elsewhere.

The wall panel was clearly designed to be removed, but Gan didn't have the tools to do it. He pried at it with his strong fingers, feeling it give just a little. As he prepared to try again, he became aware of multiple footsteps approaching. Gan turned quickly to the sound, his hand automatically going to the handle of his gun. The corridor ahead was empty, but he could tell now that the sounds were coming from a cross corridor, a short distance away. The only doors he could see were closer to the junction than to himself, so hiding in those rooms would potentially put the group now approaching between himself and Blake. As Gan stepped back, preparing to turn and run, the first security guards appeared around the corner.

'Halt!'

The leading guard raised his rifle. Gan instinctively drew his handgun and aimed.

The guard's hasty shot scorched past Gan's shoulder as he tried to fire. A blaze of pain through his head made Gan stagger. Another rifle shot narrowly missed as he lurched to one side. Gasping, Gan pulled himself together. Holstering the gun he couldn't fire, he slipped the tube of explosives off the other shoulder. Dodging in the opposite direction, he hurled the black tube as hard as he could towards the guards. He saw the two in front duck aside as he turned and sprinted for the open door at the far end of the corridor.

The flare and splutter of rifle shots filled the corridor as Gan ran for his life, dodging as best he could. He yelped at a burst of pain from his right shoulder, but it was no more than a graze that melted clothing and scorched skin. Ahead was a T-junction. If he could reach it, he'd have a few moments to call for help. Longer, if he closed and somehow locked the emergency door. Gan was bulky but powerful, strength and long legs let him move faster than people expected. He pounded towards the end of the corridor, not frightened, but determined. Three more strides, two more...

It happened very fast. Burning agony in his left leg, just as his foot was coming down. His leg buckled and he sprawled forwards, throwing his hands out to break his fall. Gan landed just at the junction and rolled, trying to make cover. As he turned, he glimpsed Blake, racing along the corridor he'd just landed in, and almost on top of him.

'Keep moving,' Blake urged breathlessly, as he hurdled Gan's body. Gan rolled again, snapping his head around fast to see what Blake was doing.

Blake landed almost at the end of the corridor the guards were in, halting himself by throwing his free hand against the wall. Without pausing, he thrust his handgun around the corner and fired a few blind shots towards the guards. There was a cry of pain and the sound of their movement came to a disorganised halt at this unexpected retaliation. Blake withdrew his gun, and slapped at the wall control for the emergency doors. The metal door slammed down from the ceiling, closing off the junction and separating Blake and Gan from the guards. Blake blasted the control, which erupted in a shower of sparks.

Gan had managed to push himself into a sitting position, leaning against the wall. Blake turned to him, crouching down.

'How bad is it?' Blake looked at the wound on Gan's thigh.

'Painful,' Gan admitted, baring his teeth in a grimace. 'Thanks for the save.'

'Timing is everything,' Blake replied, with a brief flash of a smile.

He glanced at the emergency door. 'That will hold them for a little while, but we don't know how many more there are in the plant.'

Gan pressed his hand over the wound. There was so much adrenalin in his body that he didn't feel too much pain.

'Where's Vila?' he asked.

Blake rose. 'He's coming now.'

Gan turned his head and saw Vila hurrying towards them, looking anxious. 'Any trouble your way?' he called.

Vila shook his head. 'I didn't see anyone. Can we get out of here now?' he asked Blake, almost in the same breath.

The question was drowned out by the sound of guards hammering on the door from the other side as they tried to force it open.

Blake activated his communicator. 'Jenna, get a fix on our position and stand by to pick us up very shortly.'

'Understood,' she answered crisply.

Blake changed channels. 'Cally? We've run into trouble here. How are things where you are?'

'There are no sirens or alerts here.' Her voice was just audible to Gan and Vila above the noises from the door

'Our bombs are all set so we're about to pull out,' Blake said. 'Is Avon getting the data?'

There was a brief pause before Avon's clipped voice replied. 'I've got into the computer systems *without* setting off any alarms. Technical data on the pursuit ships is nearly downloaded, but I've also found some interesting files on Greerson.'

'How interesting?' Blake sounded fairly calm, but he glanced in the direction of the closed door as a new shower of sparks erupted from the lock panel.

'Given a little time, I think I could find something to raise interesting questions about how he's used his powers as President,' Avon replied coolly.

'We don't have any more time here.'

'Cally and I are not in immediate danger,' Avon said. 'Security will be tightened after our attacks. I don't know if I'll be able to get into this level of secure files again, not without some months of work. The information I'm getting could do as much damage as any bombs. I need another ten minutes to get it.'

'They'll be through that door in less than ten minutes!' Vila stage-whispered in alarm. 'We've got to teleport back to the ship, Blake!'

Blake nodded to Vila and spoke to Avon again. 'We'll teleport up, but keep in contact with you and Cally, and bring you up too, when you're ready. Good work, Avon.'

'As always.' Avon cut the connection.

As Blake changed comms channels again, Gan struggled to his feet, then propped himself against the wall. He caught his balance as Blake asked Jenna for teleport, and a few moments later, the corridor disappeared from around them as they dematerialised.

stage-whispered in alarm. 'We've got to teleport back to the ship, Blake!'

Blake nodded to Vila and spoke to Avon again. 'We'll teleport up, but keep in contact with you and Cally, and bring you up too, when you're ready. Good work, Avon.'

'As always.' Avon cut the connection.

As Blake changed comms channels again, Gan struggled to his feet, then propped himself against the wall. He caught his balance as Blake asked Jenna for teleport, and a few moments later, the corridor disappeared from around them as they dematerialised.

THREE

Blake was getting used to the strange, non-event of teleporting. It was like blinking, and opening your eyes again to find yourself in a different place. There was no sense of movement, or change. He was immediately ready to grab Gan's arm and support him when they reappeared in the *Liberator*'s teleport room.

'Thanks, I can manage,' Gan claimed. His face was starting to look strained as the shock of his wound began to set in, but he refused to lean on Blake's shoulder.

'Blake!' Jenna interrupted before Blake could argue with Gan, 'Zen's been intercepting messages from the security forces on Belzanko. They've seen the *Liberator* and are scrambling three pursuit ships to intercept.'

Blake muttered a curse. 'Vila, help Gan to the medical unit and take care of him.'

Vila set down his box of tools and gallantly shouldered some of Gan's weight.

'Oof, what do they feed you on, wherever it is you come from?' Vila grumbled, steering Gan up the steps to the corridor. 'And steps – in a spaceship! Who has steps everywhere in a spaceship? They built Zen, and a teleport – and steps!' The complaints faded away as they left.

Blake wasn't really listening to him. He strode across the room to lean over the console, where Jenna was studying displays.

'PURSUIT SHIPS WILL BE IN FIRING RANGE IN FOUR MINUTES.' Zen's voice came from the speaker in the wall.

Jenna glanced at the corridor, and Blake knew that she wanted to be on the flight deck, at the ship's controls.

'Can we fight them?' he asked.

Jenna shook her head. 'We could fight two, but I'm not really sure about three. And three is just what they've sent up now. They can send reinforcements.'

Blake frowned as he thought. 'Do you have a fix on Avon and Cally? We'll have to bring them back now.'

Jenna nodded. She pressed a button and a light showed on the green locator grid set into the console. 'Three minutes until the pursuit ships arrive,' she added.

Blake slid onto the seats on the other side of the console. 'Get ready to take us out of orbit,' he ordered, gesturing to the exit as he moved. 'I'll retrieve the others.'

'OK.' Jenna left at a run, blonde hair flowing with the speed of her movement.

Blake hit the communicator button. 'Avon, we've got pursuit ships on the way, too many to fight. I'm going to bring you and Cally back now.'

'I haven't got all the data yet,' Avon snapped. 'Buy us some time. Orbit Belzanko a couple of times,' he suggested.

Blake considered the idea for a moment. 'That'll give them enough time to scramble more pursuit ships,' he pointed out. 'And I'm not sure if we can pick you up while we're moving.' Another idea occurred to him. 'Are there any alarms where you are yet?'

'No.'

'So Greerson's forces don't know you're there. If the *Liberator* leaves, they'll assume we've retrieved everyone from the ground and won't be looking for you.' Blake was pretty sure Avon would refuse his next suggestion, but decided to try it anyway. 'We'll leave Belzanko, outrun or destroy the pursuit ships, and come back for you in about twenty hours. You finish getting the data, then make contact with Allston and hide with them until we return. It's that, or we all leave right now.'

'Two minutes until intercept.' Jenna's voice came over the speakers on cue.

'We'll stay,' Avon said decisively.

Blake was surprised and pleased at Avon's willingness to take risks to accomplish the mission. 'That's great,' he said warmly. 'I knew I could rely on you, Avon.'

'I just hope I can rely on you to evade the pursuit ships,' Avon answered tartly.

Blake snorted. 'I'll see you both in twenty hours,' he promised. '*Liberator* out.'

Cutting the connection, he switched to internal communications. 'Jenna, take her out.'

'We're on our way.'

Blake paused long enough to remove his teleport bracelet and replace it in the rack, before heading for the flight deck. As he moved, the quiet hum of the engines changed as the powerful ship left orbit and turned for deep space.

Cally was also surprised, and more suspicious. She stalked over to the terminal where Avon sat.

'You trust Blake to come back for us?' she asked.

'Of course.' Avon offered a confident smile. 'He needs my skills, and if he deserted us, the others would be wondering how long before he abandoned them too. They might decide to desert him first.'

Cally tilted her head to one side as she studied him. 'So your trust in Blake is founded purely on logic and practicality.'

'Those, and the knowledge that Blake is reassuringly, almost idiotically, loyal to his companions.'

Cally looked as though she didn't know whether to be cross or pleased at that. Avon's eyes glittered with amusement at her dilemma.

'It's better that they never know we were in here,' he said, more practically. 'We should leave things intact.'

Cally nodded, knowing Avon was right, but no less annoyed with him for being so. Picking up the black tube, she set about retrieving the bombs she had planted in readiness.

Jenna looked up as Blake trotted briskly onto the flight deck. After a few moments, she realised that there was no-one with him.

'Where are Avon and Cally?' she asked, leaning forward at her station.

'On Belzanko.' Blake explained the reason for the separation as he unbuckled his gun-belt and dropped it onto a seat. He paused to look at the main screen. 'Where are we going?'

'Centero,' Jenna said in the tone of someone pointing out the obvious.

Blake turned to face Zen's fascia. 'Zen, cancel the flight to Centero.'

'CONFIRMED.'

Zen was indifferent to the sudden change of plans, but Jenna had questions.

'How are we going to get back for Cally and Avon with three pursuit ships on our tail?'

'How far away are they?' Blake asked, taking up Avon's usual station.

Jenna brought up a display on the main screen, adjusting the graphic to show the *Liberator*, the local planets and the pursuit ships in relation to one another.

'Not yet in firing range,' Jenna said. 'We should be able to outrun them in a few hours, less if they give up the chase before leaving their system.'

Blake looked at her, challenging her with his eyes. 'The *Liberator*'s capable of doing more than running. We want to weaken Greerson's position, so why not take out a couple of his pursuit ships if possible? If we're away from the planet they won't be able to send up reinforcements.'

Jenna touched the instrument panel in front of her, almost caressing it. It would be risky, even with the full crew on station, but the temptation of really flying this ship, and using it as the war machine it was designed to be, appealed to her piloting instincts. She knew Blake was using her love of flying for his own ends, but then he'd given her the chance to fly this beautiful ship, and she was grateful for that. The desire to pit her skill and her ship against the enemy prevailed.

'Zen.' Jenna's voice was clear and decisive. 'Set course to 299 by 45, speed Standard by two. Execute course on command.'

'CONFIRMED.'

Blake looked across at her. 'You already had something in mind?'

Jenna smiled. 'A good smuggler always has plans ready for either flight or fight.' Setting the ship to manual, Jenna took hold of the controls either side of her seat.

As *Liberator* left orbit, the pursuit ships turned to follow. Jenna gradually increased speed to Standard by four. The pursuit ships gave chase, getting closer and closer to firing range. Vila arrived on the flight deck, reporting that Gan was comfortable. He settled at his station, his eyes anxiously following the visual of the pursuit ships, and his finger hovering close to the firing button of the neutron blasters. Jenna noticed Blake looking her way, but he didn't ask what she intended to do. He trusted her to solve the problem. It was a good feeling, to be trusted. Smiling slightly, Jenna pulled back on the flight controls and sent the *Liberator* up from her flight path.

The pursuit ships followed, widening their triangular formation. Two were flying level with one another and echoed the *Liberator*'s course. The third flew above them. It accelerated into a steeper climb, cutting across the arc of *Liberator*'s manoeuvre.

'Stand by,' Jenna warned the other two. Her eyes were fixed on the screen, gauging distances and timings. 'Be ready to fire, Vila.'

'They're behind us!' he protested, keeping his eyes on his instruments nonetheless.

'Not now!' Jenna hit full reverse thrust and pushed the ship into a dive so hard it spun around its own axis.

The view on the screen swooped as *Liberator* turned 180 degrees almost in place. The crew held on to controls and consoles as the inertial dampers fought to protect them from the sudden manoeuvre. Momentum kept them going backwards in the same direction for a few moments, though Jenna switched to forward thrust again immediately.

Vila gasped, but he remained alert enough to let off a shot as the paired pursuit ships came into sight. As *Liberator* finished her turn, Jenna levelled her to aim through the centre of the enemy formation. There was a bright flare from the screen as Vila's shot hit the lower left pursuit ship.

'I got it!' he whooped.

'ENEMY SHIP HAS SUSTAINED MINOR DAMAGE,' Zen informed them uninterestedly.

'Party pooper,' Vila muttered.

The *Liberator*'s powerful engines overcame the momentum of the previous course, and thrust her forward in the new direction. In the next moment, *Liberator* was through the triangle of pursuit ships and heading into clear space. Blake switched the view to rear scanners and Jenna began to slow the big ship. All three of the pursuit ships were turning to follow.

'Good work,' said Blake.

'There's still three of them after us though,' Vila pointed out. 'It's not my fault, I did damn well to hit one at all after being spun around like that. My stomach's still upside-down.'

'I know,' Jenna sounded confident. She rolled the ship so it returned to the previous alignment with the solar ecliptic, bringing them the 'right way up' again. She also kept watching her displays, and as the pursuit ships began to catch up, she gradually increased the *Liberator*'s speed.

Blake studied the screens for a moment, then his face lit up in understanding. 'You weren't really intending to destroy any of them, were you? We just poked them with a stick to get them to chase us.'

Jenna nodded. 'We'll get them well away from Belzanko, and any reinforcements, before we actually stand and fight,' she explained for Vila's benefit. 'We'll make them use up power before we get into a fight,' she added. '*Liberator* can outlast any pursuit ship before she needs to recharge.'

'Do you have a battleground picked?' Blake asked.

Jenna just smiled. 'Zen, execute course command.'

'CONFIRMED.'

Cally abruptly stopped pacing and spun to face Avon. 'It's been more than ten minutes.'

He looked up from the terminal. 'I know. I have the data, as I said I would.'

'Then why are we still here?' Cally began stalking towards him.

'I've been preparing our way out.' He was unflustered by her attitude.

'Our way out is through that door.' Cally stopped beside his chair. 'We need to get moving before security decide to do a full...'

Avon held one hand up to stem the flow of words. 'We have several doors to go through, and the security post at the main gate to pass. All of which will be easier if we can simply walk through, rather than trying to sneak.' He slid out of his chair and gestured gracefully at it. 'Sit there.'

Cally stared at him for a moment, then did as he asked.

Avon leaned in and pressed a couple of keys on the control pad.

'Look straight at the monitor,' he instructed. 'There's no need to smile.'

Before Cally could say anything, the terminal's display blinked, then changed to show an image of her own face, looking faintly surprised.

'Not the most flattering likeness,' Avon observed. 'But then ID pictures rarely are.'

He pressed another key. There was a hum and a mechanical chattering noise from somewhere else in the room. Cally leapt out of the chair, reaching for her handgun, then paused.

'Don't worry; the printer is not a threat.' Avon leaned over the desk to shut down the terminal.

Cally made her way over to the printer and picked up the two plastic cards waiting in the tray. One bore her likeness, the other had Avon's. Both had biometric data encoded on them, which she assumed related to the fake names on them. She looked at the ID cards in her hand thoughtfully.

'These are functional?' she asked. 'The security systems will accept them?'

Avon joined her, taking his own card. 'Anyone doing a visual check will match our faces to the faces on the cards. Computers will simply scan the data encoded and check that it matches the data in their memory banks. Both humans and computers will be satisfied that we are the people on the cards. These will also serve for identification purposes if necessary while we wait for Blake to return.'

Cally was impressed both by Avon's planning, and by his skill in being able to produce the cards. She was reassured by the fact that he was relying on them for his own safety. Avon could be guaranteed not to take chances with his own life.

'Good work,' was all she offered by way of praise though. 'Let's get going.'

Five minutes later, they were approaching the security booth by the main gate. Avon had pointed out that their two-tone hooded jackets were the same style as the ones Blake and the others had been wearing, which might raise suspicion with an alert guard. It had taken them a couple of minutes to find coats that were loose enough to conceal the hooded jackets and handguns, without looking obviously oversized. Cally had fretted at the delay, but had recognised the wisdom of Avon's suggestion and reined in her impatience.

Now Avon was wearing a calf-length black overcoat, which flowed as he walked and added to his natural air of authority. The best thing Cally had been able to find was a hip-length jacket of artificial spotted fur.

As they got closer to the booth, Cally could hear the guard talking on his intercom.

'No,' the man insisted. 'There's been no-one in through these gates for over an hour. You can check the security logs.'

Cally could hear the reply coming from the small speaker, but couldn't quite distinguish the words.

'They must have breached the perimeter elsewhere,' the guard in the booth replied. He looked up from his comms unit, staring briefly at the two approaching. 'Wherever they got in from, those stupid robots were supposed to have spotted them,' the guard added sharply.

The voice on the intercom was clearer now. 'They seem to have vanished as mysteriously as they appeared. There's no trace of them in here.'

Avon strode up to the window of the booth and held up his ID card. His face had the look of disdainful boredom to be expected from management dealing with minions. Cally suspected it was a look he'd used often. She tried to mimic it as she held up her own card.

The guard glanced at the cards, then at their faces.

The voice on the intercom spoke again. 'They're probably aiming to get out the way they came in, but stay alert for trouble. They're armed and dangerous.'

The gate guard nodded at Avon, and pressed the button to open the gates. As Avon moved towards the opening gap, there was the rumble of a series of muffled explosions from somewhere deeper in the complex. A louder echo of the same sound came from the intercom. Avon and Cally both spun to look as the guard frantically scanned monitors.

'Pankham – what's happened?' the guard yelled.

There was silence for a moment, then screams came over the intercom, the cries of momentarily delayed shock.

Avon seized Cally's arm and turned her towards the widening gates. The guard glanced up from his monitors.

'Get out!' He gestured at the gates. 'There's terrorists on the loose inside the complex.'

Cally and Avon hurried through the gates, which began sliding shut again almost immediately. They could hear the guard alternately calling for emergency services, and begging for Pankham to answer him. Cally didn't expect him to get much of an answer from the latter: Pankham and his unit must had been in the area of the plant where Blake and the others had been planting mines. It was their tough luck, she felt. They had chosen to work for a company that supported the regime of a corrupt ruler, and which profited from sales to the Federation military: death was an occupational hazard for such men. It was impossible to tell what Avon thought by looking at him. His expression, and the feel of his mind, were tightly focused and closed in.

As they stepped beyond the gates to the road, a quick glance showed that the main part of the city was quite a distance from the industrial plant, and uphill. There was a public transit stop close to the gates, and they gratefully moved into the passenger shelter. It was past the peak transit hour, but a glowing electronic sign told them that they only had a few minutes to wait until the next shuttle arrived.

They sat in silence on the hard, minimal bench of the shelter. As they waited, Avon's attention turned upwards, to the sky. Cally watched him from the corner of her eye for a couple of minutes. The tenseness left his face and there was something akin to wonder in his dark eyes as he watched the grey clouds drifting across the pale grey sky.

'Are you hoping to see the *Liberator*?' Cally asked him.

Avon shot her a scornful look. 'That would be illogical,' he replied crisply. 'Blake should have left orbit by now.'

'Then why are you watching the sky?' she persisted.

He was silent a moment, then, somewhat to her surprise, Avon answered.

'On Earth, most people spend all of their lives inside the domed cities. To look up and see sky, and clouds, is strange. If I'd succeeded with the fraud, we were going to leave Earth and live on a pleasure planet where we could look at blue skies all day if we'd wanted.'

'We?' Cally asked.

The tension returned to Avon's face and his eyes became hard. He turned away and watched the road, his posture stiff. Cally gazed at his back for a few moments, hurt at being shut out of his feelings.

On Auron, it was natural to share and sympathise with others. Avon was verbally and mentally silent, and she felt very alone as she sat next to him.

FOUR

The *Liberator* fled the Belzanko system, drawing the three pursuit ships after it. Jenna played cat and mouse with the chasers, but it was the mouse that was in control. She slowed the ship very gradually, letting the pursuit ships get just close enough to try taking a shot. The distance was great enough that Blake had enough time to operate the force wall long enough to absorb the shots. Afterwards, the *Liberator* would increase speed again, slowly at first, until the pursuit ships dropped behind. Then Jenna would gently ease down the ship's speed again.

'I want them to keep up a fast chase,' she explained to Vila during one of the slowing phases. 'I need them to keep their speed up so they drain their energy banks. If I push too hard, they'll realise they can't catch us and give up the chase too early.'

'Too slow and they'll catch us,' Vila said, looking at her for reassurance.

Jenna smiled and nodded.

'But what about *our* energy banks?' he fretted.

'Zen!' Jenna called. 'Status of ship's energy banks.'

'ENERGY BANK ONE AT TWENTY-FIVE PERCENT. DRAWING ON ENERGY BANK TWO, CURRENTLY AT SIXTY-SEVEN PERCENT. ALL OTHER BANKS FULL.'

Jenna glanced across at Vila. 'See? Plenty left. The *Liberator*'s hardly feeling it.'

'How long do you think they will keep chasing us?' Blake asked.

Jenna studied her monitors. 'Another thirty minutes, I hope.'

'OK, good work,' Blake said, smiling his approval.

'Hire a professional, you get good work,' Jenna answered confidently. Glancing at her screen, she slowed the *Liberator* again, to feed the pursuit ships the false hope that they might catch their prey.

Back in the city centre, Cally and Avon had no trouble in following their instructions to connect with Allston's people. They were escorted to the offices of a garden-design company on the fringes of the business district and were met there by Allston himself. He led them into an unobtrusive storage closet full of cleaning things, and through a hidden door into secret rooms for planning and hiding fugitives from President Greerson. Allston explained that the long, narrow rooms divided two large warehouses used to store equipment for the gardening company.

'The company is quite legitimate,' Allston explained. 'It designs and builds gardens, pays its taxes, fills in government datawork and does nothing to attract attention from the authorities.'

'Other than getting all its datawork done properly and on time,' Avon commented dryly. 'A rare thing in many businesses.'

'Not on Belzanko,' Allston told him, his expression turning grim for a moment. 'Penalties for late or inaccurate datawork are quite severe, for individuals or companies,' he added.

The resistance leader was an athletic man, only in his early forties but with a full head of striking, silver hair. He had large, expressive eyes which were very appealing, but his habit of cracking his knuckles set Cally's teeth on edge, and probably had a similar effect on Avon, from the way he narrowed his eyes at the sound.

Avon had already removed the stolen black coat, now he retrieved a memory cube from the pocket of his hooded jacket and gave it to Allston.

'This contains all the blueprints for the pursuit ships,' he said. 'There are also complete plans for the plant, including wiring conduits, service tunnels and sewers.'

Allston gazed at the cube with respect, before looking at Avon. 'Thank you, thank you so much.' He broke into a wide smile. 'I promise you, we will put this information to the best use. It won't be wasted.'

'Is there any more news on the *Liberator*?' Cally asked, glancing at the monitors along one wall.

'We haven't any precise information,' Allston explained, leading them to a conference table with chairs. 'Your ship isn't broadcasting, not that we can pick up. The messages from the pursuit ships are highly encrypted, of course. We can establish their approximate distance from Belzanko from the time delay in responding to messages from headquarters, here on the planet. The pursuit ships appear to be chasing *Liberator* out of the solar system.' He looked at the cube, then at Avon, who had already sat down. 'A highly skilled computer engineer might be able to crack their encryption techniques.'

Avon smiled lazily as he sat down with the others. 'I could do it,' he stated simply. 'However, it would take longer than the time I have here, assuming Blake returns when promised.'

With an effort of will, Cally managed to avoid scowling at him.

'I can, however, offer you an alternative.' Avon raised one hand slightly, pointing at Allston.

Allston set the memory cube on the table. 'Go ahead,' he said thoughtfully.

'There are more ways to damage a person than through military means.' Avon's voice was precise. 'Give me access to a computer and the planetary datanet and I can put President Greerson out of business.'

Allston raised one eyebrow. 'Can you, indeed?'

Avon's smile widened. 'I downloaded more than just files about spaceships while I was in Belspin's computer system. I found a lot of interesting information about their financial situation. President Greerson has left his fingerprints all over Belzanko Space Industries, and, I suspect, a few other companies. He thinks he's been very clever at using the planetary stock market for his own gain.'

'But you're cleverer?' Allston asked dryly.

Avon nodded. 'I can hit him in ways that bombs couldn't do.' He leaned back in his chair. 'But first, I'm hungry, and I imagine that Cally is too. I work better when I'm not distracted by physical necessities.'

Allston gave a short bark of laughter. 'Very well.' He turned to one of his men. 'Fram! Find some local restaurant menus. Let our guests choose something to nourish them for the work to come.'

Cally sat down beside Avon. 'You can do all this?' she asked softly.

He gave her a look that mixed confidence and contempt. 'I wouldn't offer something I couldn't deliver. If Blake messes up and gets himself and the *Liberator* destroyed, we're stuck on Belzanko, with these people. Getting rid of Greerson would be in my own best interests. If Blake does return, then I've done everyone a favour anyway.'

Cally glared at him. 'It still won't make you popular.'

Avon shrugged. 'I don't care about being popular; I just care about being alive and free. And preferably, alone.'

'WARNING. *LIBERATOR* WILL ENTER AN ASTEROID BELT IN FIVE MINUTES.' Zen's voice was loud and clear across the flight deck.

'Acknowledged.' Jenna's replied calmly. 'Return control to manual.'

'CONFIRMED.'

The chase had lasted for nearly two hours so far. Jackets and gun-belts had been tidied away and everyone had taken the chance for a quick rest and refreshments. Gan was back on the flight deck, his wound already partially healed by the ship's remarkable equipment. Now up to date on the situation, he sat at the station above Vila, monitoring any signals they could catch between the three pursuit ships.

'Those asteroids look awfully big,' said Vila, staring at the viewscreen.

'FLIGHT COMPUTERS RECOMMEND AVOIDANCE OF ASTEROID BELT,' Zen warned.

'Thank you, Zen,' Jenna answered. 'Maintaining course.'

'See,' muttered Vila. 'Zen agrees with me. Nasty things, asteroids.'

'I can be nasty too,' Jenna said, giving a Vila hard look.

Vila shrank back against his seat. There were no complaints from anyone else as Jenna steadily headed the great ship into the ring of asteroids.

The pursuit ships followed. Their much smaller size gave them an advantage amongst the floating rocks that now filled their screens. They could slip through gaps too small for the *Liberator*. Blake glanced once at Jenna, his look warm and trusting. He wasn't questioning her even now, as they headed into an asteroid belt, and Jenna was heartened by this. How much of his trust was real faith in her skills, and how much was a ploy to win her loyalty, she didn't know. She was just too cynical to believe that there wasn't some underlying motive behind his actions. Well, she would prove to Blake and to the others that she was as good a pilot as anyone, and she would start by demonstrating her skills to the pilots of the pursuit ships.

Picking a generous gap, Jenna flew the *Liberator* into the crowd of asteroids. Pulling back on the controls, she lifted the ship up and over the first rock in her path, skimming the pock-marked surface and leaving it in her trail. One pursuit ship followed her, the other two went beneath the asteroid, rising on the far side to join their fellow in a regulation, triangular formation. They caught up a little as Jenna altered course to put the *Liberator* over another asteroid. The smaller pursuit ships didn't need to alter their course as much to clear the obstacles.

This time, as the *Liberator* climbed, one of the chasers sent a plasma bolt after her. Blake was a little too slow with the force wall and the big ship rocked slightly as the bolt hit one of the lower hulls.

'MINOR DAMAGE TO SURFACE,' Zen reported. 'SELF-REPAIR MECHANISMS ARE ACTIVATED.'

'Acknowledged.' Blake answered the computer, letting Jenna concentrate on flying the ship. 'Maintaining force wall,' he added, for the benefit of the others.

Jenna turned the *Liberator*, aiming for the largest asteroid in her path. The upper pursuit ship hit with another shot, but this was absorbed by the force wall.

'ENERGY BANK FOUR AT FIFTY PERCENT,' Zen informed them.

'Their energy banks must be getting low,' Gan called, studying his monitors. 'They can't have as much power as the *Liberator*,' he added confidently.

Another shot from behind rattled the *Liberator* and made them sway in their seats. Jenna's hands remained steady on the controls, and the ship barely deviated from her course.

'They don't have to do that much damage to us,' Vila said, his voice high-pitched with nerves. 'If they make us crash into an asteroid, that'll tear us wide open. Why don't we go back into deep space?' he pleaded, glancing briefly away from the screen. 'We can outrun them. They're not going to chase us too far from their home planet, especially if they're already low on energy,' he pleaded.

'If we destroy them now, there'll be three fewer ships to face when we go back for Cally and Avon,' Jenna told him, watching the screen as they closed on the asteroid. 'Stand by on the neutron blasters,' she warned.

Again, the ship rose to skim over the top of the obstacle. This time, though, Jenna didn't resume her course but instead threw the ship into a dive that hugged the far side of the asteroid. Its bulk temporarily hid them from the following ships. As before, one pursuit ship rose over the top of the asteroid and the other two flew underneath. They were below and in front of the *Liberator* as they came out from beneath the slowly spinning rock and began to angle upwards.

Vila was ready for their appearance, and fired as they came into sight. His shot hit full on and the pursuit ship exploded in a brief, glorious shower of sparks and fire.

'Yes!' Vila sounded surprised at his own success. In the excitement of the moment, the pursuit ship seemed little more than a target in a game, albeit a potentially deadly one. It was as if he was too busy reacting to consider that the image on his screen was actually a ship with living people inside.

Jenna accelerated and flew through the space where the enemy ship had been. Debris rattled against the hull as the survivor let off a quick shot. It missed, then the two ships passed one another, the *Liberator* heading down through the belt of asteroids. Jenna turned the ship on her central axis to dodge a smaller asteroid, and pulled around in a loop back towards the pursuit ships.

'Good work,' said Blake warmly. 'Let's try to finish them before they make a run for it.'

'Already on it,' Jenna answered, smiling as the big ship responded to her controls.

'I discussed it with Blake, but he thinks the *Liberator* is too important an asset to be tied to any one place,' Cally told Allston.

They were sitting together in the second of the hidden rooms. This one was designed more as living space for people in hiding, and was furnished with comfortable chairs, a dining table, two narrow beds and had a corner closed off as a tiny bathroom.

Allston thought for a moment, frowning, then his expression suddenly opened into a smile. The effect was pleasing, like the sun coming out from behind clouds.

'I guess he may be right, especially at this stage. Hit and run attacks will make it difficult for the Federation to track you, especially after the damage you caused at Saurian Major. We knew that long-distance communications had been disrupted, but if the Federation have told Greerson why, he hasn't told the rest of us.'

Cally nodded. 'We can use the *Liberator*'s power, and especially her teleport system, to help planets like yours, as well as disrupting the Federation's ability to control. If we can pry planets free from their grasp, and weaken their grip while strengthening the opposition, then eventually we can overthrow them.'

'A galaxy of justice and democracy,' said Allston. 'That's all we want.'

He leaned back in his chair and stretched. Cally, watching him, was surprised when he gave a sudden yawn.

'We should go and see what your comrade is doing,' Allston suggested. 'Now he's had a chance to develop his ideas, he might be a bit more forthcoming about how he intends to bring Greerson down without fighting.'

Cally rose. 'Avon resents the Federation for catching him, but he isn't a real fighter,' she said. She followed Allston to the door between the rooms.

Allston looked at her thoughtfully. 'Does he do what he promises to do?'

Cally paused for a moment. 'I haven't known him long,' she admitted. 'He's kept his word so far.'

'Then we can assume he's going to bring down Greerson, whatever his motivation.'

In the office room, Avon was still working at a computer terminal. He looked up as they entered, and sat back in his chair, waiting as they approached. Although he'd only been in the rebels' base for a few hours, he looked very much at home and in command of the situation.

'How are you?' Allston asked. 'Can I get you a drink?'

Avon's expression softened. 'Well now. That's kind of you but no, thank you.'

Allston sat down in the next chair; Cally sat on Avon's other side,

'How have you been getting on with your program?' Allston asked.

Avon turned back towards his terminal, though he continued to look at Allston.

'My program works now,' he answered. 'I am refining the details.'

'How is it going to bring President Greerson down?'

'It's taken time to track down the necessary information,' Avon began, talking rather as though giving a lecture to students. 'Greerson has been quite clever at disguising his interests. When you start digging, you find a lot of companies are owned by other companies, that are part of corporate groups, and so on. Either directly, or by such indirect means, Greerson has shares in more companies than he has officially declared. And a lot of the final companies, the ones that do actual work, are the companies that get government contracts, such as Belspin.'

Allston looked happy. 'You've done good work. We suspected this sort of thing was going on, but we could never dig far enough to get real proof that Greerson was corrupt.'

'I have the proof,' Avon agreed. 'But my plan is to turn Greerson's greed against him. I suspect that he has a great deal of influence over the media, and the legal system on Belzanko?'

Allston nodded his agreement.

'So if you tried bringing his underhand practices to public attention, you would find it hard to get heard, and it's unlikely that a case would be brought at all, let alone with any chance of success against the President,' Avon surmised. He began to smile. 'My plan is to get to him through those share dealings. To wipe out his fortune and leave him vulnerable.'

'I don't see how that's going to work,' Cally objected. 'We came here to attack Greerson, not to mess around with the stock markets.'

Avon's smile became patronising. 'Attempting to attack President Greerson directly would be foolish. He must be very well guarded, or else I imagine Allston and his people would have removed him already. Even with the *Liberator*'s resources, we do not have the capability to launch an attack large enough and damaging enough to unseat Greerson. We can certainly hurt his position, but it would take a sustained series of attacks to remove him, and he would call in help from his allies in the Federation before we could finish him. And the Federation would fall over themselves to help if they suspected Blake was involved.'

'But you agreed to come here and help,' Cally pointed out hotly. 'Though all we planned to do was to weaken Greerson by attacking his pursuit ship production.'

'Blake was determined to come here, and I am travelling on the same ship, for the time being, therefore I came too,' Avon said calmly. 'And since I was coming, I thought I may as well help out, since you needed my skills. If you try to attack him with just guns and bombs, you'll be doing so without me.'

'You boast a lot about your skills, but you still got caught,' Cally said tartly. She was pleased to see the smile disappear from Avon's face. 'How can we be sure your program will work?'

'I was caught because I trusted other people,' Avon retorted. 'I shall take care of this myself.'

'How is your program going to work?' Allston asked, leaning forward.

Avon turned again to face him directly. 'I need to plant this program directly into the computers of the main planetary stock exchange. The buying and selling of shares is heavily computerised and a lot of business happens automatically. Once active, my program will submit orders to start selling shares from the companies that Greerson has a heavy stake in. Other computers that monitor the markets will notice the run of sales, and be triggered into selling their own shares in those companies. Once share sales reach a certain point, their value will crash and those companies will become worthless. That's a simple explanation, of course,' he added, his expression implying that they wouldn't understand a complicated one.

'Stock markets have to be more complicated than that,' Cally protested, nettled. 'There are humans buying and selling on the stock exchange, aren't there?' she asked Allston.

'There are, but how it works is a mystery to me,' Allston said.

Avon smiled again. 'Finance is my specialist field, remember? There are traders who buy and sell at the request of investors, or in the hope of spotting a market for themselves, but a lot of the system is automated, and computers are very good at doing what they are told, without asking questions.'

'It's a weakness you can exploit,' said Allston, cracking his knuckles absently.

'That's correct.'

'So what happens when Greerson loses the money invested in his shares?' Cally asked. 'He's still in power as President.'

'But severely weakened.' Allston answered her, his face bright with excitement. 'He won't be able to hide such a big hit to his finances, and with Avon's information, we'll be able to make it clear just how many companies he's been dealing with, the government contracts he's been giving his own companies. With millions of credits wiped off his value, he won't have the same power to control the media, or the courts.'

'I can tell you which companies are suddenly going to lose value for no good reason,' Avon told him. 'There's no reason why you and your supporters shouldn't buy into those companies while prices are at a low.'

Allston smiled. 'We could buy enough to get controlling interests in one or two important companies like Belspin. We would get a say in how the companies are run, and who they sell to.'

'Pick good companies, and you'll be making money on cheap shares,' Avon advised. 'The profits would fund your activities.'

'As Greerson is doing at the moment, but for different purposes.' Allston smiled at Cally. 'Don't you think there's poetry in that irony?'

It didn't seem as simple and certain to Cally as a military attack, but she could see the attraction of fewer people getting hurt. 'If the program works, and the markets react in the way you predict, it could bring change and save lives,' she answered.

'The program will work,' Avon repeated. 'It's up to Allston and his followers to take advantage of it.'

'Oh, we will,' Allston promised, cracking his knuckles. 'We will.'

FIVE

Liberator rose steadily through the belt of asteroids. The pursuit ship they had passed had already disappeared from their scanners, hidden by one or more of the slowly spinning rocks. Jenna took the ship round on a loop past another asteroid, that glimmered with streaks of metallic ore.

Gan concentrated hard on his station. 'I can't pick up the pursuit ships,' he said.

'Keep trying,' Blake said encouragingly. He had turned off the force wall to conserve energy.

'They'll be after us for sure,' said Vila, his fingers waiting restlessly by the controls of the neutron blasters.

Jenna deliberately swung the *Liberator* close around the asteroid as she headed back in the direction of the pursuit ships. As they came around the bulk of the rock, she saw a smaller asteroid in the path of the ship, orbiting the larger one.

'COLLISION IMMINENT,' Zen warned.

'I can see that!' Jenna hissed, jerking the ship sideways.

Everyone lurched and grabbed for consoles as the ship scraped past the small rock.

'Ow!' The exclamation came from Vila. 'I've bitten my tongue!'

'I'll bite something worse if you don't shut up,' Jenna threatened, her concentration on the screen.

As they cleared the asteroid, the two remaining pursuit ships came into view. They had joined up and were waiting ahead, pointed at where they guessed the *Liberator* was going to be. Plasma bolts filled the screen. Jenna swore. Blake hastily flicked the deflector shield on. Fortunately, Jenna's hasty dodge around the small asteroid had put them slightly off the optimal course. One bolt missed altogether, the other made a glancing blow against the shield. The big ship lurched again as brilliant light flashed through the bridge.

'LOWER HULL DAMAGED. SHIP INTEGRITY REDUCED TO NINETY-THREE PERCENT.'

In response, Jenna thrust the controls forward, accelerating the *Liberator* towards the enemy ships. Vila squeaked in alarm, but kept his eyes on his screen.

The pursuit ships drove forward to meet them, rapidly getting large on the viewscreen and scanners. As they fired, so did the *Liberator*. Plasma bolt met neutron blast in space. Viewscreen and bridge lit up and the ship bucked beneath them like a startled animal. The other plasma bolt struck a glancing blow on the small asteroid.

'Force wall holding,' called Blake.

After the head to head run, they passed above the pursuit ships.

'Stand by to turn,' Jenna warned, taking a firm grip on the controls. 'Vila, be ready to shoot.'

'Ready.' Vila's voice betrayed his nerves, but his hand remained steady.

As before, Jenna reversed the engines and pulled the controls back, spinning the *Liberator* almost in place. As soon as they'd turned, she hit maximum forward thrust to counter their backwards momentum. The starscape whirled about their forward scanner, as her stomach churned in sympathy. Vila gulped audibly, but managed to send a shot after the pursuit ships as they vanished beyond the large asteroid. The shot caught the trailing ship and it vanished in a silent explosion.

'Well done!' said Blake. 'Just one more to go.' He leaned forward at his console, his expression as intent as a hunter in sight of his prey.

'It's behind that asteroid. Scanners can't pick it up,' reported Gan.

'If they've got any sense, they're running for home,' Jenna said, pushing the *Liberator* forward.

She turned the big ship so they passed to the other side of the big metallic asteroid.

'We may get a glimpse of the pursuit ship as we clear the asteroid,' Jenna warned Vila.

'Right.'

As they rounded the rock, there was a brief flash ahead from the engines of the pursuit ship as it disappeared behind an ovoid asteroid. Vila fired reflexively, but the shot did no more than to cause debris to spout from the surface of the rock.

'Sorry,' Vila said breathlessly.

By way of reply, Jenna sent the *Liberator* on by the most direct route, aiming to pass underneath the ovoid rock.

The asteroid headed to the top of the viewscreen and vanished as they started to pass underneath. As they reached the lowest point of their dive, a plasma bolt appeared from the far side of the asteroid, almost in front of them. Vila squeaked.

Jenna swore. She threw the ship into a spin in the hope that the plasma bolt would miss. It hit a glancing blow to one of the hulls, making the whole ship shudder. Brilliant light seem to erupt around them, and once again the crew found themselves clinging to their consoles.

'Where did that come from?' yelled Gan.

'The last pursuit ship curved around the asteroid and came back at us,' snapped Jenna, wrestling for control of the ship.

'HULL DAMAGED. SHIP INTEGRITY REDUCED TO EIGHTY-ONE PERCENT,' intoned Zen, adding to the noise. 'POWER BANK FOUR AT FIVE PERCENT. SWITCHING TO POWER BANK FIVE.'

Jenna pulled the spinning ship away from another asteroid that seemed to loom up very fast.

The pursuit ship hadn't kept fleeing, as they'd expected, but had hugged the curve of the ovoid asteroid until it faced back towards their path. The smaller ship had been able to see the *Liberator* around the asteroid before they had been able to see it. As Jenna kept accelerating forward, the pursuit ship came into sight. It launched another plasma bolt, as Vila took another shot with the neutron blasters.

This time Blake flicked the force wall on in time. Jenna spun and dodged, and the plasma bolt passed by the main hull, lighting up the scanners as it passed. Vila's shot also missed, as the pursuit ship accelerated towards them. The two ships passed one another harmlessly. Jenna didn't try to flip the ship again, but put her into a tight turn around the asteroid below them.

'The pursuit ship is looping around an asteroid,' Gan reported, watching the sensors. 'I think they're coming around for another head to head pass.'

'Thank you,' Jenna answered, turning the *Liberator* as she made her own downward loop.

'They must be low on power,' Blake said, frowning at his console. 'That's why they're not running.'

'I hope so,' said Vila, his nervousness making him talk. 'The low on power thing, I mean. I wouldn't mind if they ran away. That would be better in fact. Better for them, and much better for us.'

'Vila!' Jenna silenced his chatter.

Instead of curving close to the asteroid's surface, Jenna made a wider turn, then closed in to come back at a steeper angle.

'Ready, Vila,' she called.

A moment later, the pursuit ship was in sight. Small and fast, it stayed close to the surface of the asteroid it had looped around. Its weapons were pointed where the *Liberator* would have been if Jenna had followed a similar, tight course around the reddish asteroid. Vila fired a quick shot, even as the pursuit ship adjusted its angle, tilting towards the *Liberator*'s position. The shot just missed the pursuit ship and impacted against the surface of the asteroid. Rocky debris blasted from its surface, engulfing the pursuit ship.

As the pursuit ship emerged from the cloud of rocks and dust, an explosion tore through the rear fuselage. Vila fired again.

'They *were* low on power!' Gan exclaimed. 'Their defence shield was down.'

Vila's second shot hit the crippled ship. The pursuit ship tore apart in a series of explosions. Jenna pulled the *Liberator* into a tighter climb, so they rose with the expanding explosion cloud in front of them. Debris hit the force wall and rattled the big ship, but the crew could tell it was nothing serious even before Zen's report.

'That's it!' exclaimed Vila. 'I got all of them!' He gaped at the screen as though unable to believe what he had just seen.

Blake turned to Jenna. 'It was thanks to your piloting, and tactics,' he said, smiling.

Jenna smirked, looking calmer than she felt inside. 'The battle computers are good, but they don't have a smuggler's touch.'

'There's not many who could do what you just did,' Blake said.

'That's true,' Jenna answered, slowing the big ship down as she steered it into more open space.

Blake laughed at her honest immodesty. 'You all did well,' he said. 'If we work together as a team, we're going to win.'

'Try telling Avon that,' muttered Vila.

'He knows that value of sticking together,' Gan said. 'It's safer for him, so he'll do it.'

'It may not always be safer,' Vila predicted, not looking at Blake.

'Avon's a good man in his heart,' Blake said confidently. 'He makes a lot of noise about acting on his own, but he's one of us really.'

He strode down onto the flight deck and looked up at the mottled panel that represented Zen.

'Zen, if we stay where we are, how long with it take to replenish the energy banks, and for the auto-repair systems to fix the ship?'

Zen's lights flashed before the computer answered.

'REPAIRS WILL BE COMPLETE IN APPROXIMATELY THIRTEEN HOURS. ENERGY BANKS REQUIRE FORTY HOURS TO REACH FULL CAPACITY.'

Blake stroked his chin as he thought. 'How full will the energy banks be after fifteen hours?'

'ENERGY BANKS ONE AND TWO WILL BE RECHARGED. ENERGY BANK THREE WILL BE AT FIFTY PERCENT CAPACITY.'

'Is that with the autorepair systems working?'

'CONFIRMED. IF THE AUTOREPAIR UNITS DO NOT OPERATE, ENERGY BANKS ONE, TWO AND THREE WILL BE FULLY CHARGED AND ENERGY BANK FOUR WILL BE AT THIRTY PERCENT CAPACITY.'

'That sounds better,' Blake mused.

Jenna shook her head. 'It's too dangerous,' she warned. 'If we do run into trouble, the ship's integrity is only eighty percent. I'd rather have a fully repaired ship with slightly less power available.'

'Me too,' said Vila. 'Or better yet, we wait here for as long as it take to recharge the batteries completely.'

'I can't do that,' Blake replied. 'I promised Avon and Cally I'd be back, and that's the schedule I'm sticking to.'

'It's not just your ship, though,' Jenna objected. 'There's four of us on board, and all our lives may be at risk.'

Vila nodded vigorously in agreement. Gan just watched expectantly.

Blake stepped back towards his station, his attention on Jenna.

'I said twenty hours and that's what they'll be expecting; that timing will affect what they choose to do down on Belzanko. It's also what they will have told Allston. If I don't show up on time, it's going to look bad to Allston.' His voice became deeper and more urgent; his attention fixed on Jenna more fiercely. 'This action on Belzanko is my first opportunity to prove myself directly to resistance leaders across the Federation. We've already had to pull out part of our forces early. I'm relying on Avon to do something good with that data he stayed behind for. I've got to be seen to do the job I said I would, or else I'll find it much harder to get co-operation from other resistance leaders.' Blake's eyes were glowing with determination. 'Our chance of fighting the Federation, of uniting resistance leaders and really getting something started, depends on getting the fight off to a good start. We've got to do what we say we're going to do. I've got to keep my word. Do you see that?' he demanded of Jenna.

She stared back. 'Yes. I see you have to keep your promises.'

'Good.' Blake relaxed into a smile, and the tension on the flight deck eased.

He spun around to face Zen once more. 'Zen! Recharge the energy banks and get the autorepair systems going. We're staying here for the next fifteen hours.'

Jenna hit a switch and returned the ship to automatic, before leaning back against her seat and letting her eyes close for a moment as adrenalin drained away.

'If we're not going anywhere, I'm going to catch up on my sleep,' Vila announced. He bounced down from his station and hurried away before anyone could stop him.

Gan ambled down from his own perch. 'You did a good job,' he told Jenna, with a smile.

'Thank you.' She hauled herself off her seat and looked at Blake. 'I think, for once, Vila has the right idea.'

Blake smiled. 'Don't let him hear you, it'll go to his head.'

'A compliment would die of loneliness in Vila's head,' Jenna answered, stepping down from the pilot's position and stretching. 'I'll see you in a few hours.'

Blake nodded, still bright eyed. 'I'll take first watch.'

'I'll take second,' Gan offered.

'Thank you.' Blake made a shooing gesture. 'Get some rest first.'

Gan nodded, and followed Jenna off the flight deck.

As their footsteps faded away, the flight deck became quiet, apart from the gentle sounds Zen made. Blake looked around with the pride of possession, and smiled.

*

The Central Stock Exchange of Belzanko was easy enough to recognise, and even more impressive in real life than it had been in pictures. Cally paused across the street from it, and stared in wonder at the sweeping construction.

'Hyperbolic paraboloid roof,' said Avon, halting beside her. 'Unusual on this scale, they're commonly smaller.'

The body of the building was made of glassteel, which glittered in the low, late afternoon sunshine and gave it an insubstantial appearance. The spectacular roof was of a light grey metallic material, which seemed to hang in the air, unsupported by the glass building below, and consisted of an uninterrupted double curve. The sides flowed down to within a storey of the ground; the front and rear rose high, like the prow and stern of an ancient ship. The stock exchange was four storeys at the front and back, with the peaks of the roof soaring several metres higher.

'It's beautiful,' said Cally. 'I'm glad we're not intending to blow this up.'

Avon flashed a wry smile. 'Such a shame that it is used for such a sordid purpose as a stock exchange,' he said.

Cally flashed him a look and pulled herself together. 'Let's go.' She glanced at the traffic, then led the way across the wide street.

They were wearing the coats they had stolen yesterday, with their handguns concealed beneath them. The *Liberator* jackets were rolled up small and stuffed into pockets. The ID cards Avon had forged the night before were attached to their coats. Avon was carrying a small electronic device in one hand. Cally had Avon's roll of tools with her. The double doors of the stock exchange slid open as they approached. The entrance had a waiting area with lounge chairs, a water cooler and low tables near the entrance. A glassteel wall with coloured patterns separated this part of the lobby from the rear section, which offered access to the rest of the ground floor, and to the lifts and stairs.

Avon led the way across to reception, which controlled the barrier between the two halves of the room. A man with grey streaks in his light brown hair, and an expression compounded of boredom and suspicions waited inside the reception booth. Avon showed him the screen of the electronic notepad he held.

'Where's the appropriate computer room?' he asked in bored tones.

The security guard read the notice with the fake job on it.

'There's no work number,' he said. his hands resting on the counter, away from the switch for the barrier.

Avon pulled back the notepad and looked at the screen, frowning. 'I'm just showing you what was sent to me,' he said.

Cally could feel his tension and his annoyance with the scrupulous guard, but he kept himself in control.

'I need a work number,' the guard insisted.

Avon turned to Cally, standing beside him. 'Did you get a job order with a work number?'

'No,' she said truthfully, her eyes darting between Avon and the guard. She couldn't see enough of the security guard in his booth be to able to tell if he was wearing a gun. Her empty right hand twitched, and she longed to be holding one herself.

Avon sighed impatiently and turned back to the guard. 'You can see the order is for the job to be done this afternoon.'

'I need a work number,' the guard repeated.

'It needs to be done today,' Avon said. 'Or else Industrial Copper won't be doing any trading tomorrow, and they won't be very pleased, especially big shareholders like Tory Pamson.'

The guard stroked a hand through his grey-streaked hair. 'Pamson has shares in that company?'

Avon had chosen his cover story carefully. His research into the finances of Greerson and his cronies had brought up many companies associated with members of the government. Tory Pamson was indeed a majority shareholder in Industrial Copper Ltd. He was also one of Greerson's allies, and the powerful Minister for Internal Security. As Avon had hoped, invoking his name was enough to make the security guard think twice.

'Pamson earns a lot of money through Industrial Copper,' Avon said. 'He's going to be very unhappy if that bug isn't fixed. If I don't get it right, it's my neck on the line. If I can blame someone by saying I wasn't allowed in for an hour, while I chased up a work number, then I will.' He showed his teeth in a smile that didn't reach his eyes.

'Right.' The security guard blinked rapidly as he tried to make a decision. He glanced again at the electronic notepad Avon held. 'You put your company and your name here.' He pushed forward his own e-pad and a stylus. 'Then I can say I've got your details if there's a problem.'

'That makes sense.' Avon put the name of the imaginary company on the work order and added the name on his fake ID. He handed the device back through the window of the security booth.

The guard scanned it quickly, then opened the barrier. 'Up one level, turn left, fifth room along the corridor, on the right-hand side.'

Avon nodded. 'Thank you.' He led the way deeper into the building, Cally following, her eyes alert for trouble.

SIX

They took one of the smooth, spacious lifts but before they followed the cross corridor to the left, they stopped at the window overlooking the trading floor. This was on ground level, beyond the lifts. It was a massive room in the centre of the building, inhabiting the space created between the two, high ends of the roof. The curved ceiling sloped down at either side.

From their vantage point, Avon and Cally could see most of the large room, which was undivided by pillars or walls. Electronic boards mounted on the side walls, and hanging from the ceiling, displayed current prices for shares and other commodities. There were dozens of workstations, each attended by a neatly dressed person who spoke into a headset. Sound-damping fields around each workstation kept the room quiet, in spite of the activity happening within.

Avon and Cally watched the business going on for a minute or so. Cally was the first to lose interest, having little idea what was happening. She turned away, heading to the left, as they had been told. Avon followed, his saturnine face thoughtful.

'Do we want the fifth room?' Cally asked quietly. 'Or would another be better?'

'Are any of the others empty?' Avon asked in return. 'What can you feel?'

He waited in the centre of the corridor as Cally approached each door in turn. She paused outside each one, stretching out with her sixth sense to get an idea of the number of people within. This tactic wouldn't work on Auron of course. Auronar were far more likely to notice her eavesdropping than these silent-minded humans. She couldn't pick up more than vague emotions from these strangers, but there was enough to give her a rough idea of numbers. She headed back to join Avon.

'The rooms are all occupied,' she reported quietly. 'But there's one room with only a single individual. I can deal with them.'

'Go ahead,' Avon said, holding out his left hand by way of invitation.

Cally nodded once, spun, and returned to the door with only one presence behind it. Avon followed, unfastening his black coat for easier access to his handgun. Cally didn't bother undoing the fake-fur coat, she just shoved the roll of tools into one pocket.

Wait here, she telepathed to Avon.

His eyes widened slightly at the still unfamiliar contact. Cally tapped the door control. It slid open, and she walked through briskly. Avon caught a snatch of conversation as the door slid shut.

'Hello. Random inspection of workplace facilities.'

'Workplace facilities? What...'

The rest of the other woman's reply was cut off by the closing door.

Avon glanced up and down the corridor, hearing a burst of laughter from one of the other rooms. He frowned briefly, wondering what could be funny in the computer rooms of a financial institution. Then there was a grunt and a soft thud from the room Cally had entered. He stiffened, his hand darting towards the gun under his coat.

It's all right. Cally's silent voice reached him. *Come in.*

He hit the control and slipped through the door, his eyes searching to find out what had happened.

Cally knelt near a bank of monitors, a youngish woman motionless on the floor by her side. As Avon entered, Cally began examining the unconscious woman. He hurried over and knelt beside her, his hands gently touching the woman as she lay on the floor. There was no obvious sign of injury.

'She's stunned,' Cally told him. 'It'll keep her quiet for a while.'

'Good. Let's get her out of sight.'

Avon helped Cally to drag the woman behind some workstations, so she wouldn't be visible from the door, and left her to tie the woman up, while he started work.

With his black coat hung up, Avon opened the roll of tools Cally had carried in for him, and selected a long probe. Fortunately, the woman had been working at one of the terminals and was still logged in, which saved him some time. Avon swiftly inserted the probe into a connector to start accessing the programs within.

Cally quickly had her victim bound and gagged. She too took off her coat, wanting to look the part of a worker who had every right to be there. Like Avon, she retained her gun and belt though: she wanted immediate access to a weapon, and the gun wouldn't always be immediately visible to a casual glance. She glanced once at Avon, already absorbed in his work, then began prowling around the room. The walls were lined with computers, their lights glowing and blinking in patterns that made little sense to her. The centre of the room was taken up with two banks of workstations and terminals. Avon was sitting with his back to the door. Their prisoner was on the far side of the same set of computers.

As the minutes passed, Cally too began to study the data flows on a monitor, trying to understand the information. It seemed to be a slowly scrolling list of companies, and their value, but so much was in abbreviations that it was hard for her to make sense of it. Avon had taken off a panel and was peering inside, occasionally adjusting something and glancing back at his monitor to see the effects of his work. The memory cube he had prepared with his program was set into a slot beside the keyboard he was using. Cally wanted to ask how long he was going to take, but held her silence. Talking would only slow him down.

Cally had risen again, when there was a tap at the door. Avon looked up, but Cally was already on her way to answer. She had her hand on her gun as she let the door slide partway open, and peered around. A young woman in a smart outfit peered back at her, puzzled.

'I was looking for Bel,' she explained, leaning in and trying to see more of the room. 'Is she in here? She should be.'

'She reported a fault in the system,' Cally lied. 'There was nothing else she could do today, so she went home.'

The young woman stared at Avon. 'She didn't stop and say anything to me about leaving early,' she complained. 'We were going to go out for a drink after work.'

'I don't know where she's gone,' Cally started to say, getting irritable at the interference.

Her words were interrupted by a thudding, and muffled cries from the far side of the room. Avon looked up sharply, suddenly alert. The young woman pressed against the gap in the doorway.

'What's that? It sounds like someone's hurt.'

'Come in,' Cally said, stepping aside and letting the door open.

The woman entered, turning to where the noises were coming from. Cally hit the control to close the door.

'Bel? Is that you?' The visitor sounded doubtful, and glanced at Avon in hope of getting an explanation.

A quick stride brought Cally close enough to land a hard blow on the back of the woman's head. The visitor gave a feeble cry and slumped forward. Avon jumped from his seat to catch her.

'Help me,' he snapped to Cally.

Together, they carried the semi-conscious woman behind the other set of computers, and lowered her to the thin carpet on the floor. Avon stared at her for a moment, then turned to face Bel, still tied up and gagged, but now conscious.

'That's what your efforts brought,' he said harshly, as Cally began tying up the second prisoner. He rose briefly to stand over Bel. 'By drawing attention to yourself, all you did was to get your friend into trouble. It's better not to have friends,' he told the motionless and frightened woman. 'That way, you won't try to help them, and you won't get hurt.'

'If you don't have friends, no-one will try to help you when you need it,' said Cally, shocked by his words.

'If you don't have friends, you're less likely to need help in the first place,' Avon told her coldly. He made his way back to his workstation and sat down again. 'Next time you take a prisoner, make sure they can't do stupid things,' he said.

Cally bristled. 'How much longer are you going to be?'

'Another three minutes,' he replied. 'The security on these computers is very high, so it's taken me ten minutes to get into the system. It would have taken another engineer twenty minutes,' Avon added. 'Assuming they were good enough to do it at all.'

'I'll start believing in how good you are when your program has done all you say it will,' Cally retorted.

'It will,' Avon growled. He returned to his work with sharp movements.

It seemed longer than three minutes to Cally. Eventually, Avon's memory cube began to flash. She tensed for a moment, then remembered that this was simply a signal to say to data was fully downloaded. Avon removed the cube and his probes, and began to reattach the panel he had removed.

'Everything is good?' Cally asked abruptly.

Avon nodded, looking self-satisfied. 'My program is in the computer system. When we're ready, I can activate it using a remote control.' He finished snapping the panel catches into place. 'I'll activate it five minutes after we've left this building. I'd rather leave it longer, so we're well away when the selling programs are triggered and the collapse happens, but if we wait too long, that pair...' he gestured towards the women. '...will have a chance to raise the alarm.'

Cally stepped between the banks of workstations and looked at the two women. 'These two aren't going to move for a while.'

'Good.' Avon rolled up the set of probes, and rose to put his coat on again.

Cally followed his example, shrugging the spotted coat on over her holstered gun.

They both looked around the room, to check that everything seemed fine, before leaving. The security guard at reception seemed surprised to see them again so soon. Avon told him brusquely that their job was complete and walked past.

'If there's any complaints about our work, they'll be directed at our company, not at you,' Cally added, a touch patronisingly as she made her way through the security barrier too.

'I'm not worried about *my* job,' the security guard called.

He will be, soon, Cally telepathed silently to Avon.

Avon didn't say anything, but dark humour glinted in his eyes for a few moments.

Once outside, they crossed the street and began to walk through the financial district. Avon glanced at his chronometer.

'Blake should be back very soon,' he said. He fished the conspicuous teleport bracelet out from a coat pocket and slipped it on.

Cally was already wearing hers. 'Are you going to activate the program now?'

Avon produced a small, black device from an internal pocket. A pinpoint light glowed steadily green. Below it, a clear plastic flap covered a recessed button that was the only control. 'I'll wait another couple of minutes,' he said, lowering the control box and picking up his pace again.

It had been a greyish day, and the light was beginning to fade from the sky. Already, advertisements and windows were noticeably brighter than their surroundings, and the white streetlights had come on. People were starting to leave their workplaces, filling the pavements and clustering at public transit stops. The roads were busy with vehicles. As well as private vehicles, there were public ones, goods carriers, hire vehicles, tradesmen's vans and a few vehicles belonging to the various public services. Altogether, there was a busy stream of an endless and colourful variety going past at a steady speed on the flat roads of Belzanko.

With the early evening traffic around them, neither Avon nor Cally noticed the public security vehicle until it switched its warning lights on, and cut across the lanes of traffic to approach them. As its siren gave a brief call, Cally was the first to spin around, her left hand reaching for the fastenings of her furry jacket.

'Do not move!' blared an amplified voice.

Around them, civilians were either freezing, or panicking, some shouting in fear or anger. As Avon glanced about, looking for a bolthole, Cally acted. She swiftly drew her gun and blasted the windscreen of the vehicle. As it pulled sharply to one side, she calmly shot up the engine compartment. People on the pavement screamed and fled. Avon opened fire too. For a few seconds they stood side by side and rained gunfire into the vehicle. Windows shattered, smoke plumed out, and finally, an explosion shook the stranded vehicle where it had stopped in the street. The people inside had no chance to return fire.

Cally was the first to stop shooting. She slammed her handgun back into its holster.

'Run!' she said abruptly.

Avon turned with her, and they fled among the shocked civilians of Belzanko.

Blake drummed his fingers on the teleport console. There was no-one in the teleport bay with him to comment on the display of nervous energy. Jenna was piloting the ship, and after her masterful display in the asteroid belt, Blake knew he could leave things in her capable hands. Vila and Gan were on the flight deck with her, both happy to follow her commands as they made a fast approach to the planet.

'Scanners are clear at the moment.' Gan's voice came over the intercom.

'Keep listening for messages from the ground,' Jenna warned.

The *Liberator* was coming in to pick up Avon and Cally. Blake was on standby to operate the teleport when they got a signal. He was watching the signal locator, between listening to the conversation from the flight deck and responding occasionally.

'We're within range of the planet's sensors,' Vila reported, sounding as though he'd rather be elsewhere.

'We can outfly any of the pursuit ships,' Blake reassured him, looking up from the displays.

'And outfight them,' Gan added, his voice made slightly tinny by the intercom.

'So there's nothing to worry about,' Blake answered.

Silence fell for two minutes as they swept in fast towards Belzanko. There was no feeling of movement in the teleport room, but the strategy had been agreed on during the flight back from the outer reaches of the solar system. Blake had no reason to doubt that Jenna was following their plan. Gan's voice suddenly broke the silence.

'I'm picking up signals from Belzanko.' He sounded urgent, but not frightened. 'They've spotted us and I think they're scrambling ships to intercept.'

'Holding course,' replied Jenna coolly. 'We should be over the capital by the time they get pursuit ships in the air.'

'Just so long as we get Avon and Cally quickly and can get away again,' Vila fretted.

'We could always try to slow them down by throwing you out of an airlock,' Jenna told him.

'You need me to fire the neutron blasters!' Vila objected, his voice rising.

'Your body wouldn't slow them down much anyway,' Gan said.

Blake grinned to himself as he continued to study the teleport locator. He could just imagine Vila's expression of hurt indignation.

'We need to get off the main streets,' said Cally, as they hurried between people.

'We've got to keep out of sight until Blake arrives,' Avon said. 'Preferably without drawing any more attention to ourselves,' he added witheringly.

Cally shot him an irritated look, but didn't bother wasting breath on a reply.

She passed a wide junction and began to angle towards a narrower street a block ahead. When they were out of the main pedestrian flow, Avon slowed to take the transmitter from his pocket. Holding it unobtrusively in one hand, he used his thumb to lift the clear flap, then to press the button. He grinned at Cally with black humour.

'Such a simple act to bring down a man's little empire,' he remarked.

She didn't smile at all. 'There's still work to be done here.'

Avon nodded. 'We have to avoid getting caught.'

Cally's expression turned even sourer, but before she could reply, a new engine sound became clear from very close by.

As she looked around, Avon looked up.

'A cloudskipper!' he warned.

The flier came into view above the roofline as he finished speaking. It was black and angular, spiked with sensors, lights and weapons. Engines mounted in manoeuvrable side pods could be turned to allow quicker turns and fine control in tight spaces, which made it a popular choice of flier for security forces operating in cities. The cloudskipper fired a shot into their street as it passed over, already turning in the air. The energy bolt missed Avon and Cally by some distance, blowing a hole in the road. Debris scattered into the air and vehicles swerved crazily as it rained back down again.

Avon swore, but followed Cally as they started running.

'Get to a busier area!' he shouted.

She nodded to show she understood, saving her breath for running. The security forces would be less likely to shoot into an area packed with civilians. The ominous sound of the cloudskipper's engines grew louder somewhere behind them. The fleeing pair swerved across the narrow street, darting between the vehicles stopped in the road.

Another energy bolt, a wilder shot, struck a wall a short way up on the side where they'd been. Chunks of concrete tumbled to the pavement, leaving a hole in the building.

They fled along the road, heading for a junction into a busier street. Some of the people around them stopped and looked for the cloudskipper, some ducked out of the way. No-one tried to stop them as they ran. They dashed out the far end of the small road and onto the main one. Cally narrowly missed colliding with a smartly-dressed woman, who reprimanded her sharply. Apologising breathlessly, Cally hurried off between the people on the pavement, following Avon as he wove through gaps in the crowds.

SEVEN

The thrum of the cloudskipper's engines grew loud again. Cally was following in Avon's wake as he shouldered his way fiercely through the pedestrians. Avon raised the arm with the teleport bracelet, triggering the comm button with his other hand.

'Blake? Blake! If you can hear me, pick us up immediately.' Avon couldn't keep the urgency from his voice.

There was no answer. Avon lowered his arms to move more freely.

'Blake said twenty hours,' Cally said. 'They'll be in range soon.'

'They'd better be,' Avon snapped.

He turned to check the position of the cloudskipper. The ominous black shape hung low in the sky, orienting itself towards them. Cally gasped as she saw the guns track them. She darted sideways, almost into the traffic, Avon half a pace behind her. Lightning flickered from the cloudskipper's guns. The energy bolt struck past them, among the unsuspecting civilians. There were screams of fear and agony and a sudden, awful smell of burnt meat.

Neither Avon nor Cally stopped to look. As the cloudskipper was heading along the street towards them, Cally raced back towards it. Close to, they were harder for the security men on board to see when almost underneath, and the guns couldn't reach them. As they ran, the cloudskipper fired another energy bolt. It passed over their heads, close enough for them to feel the heat, and struck the people behind them.

'We've got to get away from the civilians,' Cally shouted.

Avon didn't answer, but his shock and disgust were clear in his eyes.

Cally darted into the road, among the traffic. Vehicles were already swerving and halting at random, adding to the confusion. Avon went with her. A blue carrier slammed to a halt half a metre from him, making him dodge sideways. He bounced off the rear of a smaller vehicle and staggered to catch his balance. His heart pounding, he lurched towards a gap while Cally ran, as graceful as a wild deer. All the time, the cloudskipper was turning to bring its guns to bear on them. Avon heard the high-pitched hum of its weapons building up to fire again, barely audible over the chaos of noise around him.

He changed direction abruptly, throwing himself into the space between two high-sided carriers. A moment later, an energy bolt struck the space where he'd been. One of the carriers rocked violently under the impact. The explosion was deafening in the narrow space.

To the right. Cally's instruction was clear in his mind.

Avon went the way she told him, skidding slightly on the smooth road surface. Recovering his balance, he shot between two more vehicles and onto the pavement. Pedestrians scattered out of his way. Avon caught a glimpse of the spotted fur coat and raced after it. Above them, the cloudskipper was turning. Momentum carried it further away as the engines adjusted direction, giving Avon and Cally enough time to get off the main road.

They ran into a narrower street, bounded mainly by office blocks, with a couple of cafés breaking the ranks of monotonous frontages. There were vehicles and pedestrians here too, but fewer than on the main street. Already, some of the people were ducking back into buildings or hurrying away from the explosions they'd heard from the main street. There was more space for Avon and Cally to run, their steps loud in the enclosed space. The sound of the cloudskipper ebbed at first, but grew louder as it made its turn and pursued them.

'This side,' gasped Avon, crossing to the side of the street the cloudskipper was approaching from.

Cally darted sideways too, dodging a two-wheeled vehicle. They were in the lee of an office building, hidden from the approaching cloudskipper until it was right over them. Cally stopped dead, drawing her handgun and raising it with both hands.

'That won't bring it down,' Avon snapped.

'I can damage it,' Cally replied. 'Slow it down.'

They saw the lights of the cloudskipper before the predatory black vehicle itself came into view overhead. Aiming, with a look of fierce concentration, Cally fired two shots at one of the engine pods. Sparks flew as smoke plumed out. The cloudskipper started to turn, but the damaged side pod wouldn't move properly. The turn was wider and more jerky than before.

'Nice shooting.' Avon was grudgingly impressed.

They started running again, crossing the street diagonally in the same direction that the cloudskipper was moving, to once again be in the lee of the buildings. Over the thrum of its engines burst the piercing wail of sirens. Street vehicles were on their trail too, and not very far away. As they ran, Avon tried calling for help once more.

'Blake, where are you? We need pick-up right now!'

There was still no answer from the bracelet's communicator. Avon swore, between gasps for breath.

'Down here,' Cally said briefly, as she nipped into a narrow alley.

Avon was less graceful as he made the sudden turn, bouncing off the wall as he entered. He quickly recovered his balance and raced after Cally. Another blast from the cloudskipper struck the middle of the street they'd just left.

'This is too narrow,' Avon shouted. 'There's nowhere to dodge when they get that thing lined up on us.'

'It opens up ahead,' Cally answered, her curly hair bobbing as she ran.

There were no doors opening into the alley, so with nowhere else to go, Avon followed her. The alley gave into a small yard, bounded by buildings. Cally jinked to her left as she entered, staying close to the wall. The sirens sounded closer and the thrum of the cloudskipper's engines was getting louder. Avon moved the other way, drawing his gun as he looked about. There were no other open exits from the yard. Large gates for vehicles on the far side were closed, and had a security lock. The only other ways in and out were service doors in the buildings surrounding the yard. Avon hastily tried the nearest door, but that was locked. Cally ran to the door nearest her position and slammed her hand on the control panel. It didn't move.

She turned her back to the wall and looked up, towards the sound of the cloudskipper, her gun in her hands.

'Can you get one open?' she called desperately.

'Cover me.' Avon slapped his gun back into its holster and pulled out the gadget he'd made with Vila's help. He didn't know if it would work on this lock, but there was no point in saying so to Cally. His spine crawled as he bent to deal with the lock, turning his back on their attackers.

Cally moved sideways to join him, her eyes searching the sky.

The wailing sirens got closer still and stayed in place, the sound magnified by the narrow alley.

The lights of the cloudskipper flared at the roof edge, giving Cally a few moments' warning of its position before the flier itself came into view. She raised her gun and aimed at the spot where it would appear. Behind her, Avon took a deep breath, keeping his emotions tightly under control. His concentration on the lock was absolute as he made minute adjustments to the dials. The rippling blast of Cally's gun made him start. Looking grimmer than ever, he refocused on the job, but precious moments had been lost. Heavy bootsteps pounded along the alley towards them. The cloudskipper's engines whined as it turned towards them. Cally didn't move, didn't run for cover. She stayed, guarding Avon as he fought with the lock. Her gun blasted again and once again as she fired at the deadly fighter above them. Its searchlights swept dazzlingly across the yard as it turned.

Dodge when I tell you! Cally's silent voice was loud in Avon's mind over the noise of the flier and the sirens.

His hand trembled at the telepathic touch, but he didn't stop working. Cally fired a single, sharp shot.

Now!

As Avon straightened up for the leap sideways, the teleport snatched them away to the sudden quiet of the *Liberator*.

'Sshh! I'm trying to listen.' Cally's complaint temporarily silenced Avon and Vila.

The crew were on the flight deck of the *Liberator*, gathered around a portable speaker on the table enclosed by the padded seats.

Twenty-five hours had passed since the *Liberator*'s quick dash through the planetary atmosphere to pick up Avon and Cally. Security forces on Belzanko had launched two pursuit ships but the *Liberator* had already been over the capital city before they left the ground.

Accelerating away from the planet, the huge spaceship had left the pursuit ships behind before they could get close enough to fire a single shot. Now they were in orbit around a standard gas giant, two out from Belzanko itself. The *Liberator*'s position was in sync with Belzanko's, so they always stayed on the side closest to that planet, regardless of the planet turning below them. At this distance, the *Liberator*'s presence would be almost impossible to distinguish from the mass of the gas giant.

The *Liberator*'s comms had been tuned to the distant output from Belzanko for hours. There were a few minutes' delay between broadcast and what the crew heard, but there was plenty of news being broadcast on the planet. Avon's program had begun selling shares before they were out of orbit. As computers sold bulk quantities from certain companies, other computers picked up the sudden sales. When a trigger point of sales was reached, they automatically began selling the same shares. Prices tumbled as shares were dumped in massive numbers. The money men panicked at the sudden losses in value, and followed where the computers led. As prices slumped into a sudden, sharp decline, the financial markets on Belzanko crashed.

Journalists were onto the story almost immediately. Some, sympathisers with the rebels, had been primed by Allston to look into the ownership of Belspin and certain other companies. Belzanko's computer networks were full of details of the shareholders in major companies who were affected, and President Greerson's name came up frequently, along with several of his allies. Greerson's financial dealings were swiftly becoming public knowledge.

Gan shook his head. 'I don't understand how this works. Someone starts selling so they all start selling? It doesn't make sense.'

'It's classic crowd behaviour,' Avon said disdainfully. His gaze fell on Blake briefly. 'They think someone is leading, so they follow without knowing what their leader's real motives are. They are content to let someone else do their thinking for them.'

Blake looked up at him, half-amused. 'Whereas individuals like you always do their own thinking?'

'Naturally.' Avon smiled.

'The point is that it's working,' Cally said. 'The media's been all over Greerson and he hasn't been able to silence them.'

'He's issued a denial of any wrongdoing,' Gan pointed out.

Jenna laughed. 'That's as good as an admission of guilt, coming from a politician.'

'More importantly,' Blake said, leaning forward. 'He can't afford to silence the news any more. They all know that he hasn't got the money to pay them, and that his position is very weak.' His eyes were bright with triumph. 'He doesn't scare them any more.'

Cally had been listening to the broadcasts, rather than the conversation. 'Two of his senators have resigned, and the senator for health has just condemned Greerson publicly.'

'Hoping to save his own neck,' Vila guessed. He took a sip from a glass of pink, syrupy liquid and sighed in satisfaction.

... have called for President Greerson to be arrested on charges of corruption. There has been no official reply from the President, but Senator Jasson has just demanded a no-confidence vote. Reports from Government House indicate fierce debate during this emergency session.

The *Liberator* crew listened to the report attentively. Events on Belzanko were moving fast and it seemed clear that President Greerson's control was crumbling.

'This is what happens when dictators hit trouble,' Blake said with satisfaction. 'The more you oppress people, the faster they rise up as soon as they have a chance.'

'And we helped give them that chance,' Cally said, looking at him.

'It's still only a chance, though,' Avon remarked. He straightened up and folded his arms. 'Nature abhors a vacuum. When one dictator leaves a space, you often find another dictator rushing to fill it.'

Cally twisted around to look up at him. 'Allston's ready to move in.'

Avon just shrugged. 'And I'm sure he'll be fine.' He sounded utterly uninterested. 'There's no point in us going back and supporting him.'

Gan looked at Blake. 'It's very chaotic down there. Do you think there will be real change, or will some other tyrant seize power?'

'It's up to the rebels.' Avon answered him first. 'We've given them a chance.'

Vila nodded. 'We've done our best. I mean, there's only six of us after all. I'd like to help out, you know I would, but there's only so much we can do.'

'Very little indeed, if you're the one doing it,' sniped Avon.

Blake looked thoughtful. 'I promised to help the rebellion on Belzanko.'

'Which we have,' Avon pointed out.

'But as Gan says, there's no point in just swapping one dictator for another,' Blake continued. 'It's not just the future of Belzanko that's at stake. We need to achieve a clean victory here so we can gain the trust of rebel groups on other planets.' His head lifted as he spoke with increasing emphasis and certainty. 'Our goal is to bring down the Federation and this is the first step. We *have* to get it right.'

'So you want to go back to Belzanko then?' Jenna asked, her expression reserved.

'Yes.' Blake's answer was decisive.

'But what can we do?' Vila gestured vaguely with the hand that was holding his luridly-coloured drink.

'That depends on the situation when we get there,' Blake told him, standing up briskly. He turned to face Zen. 'Zen, take us back to Belzanko, speed Standard by four.'

'CONFIRMED.' Lights flashed on Zen's mottled fascia as the computer silently issued commands to the navigation computers.

There was a momentary gleam of triumph on Avon's face. It vanished so fast that Jenna half-wondered if she'd imagined it.

'Call me when you know what it is we're going to do for the good people of Belzanko,' Avon said, turning away.

Jenna watched thoughtfully as he left the flight deck.

As the *Liberator* approached Belzanko, Jenna was waiting impatiently outside the door to Avon's quarters. When he opened it, Jenna walked straight in without waiting for an invitation. Avon backed up a couple of spaces and looked at her with an expression of mild curiosity. He'd found a new tunic to wear, in dark blue-grey with exaggerated shoulders edged with a broad, paler stripes. It made him physically more imposing, and the geometric design suited his angular personality.

Jenna registered the new clothes with one glance, then stared him straight in the eyes.

'Congratulations,' she said dryly.

'On choosing some new clothes?' Avon enquired.

Jenna shook her head. 'On the way you manipulated Blake into going back to the planet.'

Avon studied her for a moment, then broke into a smile. 'Why would I have done that?' he asked, raising his right hand slightly to point in her direction.

Jenna folded her arms as she faced him. 'You like money,' she stated. 'You got caught trying to embezzle millions of credits from the Federation banking system. You've just been interfering with Belzanko's financial system. I can't believe you did that without creating the opportunity to make some money for yourself. You need Blake to return so you can get at that money because you can't establish a secure and discreet link from this far out in the system.'

'People have lost fortunes on Belzanko,' Avon pointed out. 'They have not been making them.'

'Someone who's clever with money and computers, and knew that the crash was coming, could have made money somehow,' Jenna insisted.

'Why, I'm pleased to know you think so highly of my skills, if not my morals.' Avon's eyes sparkled with wicked humour.

'You're a self-confessed criminal, Avon. I've never had any doubts about your morals.'

'So says the convicted smuggler.'

Jenna refused to look abashed. 'So you don't deny that you've made money on this?'

'The *Liberator* has a strong room with millions of credits worth of various currencies,' Avon pointed out. 'Why would I wish to acquire more?'

'Because it would be your money alone,' Jenna answered promptly. 'No-one else would know you had it, or how much you had. It would give you the freedom to leave Blake any time you wanted without the humiliation of having to ask him for a share of the *Liberator*'s money, or the trouble of stealing it, and being chased by Blake as well as the Federation.'

Avon smiled. 'From your prompt answer, I suspect that you have thought about the consequences of taking money from the *Liberator*, yourself.'

Jenna looked him in the eyes. 'Don't change the subject. You exploited the situation on Belzanko to make a fortune for yourself, didn't you?'

Avon shrugged. 'I kept my word. I helped Allston and exposed

Greerson for what he is. Why not take a reward? I'm not taking money from the resistance.'

'I don't think Blake will like it. He'll probably insist that the money goes to help the rebellion.'

'Blake doesn't need to know.'

'And what will you do with the money?' Jenna asked, confronting him directly. 'Is there enough for you to leave and set up somewhere on your own?'

Avon's expression remained carefully neutral. 'I don't know how much there is.'

Jenna studied him a moment, then lifted her chin as she spoke. 'I think I should tell Blake about this.' She turned towards the door.

'Blake doesn't need to know,' Avon repeated, following her. 'I'm sure we could come to some mutually agreeable arrangement on that.'

When Jenna turned back, he was standing right in front her. She tilted her head back to look him straight in the face.

'Are you offering me a bribe for my silence?'

'If you want to call it that. It could be millions of credits.' Avon's voice dropped as he enticed her.

Jenna continued to stare at him. The silence was interrupted by Blake's voice coming from the comm on the cabin wall.

'Jenna? Where are you? We're approaching orbit and we need you on the flight deck, please.'

Jenna turned and pressed the button to answer. 'I'm on my way.'

She spared Avon a brief, enigmatic glance, and left.

EIGHT

Everyone else was already on the flight deck when Avon arrived, a few minutes later. Jenna was at her station and kept her eyes on the displays as Avon jogged down the steps onto the deck. Vila, Gan and Cally were also at their posts, alert for any sign that they had been spotted as they approached the planet.

'I was just about to ask you to come,' Blake said, moving towards him.

'Well, I'm here,' Avon replied succinctly, sliding into his seat. 'And keen to find out how exactly you are planning to help Belzanko's resistance.'

'That's not why I wanted to speak to you.' Blake moved alongside him, his hands on his hips. 'Is it true that you've managed to make millions of credits for yourself while you were manipulating the stock markets?'

'Millions!' Vila interrupted, looking across at Jenna. 'You didn't tell the rest of us it was millions!'

'Oh, Avon never does things by halves,' Blake said, keeping his eyes on Avon's face. 'Especially when it comes to money.'

'That's why you wanted to stay longer on Belzanko, isn't it?' Cally accused Avon. 'It wasn't just about getting the data on the ships. You had a plan for bankrupting Greerson whilst making yourself a profit on the side, and you needed time to develop your more complicated program and to insert it into Belzanko's financial system.'

'And you weren't going to tell the rest of us about it, either,' Jenna added.

Avon neither denied nor confirmed their accusations. He simply looked at Blake.

'If I were to profit from the situation on Belzanko, why should it be any concern of yours?' he asked coolly.

'Because we're a team,' Blake insisted. 'We live together and we work together. We agreed to share the wealth that's on this ship.'

'If I had earned myself a sufficient fortune, I could take that when I go, and leave everything we found here with you,' Avon said. 'You would lose nothing.'

'I'd lose you,' Blake replied.

'That would be your loss, not mine.'

'You'd lose something too.' Blake fixed Avon with an intense look. 'You'd lose the chance to fight the Federation and their corruption, to take revenge on the system.'

'I'd rather just forget about the Federation and spend the rest of my life on a neutral planet, so wealthy that no-one could touch me.'

Blake shook his head slowly. 'You'd be bored within a year, Avon. And you'd regret leaving us and losing your chance to be part of history.'

Avon didn't answer immediately, but his dark eyes briefly turned vulnerable. Then the shutters came down and he was brittle once again.

'I'm not after glory, Blake. That's your path.'

Blake was about to reply when Zen interrupted.

'*LIBERATOR* IS RECEIVING A MESSAGE FROM THE PLANET.'

Blake turned away and spoke as he moved forward. 'Put it on visual, please.'

Everyone's attention was diverted to the main screen as an image blossomed on the fascia. It was Anwar Allston, standing in an office. Sunlight flooded through a window behind him and sparkled on his silver hair. He smiled as he saw the *Liberator*'s crew.

'It's good to see you all.'

'And you,' Blake answered. 'What's the situation on the ground?'

Allston smiled, radiating confidence and charisma. 'Better than we'd ever hoped for, thanks to you and your crew. Greerson and half a dozen of his closest political allies have been arrested on charges of corruption. The media have already convicted him, even the ones he used to bribe and threaten into silence. In fact, they're the most strongly against him now.'

'If he's going down, they don't want to be associated with him,' Blake commented.

Allston nodded, and cracked his knuckles in emphasis. 'There's a no-confidence vote on the government tonight, and there's no way Greerson's cronies will survive it. There'll be elections for a new government and Belzanko's ready for change.'

'You'll be getting involved in the elections?' Blake asked eagerly.

'Of course. We should be able to make a good job of it, thanks to that donation you just sent to us.'

Blake's eyes widened, but he thought fast. 'It just got to you?'

Allston smiled. 'Just in the last few minutes.' His smile grew broader. 'Millions of credits. It was a brilliant idea, Blake, taking advantage of the financial crash to make money.' Allston laughed. 'It's such sweet justice to be using the money lost by Greerson and his friends against them. It's money that should have been in the pockets of other people, and now it is.'

Blake chuckled too. 'I can't think of a better use for it.'

'And all thanks to you and your people,' Allston said. He turned his gaze to Avon. 'You especially, Avon. You'd be welcome here on Belzanko any time.'

'I shall keep your offer in mind,' Avon said graciously.

'It sounds as though you've got things under control,' Blake said.

'Yes.' Allston glanced to one side and raised a hand in a gesture to someone offscreen. 'I'll be even busier from now on, I suspect.'

'Then I'd better let you get on with it,' Blake said. 'We've got plenty of business elsewhere, but we'll come back and help if necessary.'

'Thank you.' Allston's expression turned sober. 'Belzanko won't be producing any more pursuit ships for the Federation, but we'll have a fleet of our own to defend ourselves with. We'll need it so long as the Federation exists.'

'They can't last forever,' Blake said with conviction. 'I'm going to do what I can to bring them down.'

'With the resources you've got, you can do a lot of good in the galaxy,' Allston said. 'The best of luck to you.'

'And to you.'

Allston said his farewells and the screen went dark again.

The *Liberator* crew came down from their stations and began to relax. Blake ordered Zen to set course for Centero as Vila flopped down on the comfortable seats.

'Another day, another planet saved,' Vila quipped. 'We should celebrate. How about a drink?'

No-one took any notice of him. Avon came right up to Blake and looked at him challengingly.

'I think even Vila could guess that it wasn't you who made that generous donation to Allston.'

Blake looked straight back at him. 'I apologise, Avon. You did a very generous thing, helping Allston out.'

'He only did it because he was found out,' Jenna said decidedly. She had moved round the seats and was in front of the main screen.

Cally joined her. 'That's true, isn't it?' she demanded. 'If Jenna hadn't realised what you were up to, you'd have kept all that money for yourself. Instead, you've used it to buy your way into Allston's favour.'

Avon looked amused, but didn't deny the accusations.

Blake frowned. 'We're only going to survive if we work together as a team,' he said to Avon. 'We can't keep acting as individuals.'

Avon gestured at the two women standing together. 'I have helped you two find something in common. Neither of you trusts me.'

Jenna glanced at Cally, then looked back at Avon. 'Oh, we do, Avon. We trust you to think of yourself first.'

Avon smiled, and with a nod to Blake, left the flight deck.

BERSERKER

RA HENDERSON

ONE
UNFINISHED BUSINESS

A little way outside the range of the nearest planet's detection systems, the *Liberator* hung in space, completely inert, as if waiting for something to happen.

On the flight deck, Roj Blake's concentration was completely focused on the data pad in his hand, and had been for some time.

'Zen,' he said. 'Patch this into the main viewer.'

'CONFIRMED.'

Blake looked up at the viewscreen and watched with the other crew members as the picture of space dissolved and was replaced by a three-dimensional computer-generated image. It was a huge grey object, oblong with a vaguely trident-shaped rear end.

'Station Amber,' said Blake, gesturing at the screen.

'We've actually found it.' Cally sounded surprised.

'*Zen* has,' corrected Avon.

'I was rather hoping we wouldn't,' muttered Vila.

Station Amber was one of Servalan's pet projects. It specialised in advanced weapons development, and she seemed to enjoy boasting about the advances they were making. Until just over six months ago, she'd mentioned the station in almost every speech she broadcast. Then, suddenly, and with no explanation, she'd stopped. The station and its full complement of personnel vanished overnight. There was an instant media blackout. Even friends and families of station staff could only repeat the official explanation: that a design fault in the station had created a safety hazard and the station had been fully evacuated, its staff transferred to other projects with no access to communication facilities.

'So they towed it here,' said Gan.

'Yes.' Blake nodded to the screen. 'This sector of Federation space is off-limits to virtually everybody. If it hadn't been for the *Liberator*'s superior speed and Jenna's piloting skills we'd have been shot down before we even reached the cordon.'

Jenna acknowledged the praise with a small smile.

'Zen,' Blake called. 'Life form and environment status of the space station directly ahead.'

'NO LIFE FORMS PRESENT,' Zen answered. 'RADIATION NIL. AIRBORNE TOXINS NIL. LIFE SUPPORT SYSTEM STILL IN OPERATION. OXYGEN CONTENT IN MOST AREAS AT SAFE LEVELS. AMBIENT TEMPERATURE WITHIN HUMAN TOLERANCE. INTERNAL DEFENCE AND SECURITY SYSTEMS DEACTIVATED.'

'So the station's not *completely* shut down,' said Jenna. 'Curious.'

'It's what I suspected,' Blake said. 'Servalan announced the development of a weapon that could wipe out all resistance on the fringe planets before the station disappeared.' He looked round at the assembled crew. 'That's not something she's just going to give up on. I think something happened to prevent the weapon's completion. But Servalan doesn't let go of things easily. The station is still functioning because at some point she plans to come back for it.'

'Unless we get it first,' Gan said.

Jenna looked at the dark object on the viewscreen. 'We could go across, I suppose,' she said.

'You *suppose?*' mimicked Vila. 'That sounds dangerous!'

'So was getting here in one piece, but we made it,' said Blake. 'Everything in life is dangerous. Even having a meal – if you take into consideration choking.'

'I'll never eat again,' Vila said, rolling his eyes.

'You heard Zen,' said Cally. 'The station is safe. There's nobody there and the internal security systems have been disabled.'

'But what about whatever got the station shut down in the first place?' Vila said. 'We don't even know what that was.'

He looked at Gan for back-up, but Gan just shrugged.

'It's worth a chance,' Gan said finally. 'Perhaps the station was moved out here to give the danger time to pass on its own.'

'That's a possibility,' Jenna agreed.

'We can check,' said Blake. 'Zen, scan for potential hazards giving priority to serious threats to human life.'

'THERE IS NO CLEAR AND PRESENT DANGER ON THE STATION,' said Zen.

'Just the kind that lurks quietly in the dark and creeps up on you so you don't notice until it's too late,' said Vila.

'I vote we go and look round,' said Jenna. 'Besides, we can't just head back now. We've come so far out that the power cells are only at one-third optimum capacity. That's enough for life support, but not for the force wall or weapons. We need time to recharge, or a power source that we can siphon off.'

'Well, that's very interesting,' said Avon darkly. 'In that case, there's one other thing we need to factor in.' He looked up from the screen he'd been fiddling with. 'Did anyone know that we're being tracked by three Federation pursuit ships?'

TWO
VARIOUS PURSUITS

Drav Cashlan took two pins out of the silken fabric that hung from Supreme Commander Servalan's new dress and lifted them to his mouth. There were already pins clenched between his teeth, so he handed the surplus to his assistant, Keelian.

Cashlan smiled ingratiatingly at his prized customer. 'Now hold still please, my dear,' he twittered in a sing-song voice.

Normally Servalan was nobody's 'dear' but Cashlan was an excellent tailor and dressmaker, one of Earth's professional elite. She could just about tolerate his informality and affectionate *joie de vivre* for the sake of the fabulous dresses he made for her. Servalan liked dresses made the old-fashioned way – every stitch, every measurement made by a human being rather than a machine. There were not many people who could afford this luxury.

It was her third fitting in Cashlan's studio for this particular dress: silver for a change, shiny and eye-catching, full-length as was her usual preference, but with a slightly flared hem to make walking comfortable, and cut generously around the upper chest area to reveal a flattering cleavage. Servalan was Supreme Commander. She was tough, ruthless, confident and strong – a leader, a climber, a vertebra in the backbone of the Federation. But she was also a woman who knew the importance of a well-cut dress.

At this moment, Servalan wanted a lot of things. She wanted Roj Blake's head delivered to her by hand on a silver tray with the eyes removed and accompanied by a glass of rich, red wine. She wanted Travis to stop making excuses and do his job. She wanted the *Liberator*. She wanted this fitting to be over and Cashlan to be far, far away.

She looked at Keelian, who stood meekly beside him, quietly doing her job. She approved of this new girl. She knew that the assistant wouldn't dare to use the words 'my dear'.

'Clean pins, Cashlan,' Servalan snapped. 'How many times have I told you not to put them in your mouth? *You* may find it convenient, but it's extremely unhygienic.'

'Of course, Madam,' Cashlan grinned unapologetically. 'Shan't happen again.' He threw the pins into a small disposal unit and put his hand out to receive more. 'Clean pins, Keelian.'

'It had better not,' Servalan said firmly, as Keelian obediently handed Cashlan the pins. 'I don't want my outfits to stand as examples of your oral care. Goodness knows what goes into that mouth besides dressmakers' pins.'

Cashlan was about to protest, but the door alert chimed. 'I wonder who that can be?' he declared.

Servalan's irritation was turning into anger. 'You did tell your staff you were not to be disturbed?' she asked.

'Of course!' blustered Cashlan. 'Keelian, go out and tell whoever it is that I'm extremely busy.'

The young girl trotted to the door and pushed the button to open it. When it slid away to reveal a man in Federation military guard uniform, Servalan made no attempt to suppress her groan of annoyance. This could only prolong the fitting.

'Sorry to interrupt you, Supreme Commander,' the guard announced curtly. His orders were, Servalan knew, to treat her with respect at all times but not to be soft with her. 'There's an emergency communication on the secure channel from Commander Travis.'

'Can't someone else deal with it?' she asked.

'It's a report, ma'am,' the guard explained, 'but it's locked to secure level fifteen. No-one below your rank can view it.'

A level fifteen communiqué from Travis? It sounded ominous. Clearly he'd locked the report at this level for a good reason. She dismissed the guard, then waved a hand at Keelian, who seemed to guess exactly what she wanted. The girl rushed forward with the silver box holding the clothes the Supreme Commander had been wearing when she'd arrived.

'Listen, Cashlan,' Servalan said. 'Don't lay another finger on that dress until I come back for the remainder of the fitting, is that clear?'

Cashlan gave the graceless theatrical bow of a hired sycophant. 'Of course, Madam.'

If Travis was just being melodramatic, she thought, her next dress would be made from his hide.

*

On board his ship, Travis was growing impatient. What could Servalan be doing all this time to keep her from answering his priority call? She would want to know about what he had just discovered. In fact when she finally returned to her office and read his hastily written report she would probably be angry with herself for procrastinating.

Blake was in Sector H of the Fringe Planets' Restriction Zone, a sealed-off area on the outskirts of Federation territory. The Restriction Zone was a dumping ground for failed projects, situated behind a tight military cordon. No-one was allowed to go there. No-one was even supposed to know it existed. Robot sentinels patrolled the cordon at all times, programmed to attack anything that moved. Yet somehow, the *Liberator* had outmanoeuvred them.

Travis had been tracking the rebels' ship for some time, and had been in pursuit since she left the vicinity of a small moon orbiting one of the fringe planets. The *Liberator* could move fast and she had been really pelting across space when he first picked her up. She was a long way in front but Travis had managed to project her course and knew that if he kept up he'd eventually close the gap. There were no other ships this far outside the populated areas of the galaxy, and certainly no craft for light years possessed the technology to commit such a sophisticated act of piracy. Travis wondered what Blake would want inside the cordon, though it wasn't difficult to work out an approximation of his plan. He was bound to have come here eventually. There were plenty of dangerous bits and pieces out here and a lot of the experiments related to weapons technology.

'We're approaching Sector H, Commander,' a mutoid helmsman reported. 'Sentinel L one-seven-fifty has issued a warning.'

Knowing he had only seconds to respond, Travis darted from his command chair to the helm console and punched the clearance code in. A short message of acceptance flashed on the screen and they passed through the inner cordon.

Travis returned to his seat. 'Computer link-up with all inner cordon sentinels.'

The mutoid obeyed. They always did, and that was one of the reasons why Travis always chose them rather than unmodified human crewmen.

'Sentinel R three-nine-twenty received a clearance signal on an unsecured frequency and admitted an unidentified craft three point six hours ago, Commander,' she reported.

'What are you up to, Blake?' Travis murmured quietly to himself. Blake wasn't the kind of man to choose targets according to whim; he was here for something specific. Which of the dangerous top-secret rejects was he after?

Then Travis looked at the long-range scanner and instantly knew.

Station Amber was one of the biggest and most complex space stations ever built. It was a dark grey hulk, long and rectangular with its aftersection divided up into three elongated blocks. It used to be called the Devil's Fork by some, and not just because of its shape. Travis called up the image and stared at the enormous trident on his screen.

He would need to update Servalan. If she ever got back to him.

INTERLUDE I
STATION AMBER, EIGHTEEN MONTHS AGO

'I've had enough, Servalan!' Ban Kerralin shouted, throwing his goggles on the tiled floor and cracking them.

'Supreme Commander,' Servalan corrected sharply.

'To hell with your formality,' snapped Kerralin. Hell was just an old word since the Federation abolished religion. It had no real meaning any more, but whatever it was, Servalan and her precious formalities could go there. 'You've perverted this entire project. I agreed to work on weapons that would pacify by way of remote neurological adjustment. Tissue vaporisation was *never* part of the plan. I'm dropping everything. I'm not going to do another stroke, do you hear? AE105 will never exist!'

'Oh, it will,' Servalan said coolly, not even slightly intimidated by Kerralin's ranting. 'You will do exactly as you are told. Otherwise, there will be consequences. Remember the reason you took this job in the first place? I do.'

Kerralin remembered. He had never been keen on Servalan or her ideas. He had even secretly cheered on the resistance whenever word reached him that they had struck a blow against her, but when he was offered the position on Station Amber as Head Consultant Weapons Technician he wasn't in much of a position to resist.

He'd worked in robotics and computer intelligence development on Earth and had saved every credit he made to fund the side project he was working on. It was his passion. The new type of android he was developing could, he felt certain, revolutionise the practical application of artificial intelligence to real-life situations. But no matter how hard he saved, he couldn't afford to get the project even one-eighth complete, and no-one was interested in investing in what they considered to be a fool's dream. Except for Servalan. While she wasn't interested in his side project, she *was* interested in the opportunity to exploit Kerralin's talent. She offered him the funding to work on his machine on top of his standard pay, as well as access to a fully equipped and technologically advanced laboratory. All he had to do was sign a contract to work on Station Amber for the next five years...

And now he was asking to break the contract.

'I didn't know what I was getting myself into,' he shouted. 'If I keep on, I'll be turning my back on everything I believe is right.'

Servalan perched her behind on the edge of a workstation, still smiling. Kerralin could see she was fully aware that her confidence made his blood boil. 'I think you have a great deal more than your "beliefs" to be concerned about right now,' she replied.

'My family?' Kerralin said.

'We shall see.'

'Shall we?' he asked bitterly. 'You told me they were under house arrest, but I have no way of knowing if they are unharmed. You are toying with me. Perhaps they are already dead.'

'Would you like to see them in person?' asked Servalan.

Kerralin barked out a short laugh. 'I know the Federation version of "in person" only too well: a screen between me and an empty room with a few holograms inside it. I told you, I'm not a fool.'

'You'll be allowed an hour alone with them. You may examine them to the full extent of your capacity for suspicion if you so wish.'

Kerralin was silent. His mind was reeling. Could his wife and daughters really still be alive? She seemed to be promising private personal contact, and he knew the Federation hadn't the technology to come up with anything sophisticated enough to trick him under such circumstances. After all, he was an expert, the best the Federation had. If the family he spent an hour alone with was artificial, he'd know in a second.

'Why?' he said finally. 'Why would you let me see them now?'

'So that you can see they are alive and well,' Servalan answered, 'and therefore still a viable proposition for torture and execution.'

'You really are a poisonous bitch, aren't you?' Kerralin hissed.

Servalan smiled almost sweetly. 'Oh yes,' she purred. 'Another of my self-given reputations.'

THREE
EVERY SECOND COUNTS

'Station Amber may have been completely shut down,' Blake said, 'but Zen assures me that it hasn't been *stripped* down. A tap on its generators will give us a sufficient jolt of power to get the cells to maximum in two or three hours. The pursuit ships are due to arrive in six hours. I'll go with Vila. I'm going to need his lock-picking skills.'

'Couldn't we just clear off?' whined Vila.

Jenna shook her head. 'With the power so low, our best speed would be Standard by two. Not nearly fast enough to outrun Travis.'

Vila groaned. 'So we either break into that station and take our chances in there, or sit here and wait for to be blown into atoms.'

'Which would you prefer?' Blake asked pointedly.

'I'll get my toolkit.'

'Bring an emergency air plug with you,' Blake called after him.

As Avon watched, the ends of his mouth curled into something that floated between a sneer and a smile. 'So how long have we got?' he asked.

'If we don't come up with a solution to our power problem in less than five hours, we won't have the time or speed to get away and we'll be defenceless,' said Blake.

'And whose fault is it that the power's drained?' Avon challenged. 'This sector is a long way out of our way, Blake and we've rushed here on a fool's errand.'

'I thought it would be worth it,' Blake said. 'I still do. Whatever's inside that station, it's going to be worth getting our hands on.'

'At the risk of all our lives?'

Gan and Cally appeared at the door to the flight deck in time to hear this. Blake didn't answer. Instead, he looked down the corridor they had come from. 'Vila's taking his time.'

'He was nervous when he passed me,' said Cally. 'On his way to his quarters.'

'Vila's always nervous,' Blake said. 'He should be fetching tools.'

'He was muttering something about that.'

'Good. Perhaps that means he's actually doing it.'

At that moment, Vila appeared at the end of the corridor, carrying the heavy-duty box that contained his best breaking-and-entering gear.

'I've got everything I need,' he told Blake with confidence. The only confidence he had was in his indisputable talent for thievery, Blake thought. 'Shall we teleport?'

Blake couldn't help but smile. 'I'm afraid we won't be teleporting on this occasion, Vila,' he said. 'We need to connect powerlines directly to Amber from here, and that means spacewalking.'

'Walking in space?' hooted Vila. 'There's no air out there, Blake! And it's freezing cold!'

'We have the hull suits,' Blake said.

'But why do I need to come? Can't you just sort out the powerlines and then just teleport me and Gan over?'

'We're running on minimal power, Vila. Using the teleport will drain the energy even further. Right now, we have to save the teleport for emergencies, in case one of us gets trapped in space and has to be pulled out.' He grinned at Vila's alarmed expression. 'Come on. I've got to help Jenna check the powerlines before link-up.'

'INFORMATION,' chimed the ship's computer.

'Yes, Zen?' called Jenna.

'THREE FEDERATION PURSUIT SHIPS AT EXTREME DETECTOR RANGE, ON COURSE FOR *LIBERATOR*.'

Avon jumped out of his seat, where he'd been watching the proceedings. 'Estimate time to intercept,' he snapped.

'THREE POINT SIX HOURS,' Zen replied.

'Sooner than we thought,' said Gan.

That worried Blake, but he didn't panic. There was a chance that three hours might be long enough. 'Have you calibrated the powerlines?' he asked Jenna quickly.

'They're ready for link-up,' Jenna nodded. 'But I've no idea how big a payload they can take or how efficient the transfer will be.'

'Then we'll just have to take our chances,' said Blake. 'Get a suit on, Vila. Gan, can you suit up and come with us as an extra pair of hands?'

Gan nodded. 'Of course.' He gently nudged Vila towards the corridor again. 'Let's go.'

'Be ready to start the transfer as soon as we connect the lines,' Blake told Jenna. 'We need every second we can buy.'

Servalan closed the door of her office, still annoyed at having her fitting disturbed. She found Travis's report and opened the file, punching in her personal clearance code when prompted. She expected it to be yet another of his moans about Blake evading his tactics for the umpteenth time and then sloping off in the direction of some hiding place, but it wasn't. It was something entirely different. Servalan stared at the screen. *Liberator* had moved into one of the most dangerous sectors of Federation space: dangerous to the Federation itself if anything abandoned there were to fall into hands of insurgents such as Blake and his crew.

The news wasn't good. Servalan thought for a moment, wondering precisely which of the junked experiments Blake would be interested in. Then, just as Travis had, she guessed. She made no attempt to call up any information on the 'missing' space station. It loomed large in her recent memory. In fact, the very thought of it made her shudder.

She activated her direct communications link to Travis's ship.

'Travis,' the voice on the other end of the call answered curtly.

'I've read your report,' Servalan told him, expediting formality in favour of reaching the point.

'The *Liberator* has entered the close vicinity of Station Amber, Supreme Commander,' Travis reported, a note of concern in his voice.

'I'd guessed as much,' Servalan said coolly. 'And I know what he's up to.'

Travis sounded surprised. 'Supreme Commander?'

'Blake wants the AE105.'

'Shall I engage *Liberator* now?' Travis asked eagerly. He had no idea what the AE105 was, Servalan thought, and he didn't care. He was just excited at the prospect of getting his teeth into Blake's hide.

'No, Travis,' Servalan said, with a wicked smile. 'I am commanding you to leave the sector. If Blake wants the AE105, let him have it.'

FOUR
BREAK AND ENTER

Travis was bewildered. Why would the Supreme Commander, who had herself engaged him on his current mission to permanently eliminate Blake, who knew that all of the projects in the Restriction Zone were highly dangerous, simply order him to step back and let her enemies take possession of one of these things? If any of the projects were in a usable condition and Blake and his crew managed to adapt them so that they could be controlled remotely, then all kinds of devastation could be caused. Did Servalan know what kind of a monster she could be unleashing?

Perhaps she did. Perhaps that was the very reason why she was giving this AE105 thing, whatever it was, to Blake. She'd certainly been closely involved with the project on Amber for most of its run, and she'd personally authorised its shutdown. She'd issued the report to the government about its deactivation.

'Ready to withdraw, Commander?'

Travis ignored the mutoid for a moment, pondering his conclusions. 'No,' he said finally. 'Hold position. Have our detectors picked up the *Liberator*?'

'Alongside Station Amber,' the mutoid confirmed. 'Approximately sixteen hundred spacials from our position.'

'Put her on the viewscreen,' Travis ordered quietly. 'I want to see what she's doing.'

The viewscreen lit up but showed only a colourful blur of fuzzy lines. 'Interference, Commander,' reported the mutoid.

'Blake?' asked Travis.

'No, sir,' the mutoid answered after completing a quick scan. '*Liberator* has been positioned close to the Station's hull, inside her scanner repulsion field.'

Blake was clever. He'd pulled the ship inside the field of transceiver disruption generated by all abandoned Federation bases. Or perhaps there was another reason why he was so close to the hull. He had been heading out a long distance at breakneck speed. Perhaps he'd had a breakdown and had to take cover to repair it. That would be good news if it were true. If the *Liberator* were vulnerable then the kill would be easy... Then Travis's heart sank as he remembered the Supreme Commander's orders. It was just his luck. Blake's ship was probably a sitting target and Travis wasn't allowed to shoot it down.

Vila didn't like spacewalking. Despite still being able to touch the *Liberator*'s hull, he'd felt too far away for comfort. Of course he'd guessed that he wouldn't like it, but he was too unhappy to draw any satisfaction from the knowledge that his guess had been right.

He was sure that the spacesuit he wore didn't fit him properly, though he was thankful that the seals preventing the escape of any air or heat seemed to be doing their job. Gan was behind him, also holding on to the line. Blake was pulling himself forward in great leaps and bounds, confident and determined as if he did things like this every day.

Cally was waiting at the teleport suite to pull any or all of the boarding party back up the moment any call to do so came in. Vila gripped the safety line a little tighter at that thought.

Gan could obviously tell that he was nervous. 'Blake's almost at the hull now,' he said comfortingly, and Vila could hear him clearly inside his bubble helmet. The communicator frequency was kept open so that the three could hear each other talking as if they were simply in a room together. 'As soon as he makes contact, we can get the powerlines out.'

'I hope it doesn't take long,' grumbled Vila. 'I wouldn't like to be stuck out here for hours, hanging on to this line and waiting for my air to run out.'

'It'll be all right,' Gan said calmly. 'It won't take long to connect those powerlines, and then we can start charging the *Liberator*'s cells up.'

'Get them up to maximum and get out of here,' added Vila with a forced smile. 'I feel better already.' He pulled himself awkwardly towards the enormous looming underside of the space station.

'I'm on Amber's hull,' Blake announced to both of them, and they looked down to the far end of the line to see him clinging to the huge grey shape like a spider on the underside of a gutter. 'I'll find an airlock.' Blake held on to the hull, taking advantage of its minor gravitational pull, and clambered down a little until he found what he was looking for: a sealed square aperture large enough for a man to pass through should it be unsealed. 'Get down here, Vila,' he ordered. 'I need you to help me get this hatch open.'

Vila swallowed hard and pulled himself forward, still holding on to the line, and moved just a few inches. 'I'll be all day at this rate!' he moaned.

Blake was getting frustrated. 'Don't argue, Vila,' he growled. 'We can teleport you back aboard the *Liberator* if anything goes wrong.'

'Or maybe you could teleport me back right now,' said Vila. 'I'm feeling a bit sick.'

'Gan!' Blake barked. 'Push him!'

Vila screamed as Gan barged forward and slammed into his back. Instantly he was tumbling in slow motion, head over heels through the inky blackness of space. His heartbeat quickened and he felt dizzy. He shut his eyes.

'You're right on target,' Blake told him calmly.

Vila opened them again and found he was looking at Blake, who was clinging to the roof of the space station.

Grumbling under his breath, Vila pressed his body to the station's skin and clambered down to have a look at the airlock. It wasn't long before he found the maintenance panel and cracked it open. 'It's one of the simpler external to internal communication locks,' he told Blake as he started inserting the heads of tools into it. 'That might actually be a bit of a problem.'

'How?' asked Blake.

'Well,' Vila explained, 'it's supposed to connect up to a computer for a verification signal to allow it to be opened from the outside, but if nothing's switched on in there, the computer won't be working.'

'I see,' said Blake. 'So, we could ring the doorbell but nobody would answer. Does it have to link up to a particular kind of computer?'

'No. The design's really basic. It'll take the order to open from any machine.'

'What about Zen?'

'Probably, but how would we get this lock and Zen to communicate with each other?'

Blake started to slip his teleport bracelet off. 'Avon. Can you patch Zen into my teleport bracelet?'

'Give me a moment,' said Avon. 'Zen, scan for teleport bracelets outside *Liberator*.'

'THREE LOCATED.'

'Blake,' Avon called. 'Transmit your bracelet's frequency test signal.'

Blake checked his bracelet and found the control sequence required. 'Should be transmitting now.'

'Zen,' Avon said. 'Lock on to the nearest frequency test signal.'

'CONNECTION ESTABLISHED.'

'Zen,' Blake called. 'Can you hear me?'

'FREQUENCY CLEAR AND TRANSMISSIONS RECEIVED AT OPTIMUM CAPACITY.'

Blake handed his bracelet to Vila. 'What do you think?'

For the first time all day, Vila smiled. 'Should be easy,' he said cheerfully. With a flurry of hands and tools, he quickly wired the bracelet into the locking mechanism. As he worked he asked, 'One thing, though. If we've got to connect up these lines inside the station anyway, why didn't we just teleport in, hook them up, recharge our cells and teleport out?'

'Because we could teleport ourselves in, but not the powerlines,' Blake answered. 'They'd need to be threaded through one of the airlocks from outside.'

'Ah,' said Vila. Then he glanced over his shoulder at Blake. 'But if these are running through the airlock, how will the door shut? All the air could escape.'

'That's why we've brought the emergency air plug. Once we're inside, we can plug one of the internal corridors. The plug will fit itself around the powerlines without any air getting out.'

'That means we won't be able to go back out that way,' Vila said.

'We'll worry about that later, Vila,' Blake said hastily.

Vila stopped fiddling with the locking mechanism. 'I think that's about as good as I can get it.'

'Zen,' Blake said. 'Order this lock to release for access from outside.'

'CONFIRMED.'

There was a loud clunk and the airlock hatch slid open.

FIVE
STALEMATE IN SPACE

Jenna released the powerlines the moment she was asked. They shot into space towards Blake's position and their connector heads clattered against the hull of Station Amber. Gan collected the heads and pulled them through the airlock to be linked up.

'Where are those ships, Zen?' she asked.

'PURSUIT SHIPS ARE HOLDING POSITION.'

Jenna hadn't been expecting that. 'Are you sure?' she asked.

'CONFIRMED,' said Zen.

'It's a machine,' Avon reminded her. 'It can't lie.'

Jenna knew that. She knew that Zen was a highly sophisticated computer, far more sophisticated than anything she or anyone on the crew could grasp, even Avon, but she also knew that the information it had just given her was very strange indeed. 'Why are they standing off?' she asked Avon. 'We're sitting targets. They could fly in and pick us off easily.'

Avon seemed to ponder the question. 'Perhaps they're trying to work out what we're doing,' he murmured. 'Or perhaps they already know.'

Could the Federation have known that Blake was looking for Station Amber and set a trap for him? Jenna wondered. It was unlikely. Even Servalan and Travis did not know the full extent of the *Liberator*'s capabilities, and the fastest of the pursuit ships could not catch her – even at less than maximum speed. It had to be something else. Something suspicious.

The rounded metal shells of the connector heads hit the hull just a short distance away from the airlock and then floated a little way back out into space. Gan managed to grab the powerlines before they drifted too far away, and he pulled them into the hatchway towards the inner door of the airlock.

'This one's easier,' said Vila. 'It's just a standard pressurise-and-release system. We can trick it into thinking the outer door's closed, so it will let the inner door open.' He probed the small computer pad next to the door with his tools. 'Find something to grip onto.'

Gan was still holding the safety line. 'How about this?'

'No. When the door opens there'll be a gust of air. Even if you hold on to that line you'll still be blown all the way back to the *Liberator*. You need to hold on to something that's part of the station.'

'Or I could just get clear of the blast,' Gan suggested.

Vila was surprised. 'I hadn't thought of that. Shame I can't join you. Someone's got to open the door. Take Blake with you, though.'

Gan ushered Blake out of the airlock and back onto the hull, hoping that the column of escaping air would blast out of the hole in a straight line and miss anything at right angles to it.

They waited in silence.

'Are you all right, Vila?' Gan called at last.

'Fine,' Vila said. 'I flattened myself against the outer door. I thought the pressure would crush me for a minute. I have to say I'm surprised it was all over so quickly. That can't have been all the air from the ship.'

'I'll bring Blake and the powerlines round,' said Gan, and he took Blake's arm again and led him up to the airlock. The party of three entered the airlock reception unit, a small semicircular room with three doorways leading to corridors in other directions. Guided by Blake, they headed through one of the doors into the corridor beyond and found it to be a dead end.

'Let's try one of the others,' Vila suggested, starting to turn back, but Blake grabbed his arm and pushed him towards the blind end of the cul-de-sac. He pointed to a panel next to the blank wall. 'Oh!' exclaimed Vila. 'Of course! That's why the air escape cut off so fast. It's a safety system. When there's air escaping, these bulkheads close to cut it off.'

'I'll close the door at the other end,' said Gan and marched down towards airlock reception. He found the control and the door-to-airlock reception buzzed almost shut. The thick power cables stopped it from closing completely.

Vila pulled out the emergency air plug, a grey-white object the size and shape of a beach ball. He held it up in one hand and punched it hard with the other, then scrambled clear as it self-inflated, rapidly moulding itself to the corridor walls, the door and the cables, sealing the gaps and excluding any further escape of air.

He sank down as the pressure normalised and Blake unclipped the seals on his space helmet and took it off, indicating that the others should do the same. He looked back at the way to airlock reception, now blocked by a huge inflated cushion of thick greyish polymer. That part of the plan had worked better than he'd hoped.

'Well done, you two. Now let's get on with it,' said Blake. He started towards the other end of the corridor. 'Have you still got the cables, Gan?'

Gan held both the connector heads in his left hand and raised them to show Blake. 'Where do we connect them?'

Blake motioned for the others to follow him, looking around. 'Well, there must be an emergency generator nearby. All the main power's disconnected – that's why there are no lights, but something did close those bulkheads. All we've got to do is find it.'

Vila opened his toolbox and started unfastening the bulkhead release switch from the wall. 'I'll run a circuit trace,' he suggested. 'If I find out where this switch gets its power from, you can go right to the source.'

'Perfect,' said Blake. 'I don't have a bracelet any more, but if Gan comes with me then you can call him as soon as you work out where the power's coming from. In the mean time, we can search the station, see what's here. All right?'

'Fine,' Vila said, his concentration fixed on the task of tracing the circuit in the door panel. 'I work better on my own anyway.' As Blake and Gan started off, he called after them, 'But do me a favour, will you? If you find a power switch, make sure you don't turn on any security systems.'

Gan's bracelet chimed.

'We're here,' said Blake. 'What is it?'

'Zen says the Federation pursuit ships have stopped moving,' said Jenna. 'They're just holding their position.'

Blake was surprised. 'Are you sure?'

'No, but Zen is, and he's not usually wrong.'

'How long have they been there?'

'Zen reported it about twenty minutes ago.'

'Twenty minutes?' said Blake, astonished. 'And you're sure they can pick us up on their scanners? The damping field of the station would affect them getting much idea of our movements, but they should still be able to see the *Liberator* on their viewscreens from fourteen thousand spacials.'

'Zen says they have scanned us,' said Jenna. 'They definitely know we're here, but they're just sitting there.'

Blake bit his lip. 'Now why are they doing that?' he murmured.

Back at her headquarters, Servalan was wondering the same thing. She had ordered Travis to leave the sector. She knew that he was given to disobeying orders, but Servalan was not in the mood for having her orders disobeyed, even by him. She tried his direct channel again, but there was only static.

Her intercom buzzer sounded and she pressed the button. 'What is it?' she snapped crossly.

'Keelian Vardor is here, Supreme Commander,' the secretary announced. 'She has some new material samples to show you.'

'Keelian?' Well, that was quite different. Servalan was starting to like Keelian. The girl was obedient, respectful and humble, but without the irksome grovelling qualities exhibited by the likes of Cashlan. She was as a young person of her limited status should be in the presence of the Supreme Commander, a fine example of a Federation citizen. Keelian, Servalan thought, had potential.

The *Liberator* was quiet. Jenna stared through the viewscreen worriedly at the three pursuit ships, wondering what – if anything – she should do. She decided to be ready.

'Zen, put up radiation flare shields,' she said.

'Don't,' said Avon. 'The pursuit ships present no current threat. The shields will increase the loss of energy from the power cells.'

'We could bring the battle computers online,' Jenna suggested.

'No,' replied Avon. 'That will use up power too.'

'So we just stare at these ships and wonder what they're up to?'

'While they stare at us and wonder what we're up to. It's a classic stalemate.'

'Until they decide to make a move. They don't know our power's virtually drained.'

'That depends on the kind of move they decide to make,' Avon said thoughtfully. 'Perhaps the *Liberator* won't be the next piece on the board to be taken.'

SIX
RACE AGAINST TIME

The two mutoid crewmen fastened their spacesuits and put on their helmets. Travis fitted his own spacesuit and fixed the seals before checking the communications unit.

'Can you both hear me?' he called.

'Yes, Commander,' two mutoid voices chorused almost in harmony inside his sophisticated space helmet.

'Good,' Travis said. 'Move out.'

He watched the mutoids march ahead of him towards the airlock hatch and followed them. They clambered inside the cramped space, sealed the inner door and waited for depressurisation.

'Why do we not dock, Commander?' asked one of the mutoids.

'Blake didn't dock, did he?' Travis replied. 'He has something in common with the Supreme Commander that we don't: he knows exactly what's on that station and how dangerous it is. I don't want our ships too close.'

'Blake has a teleport device,' the mutoid reminded him.

'But he hasn't used it,' Travis said. 'At the extreme range of our scanners' penetration of Amber's damping field we picked up three life forms loose in space. One of them will surely be Blake. He felt the necessity to spacewalk, and so do I. You have to think like your enemy if you're going to beat them.'

The outer airlock hatch opened and they clambered onto the hull of the pursuit ship. Travis looked out across space. Fourteen thousand spacials was a long way, but it would be worth it. He gripped the control handles of the jetpack he wore on his back.

'Go,' he ordered his mutoids. 'Try to keep out of sight of her scanners and head for the station.'

'Yes, Commander,' the near-harmonious chorus came again and the two mutoids suddenly vaulted into the blackness above, each catapulted on a column of flame, and plunged towards the underside of the *Liberator*.

'I have you now, Blake,' Travis said quietly with a vicious smile. 'There's no escape.' He pulled on the handles at his sides and blasted himself after the mutoids.

*

'INFORMATION.'

Jenna looked up. 'Yes, Zen?'

'THREE LIFE FORMS APPROACHING STATION AMBER.'

'What?' Jenna was shaken by the news.

Avon gave her worst fear a voice. 'They must be from the pursuit ships,' he snapped. 'For some reason they've decided that firing on us would be unwise, so they've sent a spacewalking party to try to hunt Blake down in person. Zen, analyse the life forms.'

'ALL THREE LIFE FORMS ARE ESSENTIALLY HUMAN,' Zen reported, 'MODIFIED WITH TECHNOLOGICALLY ADVANCED APPARATUS.'

'Travis and a couple of mutoids, no doubt,' Avon said dourly. 'How long will it take them to reach the station? Surely a spacewalk over fourteen thousand spacials should take quite a while.'

'ALL LIFE FORMS ARE USING CHEMICAL ROCKET PROPULSION AND WILL REACH STATION AMBER IN POINT NINE HOURS.'

'Jenna,' said Avon urgently. 'Call Blake quickly and tell him if he doesn't get back here in fifty minutes he's a dead man.'

Jenna was already on it. 'Gan? Blake?' she called desperately. There was no answer. 'Gan?' Still nothing. 'Vila? Vila, this is Jenna. Can you hear me? *Liberator* to boarding party, can you hear me? Gan, Vila, answer me!'

'There's no response,' Avon interrupted before she could press further. 'Don't waste your time. Zen, why aren't the communicators working?'

'A LOCALISED INCREASE IN RADIATION IS AFFECTING TRANSCEIVER SIGNALS.'

'They must've got one of the generators on,' Avon said. 'But it's leaking radiation and that's affecting the detectors as well as the communications.'

'Will it affect the teleport?' asked Jenna.

'Inside the radiation field, yes,' Avon answered. 'If they can get outside its influence we should be able to pick them up, if they're not dead already.'

*

Vila was slow in reaching the emergency generator plant. He had managed to trace the circuits in the bulkhead system to their power source so he could give Blake and Gan a location fix from the circuit mapper. Vila had been walking to meet them, following directions from Gan, but when they fired up the generator the radiation cut communications. Vila was left halfway to his destination with no idea where to go.

He put his space helmet back to provide protection from the radiation leak. He tried a few corridors until he spotted a light and heard machinery humming, and then he'd followed those signs of life to their source.

Blake and Gan were inside the generator plant, helmets on. Blake was trying to patch the leak in the large glowing cylindrical power converter at the centre of the small room. Gan was lashing the connector heads of the powerlines to a coupling in the wall. Vila quickly opened his toolbox and rushed to Blake's side to help him.

Comforted by the protection of his spacesuit, Vila tackled the leak with considerable aplomb. After a few minutes the radiation readings on the computer bank above the leaky instrument started to descend. Blake watched the readings intently until the marker registered a low level, then risked taking of his helmet again.

Vila pulled his off too, and as he did an urgent voice filled the room.

'This is Avon. Can you hear me? Blake!'

'I hear you, Avon,' Blake answered. 'There was a radiation leak but we've patched it up. I'm afraid you're going to have to send over another communicator, though. I left mine behind.'

'I can send one now,' said Avon. 'Are the powerlines connected?'

'Yes.'

'Good. We don't have much time, Blake. Zen detected three life forms with jetpacks heading for the station. They'll be there in less than forty minutes.'

'Right,' said Blake. 'I'm sure we can give *Liberator* enough charge to get away in that time.' He grinned. 'The question is, what shall we do while we're waiting?'

Vila groaned. 'You're not suggesting what I think you're suggesting are you?'

'Twenty minutes is long enough to have a search around,' said

Blake. 'We passed by a big laboratory on the way here. I'd like to take a look. Coming?'

'Blake,' Vila said urgently. 'The damaged area of the generator. The bit that was causing the radiation leak. Did you notice anything odd about it?'

'No. What?'

'It wasn't accidental damage. Not the kind of thing you'd get from a technical fault or something. The conduit housings were disfigured as if they'd been melted.'

Gan pointed up. 'Look,' he said. Many of the lights in the corridor had come back on. 'The generator wasn't the only thing that was damaged.'

Blake looked all around him in stunned silence. The corridor walls, floor and ceiling were blistered, potholed and cracked, some sections of the internal architecture barely recognisable.

'Perhaps we're starting to get an idea of why this station was shut down,' said Vila.

INTERLUDE II
STATION AMBER, SIX MONTHS AGO

Another section of the corridor wall exploded, showering molten metal and polymer in all directions. Servalan was still on the floor, face down, trying to avoid being spattered by the seething hot droplets, trying to keep clear of the smoke that seemed to be filling every inch of corridor space.

How had it happened? Ban Kerralin was an expert. He was supposed to be brilliant. How could the machine have gone haywire so close to its final testing stage? It couldn't have been an accident. He must have sabotaged the machine and set it loose on the station to kill anyone in its path.

Alarms were going off everywhere, their deafening howl drowning out all but the sounds of explosions. Servalan looked up and saw the booted feet of a guard running by.

'Guard, come here!' she shouted. 'Come here at once!'

The man stopped and turned. At first Servalan thought he wouldn't see her and would leave her behind. But he crouched down beside her head. 'Supreme Commander!' he gasped. 'I thought you'd been killed, ma'am. Are you all right?'

'I just need to get out,' she answered and thrust her hand into his. He pulled her up and she immediately started to cough. The guard unhooked a remote control from his belt, and closed one of the emergency bulkheads to stop not only the smoke but also the machine getting through. Not that a mere emergency bulkhead could do much about the latter, Servalan thought bitterly.

'Where's Kerralin?' she demanded as they ran.

'I think he's dead, ma'am.'

'But we need him to deactivate the machine before it kills us all!'

'There's nothing we can do. We're evacuating the station and activating the self-destruct.'

Servalan shook her head. 'The machine knows how to operate all the computers by remote control,' she told the guard. 'If you arm the self-destruct, the machine will shut it down or jettison it.'

'And then what will it do?' the guard asked worriedly.

'And then,' said Servalan, 'it will hunt me down and kill me. And once it's killed me it will kill the first person it saw after it saw me, and then the first person after it saw him. And so on.'

'It's got a *queuing* system?'

'It's not designed to wipe out people indiscriminately,' said Servalan. 'It's designed to intimidate. Imagine an unstoppable machine loose on your planet, killing each and every citizen one by one. As soon as you've seen it, that's it. You are somewhere on its list. You know it's going to hunt you down, but you don't know when. The only way to stop it is to give in, to beg to have it turned off.' Her smile was chilling. 'An effective way to stop a rebellion, I think.'

'Who do *we* beg to turn it off?' stammered the guard.

'Ban Kerralin,' snapped Servalan. 'He's the only one who can stop it. And you've just told me he's dead.'

There was a flash and the recently closed emergency bulkhead split in half, smoke pouring through. Servalan ran without looking back. She knew all too well what was coming for her.

The giant metallic blue sphere of the AE105 crashed through the broken pieces of the fallen door and fingers of blue light trickled over its surface to form a single bright ball a couple of inches from it like a small star orbiting a huge planet. It was preparing to fire.

Servalan tripped on the hem of her dress and hit the deck again. The machine couldn't halt its attack process at such a late stage. It fired. A flash like a streak of brilliant blue lighting connected with the body of the guard, and that body turned into a cloud of vapour instantly. The vapour mingled with the smoke and the guard was lost forever.

The machine was suddenly still, hovering ominously in the corridor. It had accidentally killed someone a long way down the queue. It was confused – momentarily – but it wouldn't take long before it reset itself.

Servalan lay still on the floor, hidden from its detectors under the sheet of smoke from the corridor damage. Some more guards would appear soon, the machine would start killing them and she could make a getaway. Things were going to be fine. She had thought of a way she could immobilise the AE105.

She just needed to get through the next few minutes unharmed.

SEVEN
POTENTIAL

'There we are,' Drav Cashlan simpered, stepping back and resting his hands on his hips. 'Absolutely perfect! You look a picture, truly a picture! Doesn't Madam Servalan look a picture, Keelian?'

'The Supreme Commander looks very beautiful,' Keelian said, lowering her eyes respectfully. 'The dress fits and suits her well.'

Servalan smiled as she looked into the mirror Cashlan had set up in her office. The dress was complete, every stitch sewn, every rough edge trimmed neat. The material glittered and shimmered under the bright lights of the office, and Servalan was pleased. She was also pleased with Keelian's attitude.

'Thank you, Keelian,' she said, looking at the girl. She could not tell her that she looked nice too. Keelian was short, plump and plain. She wore a dowdy grey pinafore designed for working. She was young though, and still developing. If she lost some weight, learnt how to use make-up and did something about her hair she might look rather sweet. But Keelian would never be beautiful, Servalan thought. The girl just didn't have the features for it. Provided her development went in the right direction, by the age of twenty she might just about manage pretty.

But looks weren't everything. Keelian's words were good ones and well used. Through all the fittings for this dress, the girl's respectful attitude had helped temper Servalan's annoyance at Cashlan's irritating chatter. Great care had been taken by her to avoid informality and insult towards the Supreme Commander. Perhaps Keelian might have a better contribution to offer the Federation than that of a mere dressmaker's assistant. Perhaps she could be a good secretary. Servalan decided on something then and there.

'I want you to stay here, Keelian,' she smiled at the girl. 'Cashlan, you may go. Payment for the dress will be credited to your account within the hour.'

She could tell that Cashlan's smile was fake.

'Of course, madam,' he stuttered. 'But I shall need Keelian. I have other dresses to make.'

'You have other seamstresses as well, Cashlan,' Servalan said.

'Ah,' Cashlan said in a plaintive tone, putting an arm around little Keelian's shoulders and gently squeezing her in a show of affection. 'But none so nimble-fingered, so patient and so totally devoted as dear Keelian. Won't you let me have her?' He looked at Servalan with pleading eyes.

'This is an executive decision on behalf of the Federation government,' Servalan told him flatly. 'Will you protest and risk a charge of insurgency?'

Cashlan's face went white. 'Er, no, Supreme Commander,' he stammered. 'Of course not.'

Servalan smiled venomously. 'I find it fascinating the way fear induces respectful formality, don't you, Cashlan?'

'Oh, quite, madam. Quite.'

'Keelian will be returned to you when I have finished with her, provided she has no other duties. You will be informed.'

'Of course, madam,' Cashlan nodded and quickly scurried out of the door.

As Servalan closed it, Keelian looked shyly at her. 'Is something wrong, Supreme Commander?' she asked. 'Have I offended you?'

Servalan took her hand. 'On the contrary,' she smiled at the girl. 'Come and sit down. I have a proposition for you. One that may change your entire direction in life.'

Keelian obediently sat in the chair opposite the desk and patiently waited for Servalan to sit before asking, 'Supreme Commander?'

'Keelian,' she said in the kind of voice a proud mother might use to congratulate an exceptionally good child. 'I think you have it in you to be much more than a seamstress and errand girl to Cashlan. I think you have the potential to work for the Supreme Commander.'

Keelian's eyes were like saucers. 'For you?'

'You'll need training of course,' Servalan said. 'I assume you accept?'

Keelian smiled. 'Oh yes, Supreme Commander,' she said. 'Yes I do.'

EIGHT
LET HIM HAVE IT

As soon as Vila forced the door of the laboratory open, the boarding party entered and began to search.

Blake switched over to auxiliary power so that the systems would take the energy they needed from the recently activated generator, then turned on the computers. He began to search for any details on the weapons being developed at Station Amber. Gan pulled open cabinets and drawers, stuffing data crystals into his pockets to take back to the *Liberator*.

'It looks like the weapon being developed in this lab was called Assault Engine 105,' Blake said. 'The vault that should currently contain it is through there.' He pointed to a large double doorway at the far end of the long rectangular laboratory. 'It's hard to tell precisely what it was, all these files are encoded. But if the name's anything to go by it's obviously a weapon and the schematics show it to be a small sphere. It looks like it's small enough to carry by hand.'

Vila scurried towards it. 'I'll have a look at the lock.'

'Blake,' Gan called from near the back of the room.

Blake walked up to him and was handed a small white plastic parcel. There was a label on it with only two words that read: 'Open me.' Blake looked at it in surprise. Quickly he ripped open the package and pulled out what was inside: a small black oblong of some crystalline material.

'A micro holograph projector,' Blake said. 'And I thought no-one used them any more.' He tossed the little block of crystal into the air and Gan caught it. 'The *Liberator* should have enough charge now for us to use the teleport. Gan, take this to Avon and see if he can get it working. Give him the data crystals you found, too.'

Gan nodded. 'Cally,' he said into his bracelet. 'Bring me back.' A greyish halo outlined his figure for a moment and he faded away, the halo snapping like a rubber band and blinking out of existence.

Blake turned to his other companion. 'Vila, how are you doing with that lock?'

*

'This must be where Blake got in,' Travis announced to the two mutoids as he examined the airlock hatchway. 'I wonder how they stopped the air escaping. No matter.' He glanced at his crew of two. 'We won't go in this way,' he added. 'It'll be too dangerous. Blake might have set traps. After all, *Liberator* would have been able to see our ships.' He clung to the hull of Station Amber and started to climb up it. 'Look for another airlock.'

Travis had noticed a cable snaking out of the airlock and winding up through space towards the *Liberator*. He now knew why they had just been sitting there: they were siphoning off power from the station's generators. That of course meant that Amber's power, or at least some of it, had been turned back on, and the airlocks would open when asked to. Travis climbed up the hull and found the two mutoids standing on the top side of the station, looking down at a hatch.

'Get it open,' he ordered and the mutoids set to work.

Inside the station, the corridor was empty, though a few dim lights were on. Travis looked left and then right, wondering which way to go, where to begin his search of the station. 'Life signs?'

One of the mutoids held a portable scanning device in her hand. 'A mild radiation leak is affecting the detector, sir,' she reported. 'It's hard to say.'

A radiation leak. That would be from whichever of the generators Blake had managed to get working. He would be near to that. 'Can you pinpoint it?'

'Three decks down,' the mutoid answered, waving her scanner about. 'Maximum Priority Research Level, corridor forty-nine. It's not far from the sabotaged airlock, sir.'

Travis smiled coldly. 'Of course,' he said. 'Let's get down there. We don't want to give Blake enough time to do anything dangerous.' He indicated for the mutoid with the scanner to lead the way.

It didn't take Avon long to get the micro holograph projector working. He listened to the message with growing concern then, quickly and methodically, he started to scan through the data crystals Gan had brought, each new bit of information confirming what he already suspected.

They should never have gone to Station Amber.

He pressed the communications button on the control panel nearest to him.

'Blake? Your time's up,' Avon said. 'Cally's about to bring you back. But before she does, I need to know if you've found a weapon yet. The... AE105.'

'It's in the vault here. Vila is just picking the lock.'

'Then tell him to stop at once. I want you to leave it alone.'

'Leave it?' Blake protested. 'But that means we'll have come all this way for nothing!'

'That's a good deal better than coming all this way for an early grave,' Avon retorted. 'If you want to go ahead and release that thing, at least give me fair warning so that I can jettison the powerlines and leave you to die. I don't feel particularly enthusiastic about sacrificing my life for your unrealistic ideals.'

'Are you sure you're not over-reacting?' Blake asked. 'What is it?'

'A merciless killer,' Avon said bluntly. 'It vaporises every living thing it sees, one by one. It has no automated stop cycle, which means it won't stop killing until it's killed everyone except Ban Kerralin, its creator, who is already dead and therefore not much help. The moment you open that door it will kill you.'

Blake sighed. 'All right. We're coming back.'

Avon smiled with mild satisfaction, but his moment was spoiled by a sudden excited cry of, 'I've got it!'

'No, Vila!' Blake shouted urgently, running to the laboratory exit. 'Get away from the doors, quickly.'

The doors were slowly opening, revealing a glimmer of bright blue beyond. 'I think it's too late,' Vila said.

Blake used his bracelet. 'Cally, get us out of here!' he roared.

The door to the laboratory burst open and in marched Travis and two mutoids, all three pointing guns at Blake and Vila.

'You're not going anywhere, Blake!' Travis snapped as the two men teleported back to the *Liberator*, disappearing from view.

The AE105 floated into the room. It registered five life forms as soon as the vault had opened and created a queue accordingly. It targeted the first on the list, then scanned for a power source and located the generator. Quickly, it translocated the power directly to its conduction frame and charged itself up. Trickles of light began to dance over its surface and it floated towards the life form. Then, the blue ball unleashed a bolt of energy that reduced the life form to a cloud of airborne particles.

As expected, the other life forms in the queue turned and ran. The AE105 followed close behind.

Avon was waiting with Cally at the teleport suite when Blake and Vila materialised.

'What happened?' he demanded.

'The weapon got out,' Blake answered. 'Just as Travis and his mutoids turned up.'

'So it *was* Travis's ships that were following us,' said Cally.

'I think Travis may be dead,' said Blake.

Vila smirked. 'Well that's good, isn't it?' he said. 'One less thing to worry about!'

'You have no idea how much there is to worry about thanks to you!' Avon shouted.

Blake pushed his way between them. 'All right, Avon,' he said quietly.

'What's the matter with *him*?' Vila huffed.

'That thing you let out is deadly,' said Avon. 'It has virtually impenetrable shielding, an infinite range of mobility and a self-recharging power source. It can turn any living organism into a puff of smoke and it kills whoever it sees one by one.'

'Lucky that it didn't see us then,' said Vila.

'Of course it saw you,' snapped Avon, 'and that means you are on its kill list. It has some kind of bizarre queuing system. It must have registered Travis and his mutoids first, otherwise it would already be on its way over here. But once it's killed them, it will come after you and Blake. Nothing will stop it.'

'It won't be able to find us,' said Blake.

'Really?' Avon asked. 'It will have registered the particle disruption caused by the teleport.'

'Well then let's disconnect the powerlines and get out of here, fast,' said Vila. He darted out of the teleport suite, heading for the flight deck.

'It's not that simple,' said Avon, following him. 'Even if we do manage to get away completely, it won't stop. It will search for new targets so it can reset its queue.'

Vila frowned. 'You mean, it will look for populated planets?'

'I think so,' said Avon. 'We will effectively be signing the death warrants of millions of innocent people.'

'We've got to stop it!'

'I admire your optimism,' Avon said with a humourless smile, 'but I'm not stupid enough to share it.'

They reached the flight deck, where the rest of the crew were waiting.

Jenna was at her station. 'What's happened?' she asked.

'We've let loose a berserker,' Vila told her.

'Berserker?'

'Vila seems to think this weapon deserves a pet-name,' Avon said. He grimaced. 'I suppose "Berserker" is as good as any.'

'INFORMATION,' chimed Zen. 'ONE LIFE FORM IS LEAVING STATION AMBER AND HEADING TOWARDS THE FEDERATION PURSUIT SHIPS.'

'That's bound to be Travis,' said Jenna. 'He's escaped.'

'Not for long,' said Avon. 'That machine won't stop until it has hunted him down.'

'Then what?'

'Then it's coming for us.'

NINE
RUN, TRAVIS, RUN!

Travis and the second mutoid ran from the laboratory in different directions and, to his relief, the machine followed the mutoid. Running through the corridors, Travis managed to stumble across the place where Blake had entered the space station and stopped, momentarily confused by the large inflatable cushion. Then he put his space helmet on and aimed the finger of his artificial hand. The laseron destroyer flashed, the cushion deflated and, in a howling wind, Travis was shot out into space.

Propelled by his jetpack, Travis wasn't running away in the physical sense – he wasn't using up any of his bodily resources to gain distance at great speed – but nevertheless he was breathless by the time he reached the hull of his ship. It wasn't the ship he'd arrived in: that one, now that the mutoids had been killed, had nobody to pilot it, so Travis made for one of the others.

As he neared his ship he heard an explosion and looked back to see that the hull of Station Amber had ruptured. The AE105 had smashed its way out, and was still on his trail, heading towards him through open space. This puzzled Travis, because the *Liberator* was nearer and still tethered, a much easier target. Thoughts tumbled around in his head as he sped towards safety. Why was this machine hunting him down? Had Blake somehow programmed it to steer clear of him and his band of rebels?

Travis was inside the pursuit ship in seconds, locking the hatches and taking control.

'Commander Travis,' a mutoid said as he entered the small command area.

'Who else were you expecting?' Travis said bitterly. 'Course for Eurydice, maximum speed. Get us out of here.'

The mutoid started to plot the course on the console.

'*Now!*' screamed Travis.

Blake's crew watched, with a mixture of fascination and terror, as the Berserker ignored the two static pursuit ships and single-mindedly headed for the third ship that was already streaking away.

'Travis must be on that ship,' Blake said. 'He'll try to find shelter.'

'The nearest populated planet to here is the one we set out from, Eurydice,' said Jenna. 'There are about three billion people there.'

Avon looked accusingly at Blake and gave him a vicious smile. 'And *you* let it out.'

'I won't have those deaths on my conscience,' hissed Blake, turning his eyes away from Avon.

'You haven't a choice,' Avon replied crisply. 'There is no power in this galaxy, or probably any other, that can stop it now. Face it, Blake. This is a mess of your own making, and you can't clear it up.'

Blake wanted to hit Avon, but he knew that it wouldn't do any good. Instead he perched himself on the edge of one of the consoles and tried to think. He saw the micro holograph projector and picked it up.

'So this was a message?' he asked Avon. 'This was what warned you about the Berserker?'

'You are welcome to listen yourself,' Avon said. He took the projector from him, lay it on top of a table and tapped it twice with the tip of a finger. It glowed bright blue-green, and a figure materialised hovering an inch above it. A man with long black hair and a beard, broad-shouldered and fat, wearing shabby clothes.

'Hallo,' the figure grinned. 'My name is Kerralin, Ban Kerralin. I'm supposed to be Head Consulting Weapons Technician at Station Amber, though I've a feeling that by now my contract will be under review. You have put me on the floor, haven't you? Only if I'm standing on a table right now I must look quite silly. Don't suppose that matters now, though, because if you can actually see this and hear what I'm saying then I'm obviously dead, hence the contract review gag. I do hope somebody got that. Might as well go out on a laugh, and at least I don't have to listen to Servalan any more.' He suddenly looked frustrated. 'And why in heaven's name am I asking you anything? It's not as though you can give answers that this recording would be able to hear. But I'm rambling, aren't I?'

'Just a little,' said Vila, soothingly. Cally frowned and shushed him.

'Anyway,' the holographic figure continued. 'I've got to put you in the picture about the AE105. Keep away from it. It's unstable. It'll kill anything it sees. Now that I'm dead, absolutely nobody is safe. I'm sorry... But Servalan altered the course of my work.'

'Sounds like Servalan,' said Jenna.

'The AE105 was supposed to emit a pulse that pacified the mind by subduing certain neural activity in the brain,' continued the figure. 'Servalan held my family to ransom and forced me to modify it. She had me replace the neuro-inhibitor with a tissue vaporiser. Do you know? She even let me see my wife and kids safe and well, and as soon as I'd finished the adaptations to the unit she sent them off to be re-educated anyway.'

The hologram gave a hollow laugh, and the crew of the *Liberator* exchanged glances.

'So, the thing is, I sort of lost my temper and removed its safety features,' Kerralin said. 'All but one. The only safety cut-out it has is an integrated command that registers on sight of me. It can't kill me. But if I'm dead, everybody's had it. It can self-charge its power cells from any source of energy. It can even convert raw energy into usable power. If it's a bit tired it can go and sit near a star until it livens up again and then just carry on with its job.'

'Is this guy crazy?' Vila asked, tapping the side of his head.

'Its only order is to kill absolutely any living thing on sight, one by one. It makes a queue – first come, first served. The only thing that can slow it down is interference with its queuing system. If it somehow loses all trace of the first person in line, or if it kills someone out of turn, it resets and then the next person it sees will be number one on the list.'

'I'd have to say he doesn't sound completely sane,' said Gan.

'I'm sorry it's so indiscriminately destructive. I was hoping it'd do Servalan. If it hasn't, then don't worry. I've got a bit of a plan B that won't be nearly as easy for her to escape.' The figure laughed.

'What's he talking about?' wondered Jenna.

'I wondered that. But surely something trying to kill Servalan is the least of our troubles,' said Avon.

'I hope it doesn't do you, whoever you are,' said the hologram. 'I hope you've got the good sense to leave well alone. Look after yourself. I mean it. I'm... sorry.'

And he was gone.

'If it's that powerful,' said Jenna slowly. 'How did it come to end up in that vault? Why didn't it just blast its way out and get back to looking for Servalan?'

Blake shook his head. 'I don't know, Jenna. That's a temptation even I couldn't resist.'

'Or any of us,' murmured Vila. 'Would you stay at home when you could be out caving Servalan's head in, Jenna?'

'Probably not,' Jenna said with a smile.

'There had to be a way of keeping it inside,' said Blake. He picked up the micro holograph projector and studied it intently. 'Of course...' he said, suddenly.

'Of course what?' asked Vila, but Blake wasn't listening.

'Zen!' he shouted. 'Connect to Station Amber.'

'CONNECTION ESTABLISHED,' Zen reported.

'Scan the vault we found the machine in for holographic equipment.'

'A HOLOGRAPHIC PROJECTOR IS IN THE VAULT.'

Blake's eyes were alight. 'Is it still operating?'

'IT WAS DEACTIVATED AUTOMATICALLY WHEN THE VAULT DOORS OPENED.'

'How is it programmed?'

'SIMULACRUM LOOPED FOR CONTINUOUS PLAY.'

'Can you download the simulacrum and play it back for us?' Blake picked up the micro holographic projector and switched it off with his thumb. 'Patch it into this unit.'

The lights on the projector blinked on and off fast, then the figure of Ban Kerralin returned. But this time, it was a different recording of him. It wasn't smooth. The words were in different tones, spoken with different inflections. They had clearly been cut from other audio recordings and stitched together.

'You will... not leave... this... room,' Kerralin said in odd pitches and paces. 'You will... not attack... anyone.' He repeated the two crudely edited sentences over and over.

Vila stared at it. 'So that's how they stopped it getting out,' he breathed. 'I'm guessing they couldn't order it to self-destruct, so this was the next best thing. Lock it up, close down the station and drag it far, far away.'

'And we just *had* to go looking for it,' said Gan.

'And we're going to again,' said Blake, grimly. 'Avon, could you reprogram this hologram? Make it say something else? Tell it to switch itself off.'

'It's possible,' Avon said quietly, picking up the projector. 'Zen, can you reconfigure this simulacrum and synchronise the movements of the mouth with an open-input speech synthesiser?'

'IT REQUIRES MANUAL REPROGRAMMING.'

'Using recordings of this simulacrum and the previous one, are you able to reproduce the voice of Ban Kerralin in the speech synthesiser?' asked Avon.

'NINETY-THREE PERCENT MATCH.'

'That should be good enough,' Blake said decisively. 'Jenna, how's our power?'

'We reached optimum half an hour ago,' Jenna replied confidently.

'Good,' said Blake. 'Sever the powerlines and the safety cable. Zen, set a course for Eurydice. Standard by twelve.'

'Status report,' Travis ordered as his ship sped towards populated space.

'Weapon still in pursuit, Commander,' the mutoid reported. 'Disturbances in the energy signatures of local stars suggest that the machine is drawing power from them as it passes by. Its speed is increasing exponentially.'

'Estimate time to planetfall on Eurydice,' Travis ordered. His only hope now was to land on a populated planet, he thought. He could hide in the crowds and hope that it would eventually get bored and give up searching for him.

'Planetfall in approximately two point seven one hours, Commander.'

'How long before it catches us?'

'Approximately one point nine hours, Commander.'

Travis panicked. 'Increase speed!' he yelped.

'We're at maximum now, sir,' the helmsman replied.

Travis thought fast. He'd be cutting it a bit fine, but he might just make it to Eurydice in one piece. He alone. 'Continue on course,' he ordered.

TEN
QUEUE-JUMPING

'What you're suggesting,' Avon said quietly, 'is that we all assist you in committing suicide.'

'What I'm suggesting,' Blake countered, 'is that we make an effort to stop the Berserker killing millions of innocent people. What I'm suggesting is that we don't give up the fight just because the odds aren't in our favour.'

'But it's not *our* fight, is it Blake?' Avon snapped. 'It's yours. If you cast your mind back to the point at which we embarked on this idiotic mission, you will recall I wanted nothing to do with it.'

'Nor me,' added Vila, but hung his head like an ashamed schoolboy when Gan gave him an admonishing look.

Jenna wasn't so easily cowed. 'I think Avon's right, Blake,' she said, looking uncomfortable about agreeing with Avon – and even more so about taking his side against Blake. 'It's far too dangerous.'

Blake looked shocked. 'But it's going to come for us anyway. For me and Vila.'

'That's unlikely,' said Avon. 'Once it's reached Eurydice, it's bound to reset its queue.'

'And kill millions,' said Blake. 'Look, without the *Liberator* we stand no chance of destroying it. We need high-powered weaponry to break it up once we've deactivated it.'

'*If* it can be deactivated,' Avon interjected.

'It's a chance we've got to take,' Blake said firmly. 'Vila, you and I have got to go down to Eurydice to stop it resetting itself.'

Vila looked startled. 'What? Why me?'

'Because you're on its hit list,' Blake explained. 'You and I were within its detection range when it was released from the vault, so it's almost certainly registered both of us. We have no way of knowing who it saw first, you or me, so we've both got to get off the *Liberator* before it comes to kill us all.'

'Oh.' Vila opened his mouth to say something, and then shut it again. Slowly, he stood up and made for the weapons rack. 'I suppose we'd better go, then.'

'Good man.' Blake turned to Zen's configuration display. 'Zen, estimate time to orbit of the planet Eurydice.'

'APPROXIMATELY TWO POINT FOUR HOURS.'

Blake looked at Avon. 'Will that be sufficient time to finish editing the simulacrum?'

'I could do it in half that time, perhaps less.' Avon's answer betrayed no note of arrogance, he was merely stating a fact. 'There is one other possibility, though.'

'Which is?'

'There could be a weakness in the AE105's computer. Perhaps if you keep its attention diverted, I could locate that weakness and exploit it.'

'There isn't time, Avon. Are you sure there *is* a computer weakness.'

'Not completely sure, no. But I think Kerralin's original message was intended as a clue to it. The man may seem shabby and eccentric, but if I'm right then he has to be given an award for both his cunning and his sense of humour.'

Blake sighed. 'There's no way we could distract the Berserker for long enough. And while it's chasing us it will destroy everything in its path. What if it kills someone by mistake? Does it register that kill and reset its queue?' He turned to see Vila lurking behind a chair, obviously hoping he would be forgotten. 'Go and get ready to teleport,' he ordered. 'Now.'

Jenna looked sternly at him. 'Are you sure you want to do this?'

'As you said, Jenna, Avon's right. This is my fault, and that means it's my problem. I probably can't do much about it, but at the very least I intend to try.' Blake turned and left the flight deck, heading to his cabin to prepare himself.

Avon waited for him to leave.

'Jenna,' he said quietly. 'Once he's teleported down, break orbit but stand off just outside range of the AE105's detectors.'

Jenna was surprised at the instruction. 'Why?'

'I want to test my theory,' Avon replied, and said no more.

Travis was on edge. The fingers on his still-human hand were twitching. He was impatient to get started even though he didn't relish the task that lay ahead. He relished even less the possibility that, if he did not take the necessary action, the machine would catch up with his ship and certainly destroy him. He checked the fuel gauge on his jetpack. He had about a six-minute burst left. It would have to do. At least he had plenty of oxygen.

'Time to orbit?' he demanded.

'Forty-nine point four minutes, Commander,' the mutoid answered.

'Status of the weapon.'

'Still in pursuit, sir.'

'Time to contact?'

The mutoid checked the computer. 'At present speed and trajectory, fifty-seven point seven minutes approximately, sir.'

Travis closed his eyes for a moment and took a deep breath. He tensed, prepared himself, and waited.

'We're nearly in orbit,' announced Jenna. She glanced down at Avon, who sat probing the holograph projector with a special tool. 'Is it ready?'

'It's been ready for thirty minutes,' Avon replied dourly. He stood up and resealed the unit. 'I was just narrowing the pulse transduction conduits to make it a little more efficient, as I had time.' He laid it on one of the consoles in front of Zen's main screen. 'Status of the new simulacrum program,' he called to the computer.

'COMPLETED,' Zen said.

'Connect and transfer,' Avon commanded.

Zen gave a little chime. 'DATA TRANSFER COMPLETE.'

Blake and Vila entered the flight deck. They had both changed clothes and now wore thicker brown leather tunics, protective bands over their forearms, and combat boots. Blake marched to the armoury rack and took a weapon belt, strapping it on. 'Any sign of Travis's ship?' he asked.

'ONE FEDERATION PURSUIT SHIP HAS ENTERED EURYDICE'S ORBIT. BATTLE COMPUTERS ONLINE.'

Blake nodded. 'Are there any other hostiles in the area?'

'ONE UNIDENTIFIED DEVICE IS FOLLOWING THE TRAJECTORY OF THE PURSUIT SHIP.'

'The Berserker,' said Blake. 'Stand by for further instructions.'

'CONFIRMED,' said Zen.

Avon held up a hand in front of Blake. He was holding the shiny-surfaced holograph projector. 'It's ready.'

Blake looked around the flight deck at the rest of his crew. 'You all know this could well be the last time you ever see me,' he said. 'I don't want this to be an unnecessarily dramatic moment, but I do want you all to know that I appreciate everything you've all done to help me. I know you don't all share my ideals and for the most part haven't had anything to gain by doing me any favours, which makes the fact that you did help me all the more surprising and impressive. If I die, all that I ask is that you...'

Jenna interrupted with a kind smile. 'Don't worry, Blake,' she said. 'We won't forget you.'

'Or me I hope,' Vila said sadly.

'You'll be back,' said Gan. 'We'll be waiting for you.'

'Thank you,' said Blake. 'Cally, can you teleport us to the surface, please?'

'Of course,' she said, moving towards the corridor.

Avon had finished what he was doing and handed the holograph projector to Blake. 'Make it count,' he said.

'I plan to,' Blake answered simply.

He and Vila followed Cally into the corridor.

It was time. Travis climbed into the airlock hatch and pulled on his space helmet. His life-support units automatically cut in and he initiated the hatch release sequence. The inner airlock hatch opened and he entered and closed it behind him. It was at times like this that he envied Blake the *Liberator* and its teleport facility.

He watched the gauge until it registered total depressurisation and then opened the outer airlock and clambered out onto the hull of his ship. He didn't bother to slam the hatch down – the ship was about to be destroyed anyway. He had ordered the mutoids to break orbit and move just inside atmosphere, and once on the hull he could see the blue sky and clouds of Eurydice's technologically modified, human-friendly atmosphere stretching out ahead of him.

He wasted no time firing his rockets and heading for the ground below, curving his trajectory so that he would not plunge into seas or crash into mountains but instead soar over land and sea until he found a safe place to alight. He knew his fuel would not hold out for long, but he was expecting some help in making a little extra distance soon. The AE105 itself would do this, even though it did not intend to.

Travis heard the explosion of his ship, destroyed by the weapon, and a few seconds later felt the shockwave hit him and kick him hundreds of miles across the sky in seconds. He instantly shut off his rockets, planning to use them to steady and steer himself off the wave's impetus as it decayed. It was going to be a bumpy ride, but at least this way he would stand a chance. Fortunately the rocket-jump suit was designed to absorb most of the force from the fringe of the blast and he was close enough to its extremity not to be too concerned about the more dangerous inner belt of force. For a while anyway.

On the horizon a city rushed nearer, and Travis prepared for landfall.

Blake and Vila materialised in a small alley between two tall buildings and looked around. There was no-one there, and he activated his bracelet communicator.

'Down and safe,' he reported.

He didn't wait for an answer. Instead they headed out onto the street just in time to see Travis whoosh over their head. The airborne Commander was heading down one of the main roads towards the centre of the city, and Blake and Vila started in the same direction.

A flash of lightning whipped over their heads in the same direction that Travis had taken.

The Berserker had arrived.

INTERLUDE III:
STATION AMBER, TWELVE MONTHS AGO

'She killed them, you know,' Ban Kerralin said, as he probed inside the complex circuitry of the machine. 'Well, I say killed. Not in the physical sense, I suppose. She had them brainwashed, their memories erased. Do you know, they wouldn't recognise me now?'

The tiny precision tools went back onto the tray in exchange for different ones, which he used to poke into the machine again. 'That's as bad as death. At least, I think it is. I mean, they're not the same people, are they? The people they used to be don't exist any more and now some pre-programmed, model Federation citizens plod around inside their bodies, going about their daily lives without asking questions, without wondering why they're so docile and obedient, never thinking that it might just be nice to spit in the faces of the monsters that made them.'

Another change of tools. More probing. A part of the machine jerked suddenly. 'Oops! Sorry.' Another prod of the tools and the machine went back to normal. The engineer smiled, then sighed. 'I wouldn't want to live like that, you know,' he continued. 'Life in a permanent state of somnambulance... no. Not for me. That's why I've decided to die. I've got a plan to take Servalan with me, of course, but there's a chance that it might not work, and so you, my sweet, are my back-up.'

He closed the android's cranium up and kissed her red hair. 'Now then,' he smiled. 'Let's see how well you respond to your programming, eh?' He reached over to a computer console and typed in all of the activation codes. The screen flashed up a message that a voiceprint would be required to complete the activation sequence. 'Activate,' he said.

The android's eyes were shut. 'Please wait,' it said in a sweet, gentle voice. 'Assimilating local data.' It was quiet for a moment. 'Ready.'

Kerralin stood in front of its seat. 'Identify yourself,' he commanded.

'I am the Assault Engine One Zero Six,' it said.

'And your purpose?'

'My purpose is subversion, infiltration and eventual destruction.'

'Destruction of what?' asked Kerralin.

'The designated subject of my attack has been registered by image print for recognition and has the name Servalan,' the AE106 informed him.

Kerralin grinned. 'Excellent. Activate Offensive Program Delta Sixteen.'

'Ready,' said the AE106.

The android opened its eyes. Its pupils dilated.

'Hallo,' Kerralin smiled as if he were addressing a whole new person.

The AE106 blushed, its cheeks flushing red as it realised it was naked. 'Who are you?' it stammered in slight panic. 'Where am I? What's going on?'

Kerralin hurriedly handed the machine a dressing gown. 'It's quite all right, my dear,' he said. 'You've had a medical examination. You're all clear, but you might be a bit disoriented. I'm sending you back to Federation Space Command shortly, and you should recover your memory on the way home.' He made a show of checking his computer records. 'Sorry, I lost track a bit,' he said. 'What's your name again?'

'Keelian,' said the AE106. 'Keelian Vardor.'

Kerralin felt a lump rise in his throat. After years of work, he had finally finished. And she was perfect. He thought of all the plans he'd made when he started working on her. All the things they would do, the places they would go. She would have made him famous. The toast of the scientific community.

But things had changed. Now there was only one plan. Only one place for this amazingly lifelike android to go.

He led the girl to an annexe of his lab where there were some other clothes waiting for it, borrowed from stores. From there, it was easy to sneak her aboard a ship. He had even found her a job for when she eventually reached her destination. The Supreme Commander wouldn't notice this plain little thing among her tailoring staff.

ELEVEN
CONTACT

Travis was slowing down, but he knew that attempting to land would be dangerous. There were buildings in every direction. He was starting to think that heading for a city might not have been the best idea, but on the other hand a hillside wouldn't have provided as much cover when the AE105 attacked. There were plenty of people in the city to hide behind.

It had occurred to Travis that Servalan had told him to let Blake have the weapon because she had gambled on it killing Blake and the *Liberator* crew destroying it in return, but so far neither had worked out.

He saw a large building ahead. It was a Federation Economic Study Centre – a college for people who would one day become politicians – and there were plenty of windows. Travis aimed for one on the fifth floor and steered himself into it. The glass shattered under the impact of his spacesuit, and people screamed and took cover under desks and tables as Travis slammed into the back wall of a classroom. He slumped down into a sitting position on the floor, a little shaken but conscious, protected by his space helmet. He pulled it off and took a breath of the local air. Students were clambering out from their hiding places, some with cuts on their hands and faces. The tutor lay spread across her desk, a spray of glass shards lacerating her throat, blood pouring into a growing puddle on the polished floor.

Travis gave the corpse a look of distaste as he shrugged off his jetpack, dumped it on the floor and marched out of the classroom.

'What was the theory you wanted to test?' Jenna sat with shoulders slumped in her navigation chair.

'Call it a contingency plan,' Avon answered, turning to Zen's screen. 'Zen, have you completed the adjustments I ordered?'

'RECALIBRATION OF THE FORCE WALL COMPLETED,' Zen confirmed. 'A LIGHT FIELD CAN NOW BE PROJECTED OVER A DISTANCE OF SIX HUNDRED SPACIALS.'

'And how far are we from the AE105's detector range?'

'FOUR HUNDRED SPACIALS,' Zen reported. 'PROJECTIONS WILL BE VISIBLE TO THE AE105 AT EXTREME RANGE, ALTHOUGH *LIBERATOR* WILL NOT.'

Jenna raised both eyebrows. 'A light field?'

'Just a minor modification to the force wall system,' Avon said. 'It might solve our problems a little more quickly than Blake's plan, and probably with less mess.'

'Isn't interfering with the force wall dangerous? Would the recalibrations reduce shield effectiveness?'

'No. Shine a torch on a wall, it's lit up, but it's still a wall.'

'And what good will shining a torch on our force wall do?'

'That depends on what shows up in the torchlight.' Avon checked something on one of the computer consoles. 'Battle computers to optimum capacity,' he ordered Zen.

'CONFIRMED.'

'Align projection field with the best possible location for detection by the AE105 and power up for activation. Clear neutron blasters for firing.'

'CONFIRMED,' Zen said again. 'ACTIVATION OF LIGHT PROJECTION FIELD WILL OCCUR IN SEVENTEEN MINUTES.'

Blake and Vila hitched a ride on a freight transporter heading into the city. Tracking Travis wasn't difficult. They followed the path of destruction made by the Berserker. There were craters everywhere, full of ash and debris, and some shattered walls and cracked building facades, but so far no bodies.

They jumped down off the transporter and Blake gave the driver a wave of thanks. The college ahead of them was a wreck: windows smashed, concrete cracked. The machine must be trying to drive Travis out into the open and destroy him or else crush him in the building's rubble, Blake thought grimly. And then it would kill everyone else.

'So now what?' asked Vila, seeming unsure about whether he honestly wanted to know the answer.

Blake looked up at the damaged building. 'We've got to get as close as we can to the Berserker,' he said. 'I hope it's still looking for Travis. It should leave the two of us alone until he's dead.'

'Well, I know you don't like him much, Blake, but let's not wish him dead too soon,' Vila replied, doing his best to smile. He looked up at the wrecked building. 'Do you think anybody died up there?' he wondered, gesturing to the floors above with a finger.

'It's possible,' Blake answered.

'Would it affect the Berserker's queuing system?' asked Vila.

Blake had no idea how the AE105 registered deaths in its vicinity or determined which deaths it was responsible for. It obviously had some kind of comprehensive logic programming. He mulled over the possibilities as he opened the front doors of the college and stepped inside. The corridor was clear, undamaged and obviously hurriedly evacuated. Chairs at the reception desk lay on the floor on their sides, drinks that had been dispensed in the small waiting area stood abandoned or spilt.

'It seems to have some form of sensory data input,' he said slowly. 'Perhaps it can scan to determine whether life forms are dead, how long they've been dead and how they died. It may only register a kill based on direct contact with its tissue vaporiser.'

Vila thought this over. 'Or, it might shoot at Travis and miss, because he ducks for cover behind somebody else. Then the person shielding him would die and the Berserker would reset the queue.'

'We just don't know,' said Blake.

'Let's hope it's got a straight aim and no self-blame complex then,' said Vila. 'It'll only kill us if it actually wants to.' He sighed. 'At least we'll be keeping it happy.'

Blake crossed the small reception area to the lift bay. All the lift doors were closed. He pressed the sensor to call the lift but it didn't light up. 'The power's down. Probably a safety precaution. Check the stairwell, Vila.'

Vila darted to a door at the other end of the alcove. 'Sealed off,' he called. 'Probably another safety precaution.' The sound of a blast roared overhead and the building shook. Cracks that had already begun to appear in the walls grew longer.

The AE105 fired and a section of the wall exploded. The life form it was hunting rolled out of the way and ran. The hole in the wall was large enough for the weapon to pass through and it did not waste time heading for the doorway. It followed its prey into the corridor, powering up the vaporiser and scanning all the time. It had extrapolated full details of its target's DNA, biorhythms and brainwaves. It was a hunter and it knew exactly what it was tracking.

'It sounds like we need to go up,' said Blake. He gestured at the lift. Vila unpacked his tools and handed Blake a mechanical door lever. Blake set to work and opened the lift doors in a few seconds.

'You know that shaft could collapse while we're in there,' Vila grimaced.

'One of many dangers we're facing right now,' Blake replied, stepping into the lift car and looking for a maintenance hatch. 'There's no way into the shaft from here. If we get this lift down we can climb the cables.'

'We're on the ground floor,' Vila said. 'Where is there *down* for it to go?'

Blake examined the controls. 'There's a pit for maintenance at the bottom of the shaft,' he said. 'It'll just be a few feet deep, but we only need a small gap.' He stepped out. 'Can you over-ride the lift control system, just enough to make it drop into that pit?'

'I think so,' nodded Vila.

There was another blast and the building shook again. The lift car creaked and Vila shuddered at the thought of being crushed as he set to work.

Travis turned a corner and ran into another corridor. There were two alcoves ahead of him, one leading to the lift and the other to the stairs. The weapon wasn't going to give up, and it was closing in fast.

He darted left, arms out to push the doors to the stairwell open, but slammed into them hard. Winded, he caught his breath and banged on the doors, grabbed the handles and shook them. They didn't budge. Travis heard a sound from behind him that by now had become uncomfortably familiar: the power-up of the weapon. He ducked quickly and kept his head down as the doors to the stairwell exploded, scattering hot fragments everywhere. Travis's suit protected him, but he knew it would not save him from vaporisation. He flung himself into the stairwell and bounded down the stairs three at a time. The machine pursued him. Sections of the stairs that Travis had already conquered exploded one by one. He took a huge leap to escape one of the deadly blasts and slammed into a wall. He was disoriented, but he managed to pick himself up. He darted onto the next flight of stairs just as the AE105 fired. The steps in front of Travis disintegrated and he fell into the empty space below, grabbing the banister rail at the last second to stop himself from plunging to the bottom of the stairwell.

The bulbous metal killing machine floated down towards him, charging its vaporiser. Travis had nowhere to go but down. It was a sheer drop through the centre of the staircase, but he could grab another rail on the way down, get to the bottom a few drops at a time. He let go of the rail.

TWELVE
PLAYING GHOST

'INFORMATION.'

'Yes, Zen,' Avon said irritably.

'LIGHT PROJECTION SYSTEM NOW ACTIVATED.'

'Let me hear it,' Avon ordered.

Zen chimed again, and the synthesised voice of Ban Kerralin filled the *Liberator*'s flight deck.

'This is my final command,' it said. 'You will relinquish all control of your systems to Kerr Avon and await his orders. You will obey any and every command given you by Kerr Avon. Respond by opening a communications channel to the nearest space vessel.'

Avon nodded briefly. 'Send it now,' he said. Then he sat back and waited for a response. He knew he wouldn't have to wait long.

Blake hauled himself up a few more inches of the cable to be level with another lift door.

'I think the Berserker is on a much higher floor,' he told Vila, who was hanging on to the cable below him. 'This is only the seventh. Travis will surely be heading downwards because he'll want to get out of the building. If we come out here, we might be able to catch them on their way down.'

He pulled the door lever from his belt and used it with one hand, holding himself fixed to the cable with the other. Once the door was open, he clambered through and helped Vila out.

Something exploded nearby, making Blake turn quickly to look behind him. In the alcove adjacent to the one that had housed the lift stood the doors to the stairwell, buckled but not breached. There was another blast and the doors cracked.

'Perhaps it's Travis,' Vila suggested. 'The Berserker would have blasted through that in a second.'

'He could be trapped in the stairwell,' Blake agreed. He drew his blaster. 'Let's give him a hand, shall we?'

'Get away from me, Blake!' Travis roared from the shaft, his voice an odd booming echo. 'I can see you. If you come near me I'll kill you.'

'This isn't a rescue mission, don't worry,' Blake answered through gritted teeth. 'Not for you in any case.' He pulled the holograph projector from a pouch on his belt. Travis fired his laseron destroyer and shot it from Blake's hand. The projector plunged to the bottom of the stairwell, a useless molten lump.

'You fool, Travis!' Blake growled. 'That wasn't a weapon. That device would've stopped the machine. Now it's going to kill all three of us, starting with you.'

There was another explosion that shook the building, knocking Blake and Vila to their knees, and the shining globe of the AE105 came into sight. It floated towards Travis, as if it was coming in close to make absolutely sure it hit its slippery prey this time.

Suddenly, there was a booming noise from the sky above them. Blake threw up his hands to cover his ears. Was it a voice? There was something oddly familiar about it, but it was so loud he couldn't make out the words.

The sound stopped as abruptly as it had started and, for a moment, the Berserker hung in the air, completely motionless.

'What's it doing?' whispered Vila. 'Why doesn't it kill Travis?'

Blake stared in confusion as the glowing machine went dark. The humming stopped and the metal sphere dropped past Travis to the bottom of the stairwell, hitting the ground floor with a resounding clang.

'INFORMATION,' chimed Zen. 'COMMUNICATIONS CHANNEL NOW OPENED BETWEEN *LIBERATOR* AND THE AE105.'

'AE105,' Avon shouted into the air, exultantly. 'This is Kerr Avon. Respond.'

'This is Assault Engine One Zero Five,' the Berserker answered in a buzzing computer voice a little grittier than Zen's. 'I am instructed to take my commands from you, Kerr Avon.'

'Deactivate your defensive shielding and weapons.'

'That command cannot be accepted,' said the Berserker. 'It conflicts with my core directives.'

'State your core directives.'

'Core directive one: I am not to accept the order to self-destruct. Core directive two: I am not to accept the order to deactivate my offensive or defensive capabilities. Core directive three: I am to obey the commands of my creator Ban Kerralin unless otherwise ordered by Ban Kerralin.'

Jenna sighed. 'You can tell it what to do, but you can't tell it to do anything that would help.'

But Avon was smiling. 'AE105,' he shouted. 'Can you accept the order to delete, in whole or part, the data in your memory core?'

'That order does not conflict with any of my programming,' said the Berserker.

'Delete the file relating to your core directives,' Avon beamed triumphantly.

'The file is deleted,' said the machine.

'Now deactivate yourself,' Avon ordered.

And suddenly there was silence.

Blake's bracelet beeped.

'Blake, come in,' Avon's voice said. 'I've shut down the AE105. I suggest you grab it and get out of there.'

'I can't grab it,' said Blake in annoyance, grabbing Vila and pulling him back into the corridor. 'It's at the bottom of a stairwell.'

'Give me its position relative to you.'

'About three feet horizontally and ninety vertically,' said Blake.

'I'll come and get it myself.'

The call ended. Blake activated the bracelet again. 'Cally, bring us up,' he snapped and, in a moment, he and Vila were gone.

In the ruined stairwell, Travis clung to the remains of the stairs, his legs dangling over the drop below.

'You won't get away with this, Blake!' he roared. 'I'll hunt you down, and when I find you, you'll wish that machine had killed you. Do you hear me, Blake? Blake!'

He knew that Blake had gone but, somehow, shouting at his shadow made Travis feel better.

Finally resting in his chair on the flight deck of the *Liberator*, Blake closed his eyes and sipped a drink while Avon explained what he had done.

'What are we going to do with this Berserker then?' Blake asked.

'I was planning to reactivate it,' said Avon. He enjoyed Blake's look of horror for a few seconds before adding, 'Just its computer system and propulsion. Then I can order it to dispose of itself in this system's sun.'

'Suicide by star,' Blake smiled, eyes still closed. 'How spectacular.' Suddenly he opened his eyes. 'Tell me, why we didn't try out your long-distance plan before I dashed down to the planet with the projector?'

'I couldn't be 100 percent sure that it would work,' said Avon. 'So you didn't want to hear about it.'

Blake winced. 'It seems to be my day for mistakes.'

'Doesn't it,' Avon replied with a sarcastic smile. 'It's a shame none of them have been small ones.'

'Let's look on the bright side,' said Gan. 'We're all safe. And so are the people on Eurydice.'

'Will the Federation send anyone to investigate?' asked Cally.

'I doubt it,' said Blake. 'That would draw too much attention. They'll probably send someone to clear up and cover up, as usual.' He glanced at the AE105 again, a memory stirring. 'Kerralin said that he'd hoped this thing would kill Servalan.'

'A man after my own heart,' Avon replied dourly. 'Although I also hoped it would kill Travis.'

Jenna knew what Blake was getting at. 'He said he had a plan B, didn't he? Something Servalan would be unable to escape from.'

'As I told you earlier,' Avon said. 'Anything trying to assassinate Servalan is the least of our problems.'

Keelian completed the last of the application forms and pushed the pad across the desk to Servalan, who gave them a merely cursory glance and smiled at her.

Keelian registered that smile in her database of images connected with the name Servalan and the orders in Offensive Program Delta Sixteen. The matches were perfect. It was the final confirmation she needed. She had already checked all other references, voice pattern analyses, motion pattern analyses and absolutely every scrap of data she had on the woman in whose office she now sat. She had been processing the data for quite some time now. It had taken a long time because she needed to be absolutely sure that she didn't kill the wrong person. That was in her programming. She was programmed to kill Servalan exclusively, with no collateral damage. When her mission was complete she would automatically deactivate herself. Her last act would be the internal distribution of a special energy pulse that would cause her systems to fuse and her computer brain to melt down so that she could never be reactivated and reused. The only thing between her and the completion of the mission now was absolute confirmation of identity, and that came a second later.

Servalan was speaking. 'Your completed application will be passed through to Administrative Training, and naturally you'll be selected for fast-track priority by my order. After that, I shall want you on my personal staff, attending to such matters as...'

Keelian leapt over the desk and grabbed Servalan's throat. Servalan started to choke as Keelian squeezed, staring in shock at the young girl's face. Keelian spoke, but not in her own voice. She spoke in another voice, a male voice, a voice Servalan thought she'd never hear again.

'You really are a poisonous bitch,' Ban Kerralin hissed through Keelian's mouth. 'Aren't you?'

Gasping for air, Servalan reached back behind her chair and quickly waved a hand over the emergency ray sensor in the wall. An alarm started howling.

Servalan felt dizzy, the room was beginning to spin as she started to black out.

Suddenly, Keelian's head exploded in a shower of sparks. Her hand flexed open and Servalan rolled out of her chair, ripping a huge portion of the lower half of her dress as she pulled herself free. The decapitated girl clattered belly-down into the office chair, smoke curling up into the air from her neck. The smoke set off the sprinklers, drenching Servalan and soaking what was left of her dress right through.

The guard that had destroyed the android held out a hand to help her up. 'Are you all right, Supreme Commander?' he asked.

Servalan wasn't all right. She was very upset. On Station Amber, when the AE105 had turned on her, she had known that Ban Kerralin wanted revenge, but after his death she had dismissed the possibility that he might yet get it.

As the guard left, effectively dismissed, she looked at the broken android lying on its side by the door and wondered if this was the last message she would ever receive from Ban Kerralin. It might not have been the only dirty trick he'd planned to play on her.

Gathering herself up, she buzzed for someone to turn the sprinklers off and noticed a light flashing on her communications panel. A message from Travis.

Servalan scowled. The last thing she needed at a time like this was to hear more of his bleating.

The message was brief and to the point, a single sentence: *Blake has the weapon.*

As the sprinklers shut off, the Supreme Commander stood dripping in her torn dress and seethed. That weapon was one of the most powerful things in the galaxy and now a band of ruthless malcontents controlled it. She would have to make a formal report to the President about this. But what could she say? Only that she didn't think for a second that Blake would actually use it. He was known throughout the Federation to be unpredictable, unstable and possibly slightly mad. But if he was prepared to mess around with the AE105, he would obviously have gone berserk.

COLD REVOLUTION

MG HARRIS

ONE

At dawn, tanks drove into the city. Troops stormed the streets. A handful of Federation supporters were executed on the spot. A dozen more were arrested. The entire affair lasted only a matter of hours. Fewer than twenty people died. Then order was restored, the parliament re-opened. That was the end and beginning of the Cold Revolution.

Blake turned from the screen. He faced the crew with an expression that barely concealed the glee he evidently felt. Avon looked away. This wasn't something he enjoyed seeing: Blake enjoying a moment of smug condescension.

'You see? Revolution doesn't always have to come about through violence. The will of the people is enough.'

Avon raised his eyes to Blake's. He gazed at him without expression. 'Almost twenty people died.'

'Yes, and that's entirely regrettable, I agree. But now Kartvel is free. The Federation left, eight weeks ago. They signed a treaty. And now there's going to be an election.' Blake allowed himself a smile. 'Even someone with your evident dislike of politics should be able to respect an outcome like that, Avon.'

'When it comes to revolution,' Avon replied, 'I always find myself wondering – *cui bono*?'

Blake grinned. Even in his cynicism, Avon found a way to hint at his own education.

'Cui what?' said Vila.

'It's an old language,' Blake replied. 'Latin. It means – who benefits?'

Avon was impressed, and raised an eyebrow.

'Revolution shakes things up,' Jenna observed, as Cally entered the flight deck, holding a tray full of iced drinks. 'No argument there. But not everyone benefits. For example, last week's revolution in the kitchen means that now we have to endure Cally's cooking for another three days. If you make a fuss about the status quo, you have to be prepared to take the consequences.'

'I was quite open with you all about my lack of food preparation skills,' Cally said. She eyed Jenna archly.

Watching them, Avon found himself quite beguiled by how easily teased Cally could still be. He took a glass from her tray and sipped it, then nodded in approval. 'Nothing wrong with this, Cally. It's perfect.'

She returned his gaze, even and serious. 'This is not where my strengths lie.'

Avon wondered how long it would take a woman of her utterly alien background to finally adjust to their company.

'Blake, are you suggesting that we could benefit from this revolution?' Gan asked.

'I wasn't going to, but now that you mention it...'

Avon took another sip of his drink, concealing his own reaction. How clever Blake could be. The more Avon saw of him, the more he realised what a formidable leader Blake might become. How well he was learning to play his little band of 'freedom fighters'. Now he even had the rest of the crew thinking his ideas were their own.

But Avon knew better. Whatever the power of Blake's charisma, Avon himself would never allow himself to be manipulated by the man. The time would come when an opportunity to enrich himself would present itself. Until that time, Avon would remain an accomplice of this ludicrously ambitious revolutionary.

'Gan's right. There may be a way to benefit.' Blake hesitated.

'Are you going to tell us how?' Vila asked.

'Well, apart from the obvious advantage of having another world break free of Federation control...' Blake started.

Jenna interrupted, 'Yes, but Kartvel? Really? Wasn't it one of the Federation's more *backward* colonies?'

'Hardly. They have a population of sixty million and a continental visual broadcasting service. They have a national airline fleet of forty aeroplanes. Their two universities are amongst the best in the quadrant. And from what I hear, they can even manage the odd bit of interplanetary travel.'

'Which is provided by the Federation as part of their treaty. And it's open only for diplomatic travel.'

'True,' Blake admitted. 'But they have to start somewhere.'

'If we're looking for allies,' Vila said, 'we might want to think about somewhere with a bit more going for it.'

Blake spoke firmly. 'All allies are useful. Believe me, Lindor was in worse shape than Kartvel. But Sarkoff was still someone worth cultivating.'

Vila shook his head. 'Your plan to reinstate Sarkoff almost got us killed.'

'You don't need to remind me of that,' Blake said. His tone had turned a little sharper, Avon noticed. It often did that, when Blake sensed resistance. Dissent usually had to come from Avon, but he wondered whether this time he might get a break. Whatever Blake was planning, the others seemed to be already on their guard.

Blake continued. 'As it turns out, the man in charge of Kartvel is an old friend of Sarkoff's.'

There it is, thought Avon. Blake was itching to play politics. Again.

Cally glanced from Avon to Blake. 'You've been in touch with Sarkoff?'

'Yes, I spoke with him briefly, yesterday and then at considerable length again today. He sends his best, Cally. As does Tyce.'

Avon said, 'It's good to know that you're tending to your carefully cultivated plants, Blake. But what's the point of getting involved with whatever is happening on Kartvel?'

'The new man is a hero, by all accounts. His name is Edu Shevard. He joined the dissident movement about five years ago. It was a brave and rather risky move – given that at the time he was a Federation officer. Reported directly to Servalan.'

'He broke ranks from inside the Federation?' Gan sounded impressed. 'That takes real courage. How did he get away with it?'

'He didn't,' Blake said grimly. 'He spent two years in a Federation prison. For quite a lot of the first year, they tortured him. I'd say he's the kind of man who'd be on our side. It's what Sarkoff thinks, too. He's been in touch with Shevard. And apparently, he has a proposal for us. He needs a favour.'

Avon glanced up. 'A favour?'

'We're just six people, Avon, when all's said and done. *Liberator* might become the head, and the heart of a movement. But we still need arms and legs.'

Avon forced himself to ignore Blake's segue into tedious rhetoric. He was beginning to recognise the tactic. It might work with the others, but someone had to question whether Blake's dreams were actually attainable.

'Do you know if they brainwashed him?' Avon's eyes met Blake's again for a moment. He saw a flash of disappointment. For a moment, Avon almost felt sorry for provoking him.

Blake shook his head slightly. 'You think the Federation turned him?'

'You'd know better than me, how persuasive Federation brainwashing techniques can be.'

'As far as I know, Avon, Shevard has shown no signs of sympathy with his former torturers. But thank you for trying to protect me from myself.'

'It's clear that you enjoyed playing the kingmaker with Sarkoff. Someone has to take care that your new hobby doesn't prove incompatible with staying alive.'

'I hate to say it but he's right,' Vila said, gloomily.

'We might need more than a month to forget when you last put our lives in danger, Blake.'

As Avon warmed to his theme, he noticed a change come over Blake – his shoulders stiffened, his jaw tensed. Blake seemed to ponder his next words with great care, eventually saying, 'I'm sorry that you don't seem to whole-heartedly approve, Avon, but on this matter I'd like you to trust me. Politics is a delicate business. There are interests to balance. We're hardly in the driving seat now, are we? Allow me to do what I know how to do – to create a base of support.'

But the eyes of Cally and Jenna were on Avon. They looked anxious, especially Cally.

In the end, Avon thought, this wasn't the most radical step that Blake could make. They had the *Liberator*, the most powerful ship known to exist in the galaxy. Yet all Blake could think of were ways to push it around a chessboard as if it were a pawn and not a queen.

'All right.' Avon nodded, once. 'Kartvel it is.'

This wasn't going to be the first time he let something go without properly opposing Blake and it wouldn't be the last. But Avon was promising himself on a weekly basis that, one day, he was going to put a stop to Blake's ill-advised antics.

TWO

'An election monitor?' Vila sounded sceptical.

'If you don't know what it means, just say so,' Avon said. 'I don't imagine they taught advanced democracy during your schooling.'

'Then perhaps you'd better explain it to me too,' Cally said, with a hint of coolness. 'I haven't much of an idea what you're talking about either.'

'When an emerging democracy holds its first genuine election, a team of monitors is sent to oversee it,' Blake explained. 'They make sure that everything done is above board.'

'How can anyone trust the monitors to do their job properly?' Gan asked.

'It's a good question. With great difficulty, would have to be my honest answer. But it's something that members of the Freedom Party were asked to help with, on occasion.'

'I thought the Freedom Party was restricted to Earth,' Jenna said, puzzled. 'And there's not a great deal of democracy there.'

Blake nodded. 'There's no amount of democracy whatsoever, Jenna. But the Freedom Party had members who left the planet and managed to find themselves on worlds where the Federation's grip was weaker. I've heard of members who helped monitor the elections on some of the distant worlds. Believe it or not, there are planets where the Federation is willing to consider proposals for secession, provided that there is demonstrable popular support.'

'And provided there isn't much going for that planet in the first place?' suggested Vila. 'So, this Shevard fellow, he wants you to monitor the election?'

'It seems so.'

'But he's already in charge.'

'He's the Acting First Minister. Which simply means that he took the reins of power after the revolution.'

Jenna shrugged. 'That sounds a lot like "demonstrable popular support".'

'Not really,' Avon said. 'Revolutions can be puzzling affairs.' He flashed a sardonic grin at Blake. 'The victor isn't always the people's choice.'

'Not in *every single* instance,' agreed Blake. 'Although I'll admit, Shevard appears to have a strong case. He didn't initiate the revolution himself. He seems to have accepted the mantle of leadership, as opposed to seeking it. From what I can tell, he even proposed other candidates as better suited than him. They're standing against him in the election, political types who've held administrative posts.'

'Shevard is not a politician?'

'He's rather new to it,' Blake said. 'He worked for years in Federation Security, a fairly minor role. Then he had his epiphany, started writing some rather influential articles suggesting that the Federation ought to respect the unique traditions of the Kartveli people.'

Vila said, 'Unique traditions?'

'He means religion,' interjected Jenna. 'Kartvel is some kind of enclave for an ancient religious sect.'

Vila rolled his eyes. 'Oh, just what we need, another mad-eyed cult leader. Just so you know, this time someone else can line up to be sacrificed.'

'No-one's going to be sacrificed,' Blake grinned, his eyes crinkling with amusement. 'It's not that kind of religion.'

'But Shevard's a religious nutcase.'

'I don't think that's it,' Blake said, pensively, 'although I haven't met the man, of course. It's more to do with the nationalism. The planet was colonised by a fairly ethnically homogenous group. Shevard – and his supporters – seem to be rather passionate about maintaining ancient roots.'

'Will you be a monitor then?' Avon was getting bored. The man had clearly decided that the way to favour amongst any anti-Federation coalition included alliances with any kind of misfits. Avon simply wanted to know the plan quickly, so that he could evaluate any personal risk and how minimise it.

'Actually,' Blake said, with a smile, 'I was going to ask you.'

Avon looked at him sharply.

'I think you're the man for this job, Avon. You know all about how democracies are meant to function. You've a keen eye and you're a good judge of people.'

Avon knew better than to listen to Blake's flattery. 'I'm not at all sure that I am a good judge of people...' he began, intending to finish with some sarcastic quip about his current company. But Blake interrupted.

'You don't? In that case, perhaps Cally should accompany you?'

Avon bit his lower lip. I walked into that, he thought.

'Cally.' Blake glanced across towards the sofas, where she was sitting with Vila. 'What do you think? They'll take care of all the arrangements on the ground. You and Avon just need to turn up and register with the official team of election monitors.'

Avon said, 'And what are we to expect from our... colleagues?'

'There'll be at least two from Lindor, we know that much. Sarkoff was one of the first regional leaders that the Kartveli contacted.'

Cally frowned. 'The Kartveli pick their own monitors?'

'They nominate. The Federation has final approval.'

'But they're all friendly with the current Kartvel administration?'

'They're sympathetic, shall we say. Most of the monitors are representatives from planets with which the Federation is allied. It's in the Federation's interest to behave legally, as well as Kartvel's.'

'Or to be seen to do so,' Cally said.

'Quite so,' Avon said. 'And we'll be the odd man out.'

Blake smiled. 'That you will.'

'But you believe we'll be safe?'

'This whole affair is under immense scrutiny. All the non-Federation worlds in the sector will be watching. Including their allies. The Federation will be putting on their "benevolent Empire" face. The big brother that would only take over a world in desperate circumstances, for the good of its own population.'

Avon sighed. 'So you think the law is going to protect us here?'

'Kartvel's laws as well as the Federation's. If the Federation were to try to interfere with the election in any way...'

'For example, killing two of the election monitors?'

'There would be an interplanetary scandal. The election would be declared null and void. No allied world would trust the process again.'

'To capture Roj Blake, it might just be worth the hassle,' Vila murmured.

'Which, I imagine, is precisely why Blake isn't going himself,' Avon said.

Blake ignored the comment. 'Once you're in Kartvel City, they'll brief you and then assign you to a programme of official visits to polling stations. If you see anything suspicious, anything that looks like the election is being rigged, or that voters are being prevented from participating, then you report it.'

'Voters?' Cally murmured.

'There were no voters on Auron?'

'There were no elections, as such.'

'I imagine with telepathy, you can make certain desires known without being explicit,' Avon said.

'We had ways of choosing our leaders, if that's what you mean.'

'What if it's a trap?' interrupted Gan. 'How do we know the Federation have really left Kartvel? If there's a chance they are still there, surely none of us should go?'

'I don't think it's a trap, Gan. I'm not trying to save my own skin here. I just think that Avon and Cally might be good at this – better than me.'

Gan didn't seem wholly convinced. 'If there's a risk, is it really worth the effort?'

'It'll do this one good to step up,' Jenna remarked, hooking a thumb at Avon. 'Perhaps he'll be less prone to making barbed comments if he has to get his hands dirty with the real business of democracy.'

For a moment, Avon was surprised. It was a sour observation, coming from someone who'd once privately shared the same reservations about Blake's grandiose ambitions. Either Blake was getting much better at influencing his crew with his revolutionary fervour, or Jenna and Blake had exchanged these views in Avon's absence. Avon strongly suspected the former.

'I don't mind doing it,' Cally said.

Graciously, Blake said, 'Thank you, Cally. I'm told that Kartvel is beautiful in winter. It's one of the earliest Terran colonies – parts of the capital city are over a hundred years old, and built in the style of ancient monuments back on Earth. It's surrounded by mountains, there are ski lodges, lakes.' He grinned. 'We wouldn't blame you for staying on an extra day to enjoy the sights.'

'Wouldn't we?' Vila said, unhappily. 'Why didn't you say there were ski lodges? I'm quite partial to a bit of mountain air, me.'

'Oh, you ski, do you?' Jenna asked, laughing. Vila turned to answer but Gan joined in with Jenna's teasing of Vila's unlikely prowess on the slopes.

'You don't have to ski to enjoy the sights,' Vila grumbled.

Avon said nothing. It wasn't the worst job Blake had ever asked him to do. He was even looking forward to the chance to mix with the other election monitors. There might even be some interesting conversation. Anyone would at least be a change from the mind-numbing tedium of listening to Vila.

THREE

Five hours later, shortly after dinner, Avon and Cally arrived on Kartvel. They landed near the spaceport and were then escorted by tram to the Kartveli Parliament. It had paid, in the past, to conceal the *Liberator* crew's ability to teleport, so Cally and Avon had called the bracelets communicators and taken their seats on the shuttlecraft that Shevard had arranged.

The day was very clear, a cornflower-blue sky that remained stubbornly light, even in the middle of the evening. Blake hadn't exaggerated the beauty of Kartvel's capital city. Buildings made from a salmon-and-grey stone, wood-framed windows and striped awnings mingled with the monoliths of glass and concrete that were characteristic of Federation architecture. The combined effect was striking, especially with the backdrop of craggy, snow-capped mountains. Between some buildings, Cally caught an occasional chink of the deep blue of Lake Paravan.

Within the city itself, there was an air of calm. Yet Cally had no trouble whatsoever picking up on a barely repressed tension amongst the city dwellers. The effects of democratic upheaval were unlikely to be visible to the uninformed casual visitor, she thought. An orderly election amongst a tidy, well-behaved electorate left only the odd discarded ballot paper. Had they arrived earlier, however, Cally reflected that they might have wondered at slick patches of a rich, dark substance on the streets outside the parliament, perhaps even have gone on to identify them as the blood of traitors – or that of patriots. The baroque complexities of another world's politics could appear deceptively simple.

Within the parliament building, they were silently divested of their weapons and teleport bracelets before a single word was spoken. Cally hesitated, but saw that the same was expected for all the monitors. The immediate presence of at least twenty armed and scowling guards inhibited any instinctive reaction to protest.

'Blake's friends don't seem very friendly,' she said.

Avon turned to Cally with a half-smile. 'This one is only a friend of a friend.'

Finally, it seemed that someone apart from the guards had noticed them. The door was opened and Avon and Cally were ushered away from the other monitors.

'Our Acting First Minister Mr Shevard will see you now.'

As they stepped over the threshold into a large, wood-panelled office, Cally was somewhat surprised to find a small, balding man, dressed in a rather drab, grey two-piece outfit, standing on his desk to reach a picture on the wall behind his chair. It was a portrait of Supreme Commander Servalan of the Terran Federation.

'Close the door, please. For one thing, there are draughts.' Edu Shevard lifted the heavy portrait from its hook and lowered it gently to the ground. He stepped down from the desk, smiling a thin smile of satisfaction. 'You recognise the picture, I'm sure?'

'For an organisation that likes to pretend that it is a conglomeration of well-meaning individuals, free of unnecessary symbols of power,' Avon said, 'Servalan is the closest thing the Federation has to an icon.'

Noting the frisson that went through Shevard as he heard this, Cally felt certain that Avon's choice of the word 'icon' had been deliberate, although she wasn't sure why it should have this effect.

'An *icon*? You're quite right,' Shevard said, after a moment's consideration. 'That's what Servalan is. To many I knew, perhaps even to me, once, very long ago, Servalan was everything.'

'But no longer,' Avon said. He was watching Shevard closely.

'Which is precisely why the separation from the indignities of the past must involve, above all, a cathartic act.'

'Catharsis is important,' Avon agreed, smiling. Cally knew that smile well enough to know it wasn't to be trusted. Avon wasn't entirely convinced by Shevard.

'Exactly. We will burn this painting in a public ceremony tomorrow morning, destroy Servalan's image as the *icon* of all that we have despised for the past fifty-two years.' He smiled. 'We will replace her with one that is even older.' Shevard opened his desk drawer, inside which lay a small painting, very dark, framed in elaborately carved, gold-embossed wood. It had the appearance of something quite ancient. To Cally's astonishment, he raised it to his lips, kissed the image once, moved his fingers rapidly across his face and chest and then kissed his own fingers.

He glanced up at them. 'Another woman,' he said quietly, but with pride, 'from another time. Infinitely more deserving of our contemplation.'

Cally stared at the painting: a woman carrying a young child. It had to be some kind of religious symbol.

'May I take this opportunity to thank you for agreeing to monitor the proceedings, dear, trusted colleagues of Roj Blake? There can be few people whose anti-Federation credentials are more worthy than yours.'

Under his breath, Cally heard Avon mutter, 'Blake will be thrilled.'

'Sincerely, I am most grateful. It's been a dream of ours, for years, to be free of the Federation.'

'You are to be congratulated,' Cally said. 'Not many worlds achieve what yours has – a peaceful transition.'

Shevard gave a modest shrug. 'We're not there yet. If the Federation decide that this election is anything but honest, they'll refuse to allow the secession. We'll be a subject world again. So you see, dear friends, we rely on your support.'

With these words, the private audience with Shevard was over. Cally and Avon moved on to the lobby of the Parliament, which was hosting a grand reception for the newly assembled monitors. Shevard's people seemed determined not to let any of them out of their sight.

Cally observed that the dress code of the 'secret' police was absurdly obvious: long leather greatcoats turned up at the collar, one hand permanently hovering by the pocket that housed the gun holster. She wondered whether she should mention it to Avon, but reflected that she was more bemused than anxious. It seemed plausible, in a newly emerged democracy, to ape the outward gestures of the exiting rulers.

Cally moved between the other election monitors, a cocktail in one hand, exchanging pleasantries as best she could. Blake hadn't explained this part of the job to her. Avon seemed perfectly at ease as he enjoyed the company of willowy, elegant women in high heels, but Cally felt distinctly uncomfortable, as well as under-dressed. To a large extent she was still taking her cues for Terran behaviour from her crewmates. Now, it appeared, she was meant to flirt. She ran her eyes across the room, waiting for someone's to meet hers. After a few seconds, she stopped, suddenly aware that one of the guards was staring at her.

He was a young man of no more than twenty, good-looking with high cheekbones and smooth skin, his fair hair slicked back underneath his bottle-green uniform cap. When Cally began to return his gaze, he approached with a full glass of sparkling wine in each hand, no hint of embarrassment.

'Hello,' she said to him with a smile, 'Are you here to see that we don't get out of control, with all this generous hospitality?'

If the guard understood her joke, he didn't react. Instead, he handed Cally some wine and took her empty cocktail glass. He leaned forward, confidentially. 'It is Zviad Khurdia who presents the gravest danger. His people will stop at nothing – they have killed thousands outside the cities. One isn't safe on half of the planet.'

'Who is Zviad Khurdia?'

'A warlord. Before Mr Shevard returned to Kartvel, our world had fallen into chaos. The Federation were no longer in control. The rule of law was in collapse. The warlords took advantage. Khurdia was the most powerful of them. He still is.'

Cally tried sending a telepathic message to Avon, to bring him over. What the guard had said was news to her. Avon should definitely hear this. But it seemed that being flirted with by not one but two tall, bleached-blonde women was preventing him from responding to her call.

'Where is Khurdia now?'

'Who knows? He went into hiding.'

'Why?'

The handsome young guard shrugged, as though it must be obvious. 'You can't stand for election if you're in custody.'

'There's a warlord standing in this election?' Cally asked uneasily. Blake hadn't mentioned it. 'Is he likely to win?'

'No-one wants to deal with a world headed by a convicted criminal.'

'True,' Avon said. He'd appeared at Cally's side just in time to hear this last quip. 'But even so, it often happens.'

With a mere glance at Avon, the young guard placed a hand lightly on Cally's arm. 'My name is Koba, Miss Cally. I'm at your service. Don't worry about Khurdia. We guarantee that no harm will come to you.' There was a hint of a military salute before he turned away.

Avon watched him leave. He turned his eyes on Cally. 'An admirer?'

She sipped her drink. 'Would it matter?'

The directness of her question seemed to take him by surprise.

'It might.' Avon's answer seemed cautious.

'Why?'

'Well now, let's see... He's a member of Shevard's security.'

'And what else? He's younger than you?'

'He's younger than *you*.'

Musing, she replied, 'I know.'

'What were you talking about?'

'A man called Khurdia. The boy called him a warlord. Avon... He knew who I was. He knew my name. I don't think he was flirting. I think he was trying to warn me that there's a chance Khurdia might try to steal the election.'

FOUR

Avon and Cally moved into the gathering. They began to ask discreet questions. It seemed that Khurdia and his followers had something of a terrifying reputation. Khurdia himself was an old enemy of Shevard's. He too had been trained by the Federation. Lacking the smooth, diplomatic eloquence of his former colleague, Khurdia had not thought to negotiate for the colony to secede. Instead he'd spoken openly against the Federation, encouraged civil disobedience. When the collapse happened, he had accumulated a considerable degree of personal power.

'The Kartveli always had a predilection for the "strong man",' Avon was informed by one of the women who'd been regaling him all evening, a blue-eyed lady of aristocratic bearing who said she was from Lindor. 'In many respects, Zviad Khurdia was cast from that mould.'

Khurdia had acquired immense folk popularity – and a Federation death warrant. Now he co-ordinated, from his hideaway in the mountains, a relentless and vicious battle of terror against the supporters of Shevard. Almost exclusively recruited from the former elite who'd served under the Federation, they had the most to lose from genuine regime change. Khurdia's support, however, came entirely from an 'honest impulse of the people'. It was suspected that Khurdia sought power at any cost, that he would rule the planet as he ruled the towns and villages into which none of the pro-democracy forces would dare to tread.

'And yet he is a candidate in the election?' Cally asked, puzzled at how someone could apparently respect their democratic system enough to use it, only to want to dismantle it afterwards.

The aristocratic woman managed a condescending smile. 'It happens. Regrettably, there's such a thing as electing to be dominated.'

When it was time to leave the reception, a squat, stocky security guard escorted Avon and Cally to an armoured limousine. He waited for them to take seats in the rear of the car, then slid in next to Avon. His body was bulky and forced them to sit close together. The car began to fill with a mild scent of sweat masked with a woody cologne. A driver wearing the same uniform as the security guard drove them from the reception to their hotel.

They travelled in silence. In the streets, tanks were still crawling over the city. Some of the remaining Federation troops were still unaccounted for, apparently. Until they'd all been rounded up, the city was under semi-martial rule. In squares and plazas throughout the city, a pro-Federation faction seemed to be vying with supporters of the warlord for open spaces in which to demonstrate. Such expressions were permitted, the driver informed them, provided they were small. They saw three minor skirmishes. In each case, the pro-democracy police usually outnumbered the demonstrators.

The limousine stopped in a central plaza. Cally peered out of the narrow pane of glass that constituted the only window in the rear of the vehicle. Above them towered a huge monument of stone, lit up by huge, orange arc lamps in the square. It didn't look like a hotel – too few windows. The door alone was at least six metres high.

She noticed Avon seemed quietly impressed. On the *Liberator*, he showed little interest in aesthetics, so his reaction was vaguely surprising.

'This is a church,' he announced. He glanced sharply at the driver, who had stepped out of the car. 'What are we doing here?'

The driver gave them a curious smile. He looked to be about forty years old, with dark, angular good looks, and the ghost of a beard. 'We pretended for years that it wasn't important, but we never forgot. Maybe these doors were closed to us,' he said, pointing at the statuesque portal. 'But inside,' he continued, tapping his own chest, 'in here, it was always open, always warm.'

Avon had grown suddenly tense. With evident restraint, he repeated, 'What are we doing here?'

'You're here to bear witness. Mr Shevard wishes you to understand the source of the change that is sweeping through the Kartveli people. The reason we must leave the Federation.'

Avon turned his gaze back on the church. 'So much stone,' he commented. 'Such expense.'

Cally's eyes followed the span of the great door. She saw seven figures carved into a wooden frieze – three child-sized, flanked by four adults. All wore crowns on their heads which were surrounded by circles as far down as their shoulders. In addition, the figures were united by the fact that they clutched in their hands a cross. A larger cross hung above all of their heads, suspended over the central figure, the young boy. All seven stared straight ahead, frozen in motionless serenity, accepting their fate, whatever it might be. She immediately sensed a tragic air about them, especially the young children.

As they went inside, they began to hear voices joined in music, hauntingly beautiful, solemn, evocative.

'It is the liturgy of Saint John Chrysostom,' explained the driver, in a hushed whisper. 'Centuries old. They sang this very music in the Church of the Holy Sepulchre the night of the Second Schism.' Seeing how little Avon and Cally understood, he added, 'In the Holy Land on Earth, when the Orthodox Church split once again.'

Avon asked, 'And this is your religion, is it? "Orthodox"?'

'Sometimes I think that the Church is the only thing on which Khurdia and Shevard actually agree.'

'They do agree, then?' asked Cally, surprised.

'They'd be fools not to. No-one on Kartvel will vote for a non-believer.'

Cally stared up at the vaulted ceiling, a vast arch lined with carved, gilded wood. There was so much about this society that she didn't understand. What could she or Avon tell them about how to conduct an election?

As they left the church, she couldn't help feeling that there was something different about the position of the limousine. She turned back to look for their driver, who'd tarried a while in some kind of kneeling ritual. Avon too, had tensed, glancing from the car to the open door of the church.

The door to the armoured limousine opened. Cally felt Avon's hand grip her arm.

Something's wrong, she telepathed.

A woman emerged from the front passenger seat of the car. She wore the greatcoat and cap of Shevard's security forces, but Cally had never seen her before. She held a blaster. It was aimed at Avon's chest.

'In the car,' she snapped. They could barely see her features, shadowed by the peak of the cap. She'd positioned the armour-plated door between her and them. Any kind of physical attack was likely to fail. Her demeanour suggested she was serious about using her weapon.

Avon muttered, 'It's a set-up.' There was nothing they could do but comply.

The stocky security guard who had waited in the car was still on the back seat, slumped against the opposite door. The only clue to his condition was a tiny bruise to the skin above the carotid artery. Cally doubted whether she herself could have made a cleaner job of it. A quick touch on the pulse points, however, revealed the guard to be alive.

Inside the car, the woman told them to strap themselves in, and kept her blaster on them as they complied. Next to her, a man in the same uniform began to drive. Cally tried to catch a glimpse of his face in the mirror, but large sunglasses obscured his eyes.

The woman said, 'We don't wish to harm you. But if you resist, we will.'

Cally said, 'If any election monitor comes to harm, the election is declared null and void.'

Avon glared at their kidnapper. Cally could sense the effort it took to conceal his disdain. 'So, you are pro-Federation?'

'You're mistaken,' was her uninterested reply.

'Then what's the meaning of this?'

'Your impressions of this world are dangerously inaccurate,' she said stiffly. 'It is necessary to take measures to rectify this.'

'So you're kidnapping all the election monitors?' asked Avon.

'Kidnapping is a very harsh word for what's happening here.'

'I'd say it's accurate.'

'It's impossible to conduct a private conversation in this city. And someone wishes to talk with you. Now be silent, please.'

The car lurched through several streets, then pulled a hard left onto a side street. The front door opened. The woman who held the gun slid closer to the driver. She was joined by another woman, this one wearing a shabby, mud-coloured overcoat. The second woman produced a gun, which she aimed at Cally.

Avon sat back and stared. 'Evidently, you mean business,' he said, with a hint of a sneer.

The driver left the city behind and took them through the valley until the road began to climb into the mountains. They rode in silence. Avon seemed distracted and Cally glanced at him a couple of times, trying to catch his eye, to detect the inkling of a plan. Tentatively, she tried telepathy.

If you want to try something, Avon, just give me a signal.

Avon ignored her, gazing directly into the blaster that stared back at them.

Once they had escaped the city limits, the car slowed as the driver opened the door and threw out the unconscious guard. The two women held guns on them the entire time. Their gazes were devoid of any feeling that Cally could read.

There could not have been more than one hour of light left and a bitter cold was beginning to envelop them. Cally reflected that she might have been wrong in her earlier judgement. The kidnappers didn't seem all that merciful now.

FIVE

Four hours later, they arrived in a small hamlet, a cluster of barns and a guest house with three apartments under gambrel roofs. The upper slopes of the gambrels were piled half a metre high with snow. The car park and all paths had been swept, but every other surface was thick with snow that glowed a lambent pink in the neon of the three streetlamps. Avon and Cally were escorted to an apartment on the second floor. The accommodation was simple but surprisingly comfortable: rustic furnishings, wood-panelled floors and ceilings, a log fire in which wedges of wood crackled and smoked.

The woman who'd held them at gunpoint for hours stood by the entrance, but didn't enter the apartment. She looked exhausted. Cally thought about attacking her. The four-hour drive back to Kartvel City was a strong deterrent, however; they'd certainly be followed, even assuming they could commandeer the car. Furthermore, she was intrigued. If they were to be harmed, it would probably have happened by now. Maybe it was better to wait and see what these people wanted.

'Please, friends of Roj Blake, your attention.' The woman spoke with a heavy accent, not the more urbane tones they'd heard in Kartvel City. 'My name is Borena. Accept my apologies for necessity of threat. Sometimes is no other way. Now, the hour very late. We expected you sooner at St Mark's. But now too late to see Zviad Khurdia. You stay here until tomorrow. There is food,' she added, opening a cupboard, 'and vodka in the freezer. You should not be uncomfortable. Shevard's people have been told that you are in no danger. They surely will contact your ship to reassure your colleagues. Truly, my friends, we simply wish to exercise our right to put our case.'

'Then we aren't your hostages?' Cally asked.

'*Hostage* most inappropriate. We are hospitable people. Permit us to entertain you.'

Avon said, 'You've begun well. I don't know when I was last kidnapped so effectively.'

'You may discuss our methods with Mr Khurdia in the morning. Now, we are all tired. I am certain you wish to rest,' Borena said. 'I wish you a good night.' She closed and then locked the apartment door from the outside.

Avon went immediately to the door and tested it. He frowned, then tested the windows. Also sealed. He began to remove his jacket. The air outside had been so cold that its metallic fibres had sharply chilled. But inside the apartment, the air was warm and smelt faintly of sweet resin.

Cally opened the fridge and brought out a few things from inside. There was a wheel of cheese wrapped in waxed paper, some sliced sausage, six blue-grey eggs, butter and a fruit that looked rather like apples. A paper bag contained a sliced loaf of brown bread.

She removed the bottle from the freezer, found two glasses and poured a measure into one. It was a very pale green colour, tasted very crisp, clean and had a smooth, grassy aftertaste. She poured out a second glass and turned to face Avon with it in her hand.

'Plan?'

'I don't think there's any point trying to escape,' he began. 'And anyway, I want to meet this Zviad Khurdia. There are a few things about this planet that interest me.'

'For instance?'

'The relative ease with which Shevard managed to persuade the Federation to let the colony secede. It struck me as odd the moment Blake showed us the broadcast. There are a fair number of these little worlds. In general, the Federation is loath to let go of any of them. In the case of Kartvel, it seems even more unlikely. Look at these mountains for example. Mountains this big often contain useful natural resources: bauxite, copper ores, precious metals.'

'Yes, I see.' Cally handed him the glass of vodka.

'Then there's the image Kartvel likes to give of itself,' he continued, 'of a religious outpost. Most people hear "religious" and they think of primitives worshipping idols. Yet what we've seen is a sophisticated culture. Certainly the type of culture that might become a threat to the Federation. It's as if the Kartveli are keen to give an *impression* of being a cultural backwater.'

'Avon, what about that painting that Shevard showed us? He treated it like some kind of holy relic.'

'The Federation doesn't generally tolerate organised, literate religion. On Earth it's illegal. Something's going on here, Cally.'

'You think we've walked into a trap?'

Avon sampled the vodka. 'It wouldn't be the first time that Blake led us astray.'

'If you disagree with him so much, why do you stay?'

'On the *Liberator*?' he shrugged. 'Survival. I'm a wanted man, what other realistic option is there?'

She shook her head. 'That might be true, perhaps, of Vila. But you, Avon? No. You're too involved for it simply to be a matter of survival.'

'Everyone needs a purpose.'

'I thought yours was to get rich?'

'The money was always irrelevant. The goal was security. To have safety, freedom.'

'And now, you have neither.'

They shared a moment of silence. Cally's eyes lowered, she began to turn away. 'We shouldn't stay up too late. We've no idea what Khurdia has in mind for tomorrow.'

'You're wrong, you know.'

She turned to face him again. 'Wrong about what?'

'I *have* safety, and relative freedom. The *Liberator* is the fastest ship in the galaxy. Some might say that I am as close to freedom and safety as you can get.'

'If only Blake didn't insist on getting in the way.'

He tried to suppress a grin. 'You may have a point. But that may not be permanent.'

'Do you see Blake giving up the *Liberator*?'

'To him it's a means to a very different end, one that might eventually be accomplished.'

'So that's a yes?'

'It's a qualified yes.'

'What about us?'

'What about you?'

'Are you going to throw us off the *Liberator*, if it becomes yours?'

He reflected. 'Tempting.'

'It's a pointless argument, really,' Cally said. 'I think Blake's a long way from overthrowing the Federation.'

'That's because you see this as a recent venture. But for Blake, this began years ago. Remember the Freedom Party?'

'The Federation disbanded them, didn't it?'

'And yet here's Blake, a convicted criminal, leading the rebellion from the galaxy's most powerful spaceship. Blake – so well networked within the community of revolutionaries and dissidents that newly elected leaders call on him for support. Insurrection isn't new to Blake, Cally.'

'It isn't new to me either.'

'Hence your great value to Blake.'

'So if you get your wish, Avon, the *Liberator* for youself, would there be a place for me?'

'I think you know the answer to that.'

SIX

When Blake had first suggested that Avon and Cally should accept the invitation to act as election monitors, he had felt rather proud of himself. He didn't usually find it easy to delegate. He told himself that it was a natural leader's fear of placing his crew in danger. But Blake understood that his true reasons were more complex.

His reservations began the moment that Avon and Cally took the shuttle to Kartvel. Avon was cunning, resourceful and strategic. Cally added bravery and loyalty to the team. But this mission was a diplomatic one, and Shevard had very clearly wanted him for the task. Now, Blake had introduced an unexpected element to the equation. A niggling instinct had warned him that the outcome of such interference would not be good. Yet he'd ignored that instinct and sent them.

Anxiously, Blake checked the logs for any missed communication. There hadn't been any word from Avon or Cally since they'd reported briefly from Kartvel City spaceport. All attempts to contact them had failed, which meant that the teleport bracelets must have been removed.

Nothing in what Shevard had told Blake about the election had warned them that this might happen. Yet later, when he'd contacted Shevard's office, they'd confirmed that indeed, all election monitors were required to respect the communications protocol: Avon and Cally were free to send any message via the official channels, he was told. Otherwise, they had to remain neutral, and therefore cut off from all off-world communication.

Vila ambled onto the flight deck, yawning. 'Any news from Avon and Cally?'

Blake shook his head.

'You reckon they're living it up in some fancy hotel suite, getting to know each other far too well, if you know what I mean?'

'I somehow doubt that,' Blake said, dryly.

'Yeah well, you would,' Vila said. 'But Avon, on the quiet I reckon, is a bit of a ladies' man.'

'Hides it rather well, if that's the case.'

'He's a bit surly with Jenna and Cally, sure. But he's not a bad-looking fellow, is our Avon. Oh yeah, I'd put a bet on him finding some pleasant female company down on Kartvel.'

'It's reassuring to know that two of your crewmates can be out for contact for this long without you getting anxious.'

'You're worried?'

Blake nodded and said, slowly. 'I am.'

'Well,' Vila remarked in a mild voice, 'maybe you should have listened to Gan. He said it was probably a trap.'

'A trap?' snapped Blake. 'Yes, of course, there's always that risk. But almost any invitation could be a trap. I checked – the other election monitors have received exactly the same treatment.'

Vila raised his eyebrows. 'Oh, you checked?'

'Despite yours and Avon's persistent doubt in me, I don't send people into the field without a pretty good idea of what they're going to face.'

Vila shrugged. Blake could see that he was simply arguing for the sake of it. He probably didn't really care much one way or the other. So long as Vila himself felt safe, he was usually pretty calm. 'What time is it, in Kartvel City?'

'Late evening. I'd have thought they'd check in with us before going to sleep.'

'Maybe they're at a drinks party. Wouldn't there be some kind of reception?'

'You're right. I'm going to call Shevard's office again, see if they can get a message through.'

'I'm going to make a hot drink,' Vila said. He turned towards the kitchen. 'Fancy a cup?'

It took a few moments to get through to someone on Kartvel who'd actually speak to Blake. Then, to his surprise, he was told that Acting First Minister Shevard himself wished to address him. When his face appeared on the screen, Blake saw at once that there was trouble. The man's voice was calm, but carried an undercurrent of urgency. 'Blake, talk to me, what have you heard?'

'Shevard, what's going on?'

'Don't be alarmed, Blake. That's the first thing to remember.'

'Alarmed? I think you should let me be the judge of that.'

'We have every assurance that Avon and Cally are alive.'

Blake blinked and drew a long, slow breath. 'Shevard, I entrusted you with the safety of two of my team.'

'And we let you down. I know. You have my most heartfelt apologies, Blake. I trusted my security forces. Most regrettably, it appears that Zviad Khurdia's supporters may have infiltrated their numbers.'

'Who is Zviad Khurdia?' growled Blake.

'He's of no consequence, really. A local warlord. Towards the end of the Federation's time here, things fell apart somewhat. Something of a power vacuum. Khurdia took control in some mountains regions.'

Vila looked doubtful. 'Yeah. Had a lot of experience with warlords, have you?'

'Primitive societies sometimes have them.'

'So that's a "no"?'

Blake shrugged. 'I don't see why it's relevant.'

'I dunno. I worry easily, you know me. People with the word "war" in their title, they especially worry me.'

'Why can't we reach Avon and Cally?' Blake asked Shevard. 'Did you take their communicators?'

'The election monitors are required to be kept in seclusion for the duration, Blake. These are the Federation's rules.'

'You might have explained that earlier.'

'Would it have made a difference?'

Blake suppressed an exasperated sigh. Shevard had no way of knowing that the communicators were also a sure-fire way of pulling any of the *Liberator* crew out of harm's way.

'What now?'

'We wait. A ransom, no doubt, will be requested at some stage.'

'Shevard, why don't you just tell me where my crew have been taken and leave the rest to us?'

'Impossible, my friend. We don't know.'

Bitterly, Blake repeated, 'You *don't know*?'

'They were taken outside St Mark's Basilica. They may still be in the city. Or they may have gone further.'

'Where?'

'Into the mountains.'

'Unbelievable.'

'Zviad Khurdia must be desperate for funds. He's not likely to harm them; he'll want you to pay some kind of ransom.'

'Was anyone else taken?'

'Just Avon and Cally. Their driver was betrayed, attacked.'

'Were they targeted – because of me?'

'Blake, all the election monitors are individuals with some connection or status. This was merely bad luck. It's a last gasp. Sheer desperation.'

Blake was silent for a moment, weighing the possibilities. Gan's warning, his own doubts about sending Cally and Avon, came to the fore. There could be no coincidence in the choice of the *Liberator* crew. He wasn't even sure he could trust Shevard's testimony thus far. Without being able to actually speak to his crewmates, Blake was wary of everything he was being told.

'Shevard, I'm going to send two more of my crew down.'

'All our shuttles are in operation.'

'We can arrange our own transportation.'

'Blake, I'm already responsible for two of your crew. I can't accept any more risk.'

'You won't be responsible – I will.'

Shevard's tone hardened. 'Regrettably, Blake, I'm going to have to forbid it.'

Blake hesitated. Vila had just walked back onto the flight deck, carrying two insulated mugs. Blake gestured at him to take them to the seating area. He ignored Vila's silent, implied question.

'At least tell me where your own men will be searching.'

Shevard shook his head, in vague disbelief. 'There will be no search. Khurdia has taken the initiative, we have to give him that victory. He's won the right to the next move. When we have some idea of what he's demanding, then we'll formulate a response.'

'And when, precisely, will that be?'

'It's late. We don't expect any news in the next few hours.'

'I want to know, Shevard, the instant you hear anything.'

'Naturally, naturally. Try not to worry. These are troubled times, but Zviad Khurdia is unlikely to risk the possibility of being disqualified from the election.'

Blake exploded. 'Kidnapping the monitors won't get him disqualified?'

'It's hard to prove they were kidnapped, unless they file a complaint.'

'I think we can assume that they will!'

'That's where you underestimate Mr Khurdia.'

'From where I'm standing, Shevard, it looks to me as though that's the exact mistake you made.' In disgust, Blake cut the communication. When he looked across the flight deck, Vila was staring at him with frightened eyes.

'So Gan was right.'

'No, Gan was not right, Vila,' Blake said, not bothering to hide his irritation. 'This wasn't a trap. It's sheer bloody-minded incompetence. Doesn't Shevard realise that the election monitors were going to be a huge security risk?'

'Pathetic!'

'What are we going to do?'

Blake hesitated. 'We'll wake up Jenna and Gan. Then you and I can teleport into Kartvel City and take a look around, see if we can find out what's going on.'

Vila's eyes registered immediate panic. 'But isn't the city locked down, during the election?'

'We'll go incognito.'

'And if we're caught?'

'Oh, we'll be armed.'

'Blake – you know how fond I am of Avon and Cally. Well, Cally, actually. Not so much Avon. But still, don't you think we should just hold off a bit, like Shevard says? No sense throwing you and me into the mess now, before we know anything.'

'Wait until morning? Avon and Cally could be dead by then.'

'Blake,' Vila reminded him, 'if we're dealing with the kind of people who'd murder them, they would already be dead.'

Reluctantly, Blake agreed, 'You have a point.'

'I'm hoping not! At least, not Cally. I like her.'

'All right, all right. You might want to remember that you owe your life to Avon, several times over.'

Vila muttered, 'Oh, you think he ever lets me forget?'

SEVEN

Avon woke to a white dazzle of light from the snow outside, which streamed through vertical blinds and into the lounge. He sat up on the sofa and glanced at the bedroom door. It was open. The faint sound of drizzling water could just be heard from the bathroom. He strolled over to the kitchen, barefoot and dressed only in the loose-fitting pyjama trousers and short-sleeved knit shirt that had been left out for him in the apartment.

Within a few minutes, Avon had made one large omelette from the sausage and eggs, and prepared a plate of sliced apples and cheese. He toasted two pieces of bread under a grill. By the time he'd put the food on the table, Cally was emerging from the bathroom, wrapped in a towel.

'You're awake. Did you manage to get some rest?' she asked.

'I'm fine,' was all he said. Avon had insisted that Cally take the bedroom, even though she'd suggested they introduce some randomised element to the choice. Cally accepted his gesture without a word.

They ate breakfast at a table made from solid, varnished wood that sat in the corner of the apartment, flanked by windows, which gave on to the steep rise of the snow-coated mountain behind the hamlet.

Avon said very little, which was characteristic of his mood in the morning. He disliked idle chat most of the time, but in the morning he refused to pretend otherwise. Cally was far from the worst offender amongst his crewmates, and now she ate in amicable silence, smiling her thanks for his efforts in preparing the food.

They'd barely had time to clear the table when they heard the key being turned in the door to the apartment. Borena had returned. She was stamping her feet, blowing into her hands.

'Cold!' she exclaimed in a friendly voice. 'So, Cally, Avon. You spent a good night?'

'Wonderful,' Avon answered in a level voice, looking straight at Borena. 'When do we meet Khurdia?'

'Mr Khurdia is at the morning service. We meet him there.'

Avon and Cally followed her into the car. After a ten-minute drive to a larger village, dominated by a steeple with a bulbous shape at its summit, it became obvious that they were going to another church.

This church had nothing of the resplendence of St Mark's in Kartvel City. The interior was simple, lacking any ornate features whatsoever. In spite of this, the spiritual ambience was somehow more pronounced. The benches were half-full and the singers stood only a short distance away from the back, by the door. Avon seemed to recognise the music, the same chanting and chorusing as the previous day. The sounds were alien to him, yet not unpleasant.

Borena left them at the back of the church and made her way towards the front, where she touched the shoulder of a grey-haired man kneeling in prayer. Zviad Khurdia stood, turned to face them and followed Borena. A noticeable number of the congregation turned discreetly to watch him pass, regarding Avon and Cally with a certain amount of curiosity. They left the church and began to talk in the cobbled yard outside.

'How do you like our church?' was the first thing he said. He wasn't a handsome man. The ravages of age had brought a droop to already solemn features, giving his jaw and eyes a mournful quality, particularly on the left side of his face. His hair was thinning, gun-metal grey and parted neatly at one side. There was the suggestion of a moustache, a narrow line on his upper lip. His neck disappeared within the bulk of a padded, forest-green jacket.

'We don't really know what to expect,' Cally interjected with a smile. 'We don't have a great deal of previous experience.'

Khurdia's gaze travelled from Avon to Cally. 'Of course not. I've been to Federation worlds. You have nothing like this.'

'Cally isn't from the Federation.'

Khurdia's surprise showed for a second in his eyes, but his lack of information didn't appear to trouble him. 'You're colleagues of Roj Blake, yes? This tells me everything I need to know about your feelings towards the Federation.'

'Did you also know that it was Edu Shevard himself who requested our presence on Kartvel?'

'It doesn't surprise me in the least. He intends to win this election as unequivocally as possible. All election monitors will no doubt be encouraged to say that there's no fraud. With you, he has the extra assurance that you, more than most, would do anything to prevent the Federation regaining the mandate to rule in Kartvel.'

'Is he going to win "unequivocally"?' Avon asked.

Khurdia's lips twitched, as though he were suppressing a smile. 'Very little in life is unequivocal, wouldn't you agree?'

Bluntly Avon said, 'What are we doing here?'

'I wished you to see the daily service, as it is celebrated in every village on Kartvel.'

'Thanks to Shevard.'

A sullen anger showed for a brief instant on Khurdia's face. 'Shevard isn't the man you believe him to be.'

'Who is?' Avon countered, mildly.

'It must be interesting,' said Cally, 'to feel some connection with something genuinely ancient, with your own past.'

Khurdia seemed relieved to have an opportunity to return to a favourite subject. 'Quite simply, that is what our life here is about. I wonder if you realise how special that makes us, within the human-populated worlds.'

'There are others, no doubt,' Avon observed.

'Oh, indeed. And do you know who has a current list of every single "suspect" world upon which religion is practised? Ask Edu Shevard.'

'You suspect the sincerity of his faith?'

Khurdia guffawed. 'Of his faith and a good deal more.'

Avon's eyes narrowed. 'What are you saying?'

'Is it not obvious? He has made a pact with the Federation. He may even be foolish enough to trust that they will honour it.'

Khurdia began to walk, leading them towards a large house on the plaza. Neither Avon nor Cally spoke for a minute, both considering the implications of Khurdia's statement.

'You see, my friends, you have been deceived. Shevard is an outsider on Kartvel. He's barely been on the planet in the past fifteen years. He may have been born here, but he's a Federation *apparatchik*. A member of the *nomenklatura*.'

'Explain, *apparatchik*, *nomenklatura*.'

'Old words, with bitter meaning for my people. Shevard was part of the apparatus of a foreign, imperial power. And not an insignificant member! Once, he was one of Servalan's closest advisers.'

'But that was before he turned against her.'

Khurdia smiled. 'My dear Avon. I took you for a man of the world! It is I who am the true choice of our people. I was on the point of gathering enough forces to oust the Federation presence myself, with the full support of the people. In an election held fifteen days before Shevard's arrival, I was elected by eighty percent of the public. Ah, but then Shevard claimed himself as the saviour of the people. Before I could be inaugurated, he engineered this "secession" from the Federation. As though we needed to secede by then! We had the best part of the Federation administration packing their bags.

'Now Shevard hovers over the seat of power, aided, I am certain, by his old friends in the Federation. It should be obvious the extent to which he is eager to ensure that the favourable outcome for him of this election is seen to be fair and just. That is why you and the other election monitors are here – you will put the final and necessary seal of approval on his new regime. And then he will ally himself with the most powerful of the non-Federation worlds: a veritable wolf in sheep's clothing.'

EIGHT

They sat outside the only café, the whole village bathed in the brilliance reflected from the snow. Despite the sunshine, the mountain air was almost painfully cold and Avon and Cally were grateful for the wood-burning brazier that provided enough heat to warm their stiffened fingers.

A young, ruddy-cheeked woman smiled as she invited them to pick from a basket of warm pastries. Avon took a flaky horn-shaped one filled with a kind of custard. He tore off a section. Hot mint tea was placed before them; on Khurdia's recommendation they'd avoided the "coffee", which was apparently no such thing.

Avon considered Khurdia's speech. 'I'm assuming you can prove what you say?'

'Given enough time I could, Avon. About my election – all you need do is to ask the people. Shevard, most certainly, will accuse me of having staged an ill-conceived and illegal election, prior to his return to Kartvel, the celebrated "dissident" now "freed". You must trust me, I was fairly chosen.'

Cally asked, 'Can you at least prove that Shevard has links to the Federation? And can you substantiate your claims that he intends to act as an informer and spy?'

Khurdia dipped a pastry into his tea. 'Mr Shevard has neither deported nor imprisoned the remaining Federation security troops. He merely "holds" them in a complex outside the capital city. In reality, they are his guests and you can be sure that he calls on them whenever he needs a few extra troops. In disguise, naturally: no-one recognises their faces, since they used to wear masks. When he takes up power, you will find that these people will be assumed into the population and will soon occupy similar roles to those they held previously.'

'You make serious allegations,' Avon said. 'You cannot believe that we'd act on your advice without evidence. You cannot expect us to trust you blindly.'

'Would that I had the time to reassure you, Avon.' Khurdia didn't seem surprised by Avon's reaction, but Avon sensed a guarded disappointment. 'But there is none. The election is tomorrow. You must trust your own instincts and you must trust *me*. Does it not strike you as unlikely that the Federation would allow this world to secede with such scant opposition? Do you not wonder about the timing? Shevard must have planned all of this as soon as he heard about my election. Then there is the question of Shevard's suddenly revitalised interest in religion. Do you suppose that a man of faith could advance anywhere in the hierarchy of the Federation?'

Cally said, 'What about his nationalism?'

'That, I suspect, is genuine enough. I believe it is the key to his motivation. I think he truly believes that after he has taken control, with the Federation's help, he will then be able to rid himself of them and personally take charge.'

'Assuming that what you say is true,' Avon said, 'what do you want us to do about it?'

'No more than your duty. Pay special attention to the conduct of the election. Report widely the truth of the fraud. Do not allow Shevard to intimidate you, as he undoubtedly intends to do.'

'So far, it is only you who has forced us to do anything against our will,' Cally commented.

'I had to see you,' Khurdia spread his palms. 'Who else but the colleagues of the most celebrated Federation dissident, Roj Blake? Your word will carry more than that of any of the other monitors. I had to tell you the other side of the story. Without any access to information, you would have no means to guess at the truth.'

'Will you now take us back to the city?'

'Eventually, my dear, yes.'

Avon said nothing. It was difficult to believe in this man as a warlord. The tranquillity of the village had quietly impressed him, as had the discreet hospitality. There was nothing about Khurdia that suggested the forceful nature that Avon would expect of a warrior. He seemed more like an academic, perhaps a senior administrator, than anything else – quite a contrast with Shevard, who from the beginning had exuded urbanity, and a familiarity with institutional power. There had to be another side to Khurdia, Avon mused. One that he was well practised at hiding. The ruthless reputation he enjoyed couldn't be squared with the character who faced them now.

'What is your personal connection with Shevard?' he asked.

Khurdia's mouth set into a hard line. 'We were boys together. We studied together. That is the way we are here on this world – we are few and consequently, we remain close. Then, Edu Shevard went to the Federation Academy. I did not. I stayed here. Shevard became Federation.'

His speech slowed down. 'When I was taken in for questioning about my anti-Federation protests, it was he who interrogated me.' Khurdia's eyes closed, briefly. 'Such horrors. Things I will never forget, nor forgive. As you see, Avon, I have some insight into what that man is capable of.'

'Shevard was tortured, too.'

A brittle smile appeared on Khurdia's face. 'Ah yes. The sheer originality of the man. He took the records of my ordeal and altered them to fit his own history.'

'We only have your word for that,' Cally pointed out.

Khurdia's smile froze, his eyes became glassy. 'A man's word is often all there is.'

Avon said, 'You have our sympathies.'

'I can rely on you?'

Avon shrugged. 'Why not? All you're asking is that we monitor the election, as we have been asked to do. If you are being cheated in any way, we will report it.'

Khurdia beamed in gratitude. It was the first time they'd seen him smile properly, and it utterly altered the man. For a second, Avon could see what others might follow in such a man. He might just be chameleon enough to be a credible leader.

'Thank you, my friend. That is all I ask.'

Khurdia saw to it that no more time was wasted. The drive back to the city would take at least four hours and the election was to be conducted the next day. They were driven to the forest at the base of the hills and then along the twisting, hidden pathway through the trees. Then, for security purposes Avon and Cally were given the keys to the car – a fairly standard Federation road vehicle. The satellite navigation was programmed to guide them back to their hotel in Kartvel City. To be accompanied further by Khurdia's men would surely have resulted in their being shot at on any approach to the city.

As they took their leave, Khurdia leaned his head inside the car.

'You will not be sorry, I promise you. I have powerful friends who will be willing to help Blake. Not Federation – other, independent thinkers like myself.'

It was only when they were once again alone that Avon and Cally began to discuss their impressions of the encounter. Cally was fairly convinced that, from the few facts of which they were actually certain, it was not possible to believe either man's story. Thankfully though, there was only one realistic course of action: to do the job they had been asked to do.

Night had begun to fall as they approached the outskirts of the city. The streetlights cast a pale russet glow over the valley as they descended from the hills. They strained their eyes looking for any potential threat from the roadblock ahead, in front of St Mark's Basilica. There must have been fifteen armed guards waiting as they slowed to a halt. They appeared to be expecting them and made some show of relief that Blake's envoys were unharmed.

Avon recognised one of the bodyguards outside St Mark's as the driver who'd been assigned to them the previous evening.

'The incident was regrettable,' the man acknowledged, drawing attention to his heavily bruised eye. 'We were betrayed from within. You see the treachery that First Minister Shevard must contend with? The battle is relentless.'

Cally corrected him. 'Don't you mean, *Acting* First Minister Shevard?'

Dismissively, he replied, 'It is just a matter of time. Khurdia has no support outside of the backward people of his mountain villages.'

'You're describing most of the population,' Cally said.

This drew a surprised reaction from the driver. 'What did they do to you?'

Avon replied, 'Nothing.' His eyes met Cally's in a calm, silent warning.

'They took you away for the night, and nothing happened?'

'We escaped,' said Avon, breezily. 'They should probably have taken some election monitors who had less experience of combat than us.'

'You don't appear to have been hurt,' said the driver, suspiciously.

Avon beamed. 'Precisely so.'

The driver didn't seem convinced. Reluctantly, he let the subject drop. There was an urgency to his manner that suggested to Avon that he was under some time pressure. As they allowed themselves to be led to another armoured limousine, Avon placed a reassuring hand on Cally's arm and briefly wished that he shared her telepathic gift. They should have left the moment that Shevard's men had confiscated their teleport bracelets. This was a far more complicated situation than Blake had anticipated.

A familiar sense of disappointment was rising within Avon. He wasn't disappointed with Blake, but rather himself. It wasn't as though he hadn't suspected Blake's enthusiasm had been misplaced – again. Yet he'd let that slip principally for the chance to get away from the rest of the crew, even for a couple of days. Avon only had himself to blame.

NINE

By the time that Jenna and Gan joined the others on the flight deck, Blake had asked Zen to search through all possible records in nearby public sector databases.

'Who are you looking for?' Jenna asked. She'd dressed quickly, Blake noticed, and had worn the same outfit three days running now. He concealed a smile. 'I'm trying to find an old friend of mine, Raisa Beridze.'

'An old girlfriend?'

Blake acknowledged the gentle prod at his reserve of unanswered questions. On the *Liberator*, it was Avon who exuded the downright icy air of mystery about his personal life, another of the many things that Blake admired about the man. Yet Blake too, had managed quietly to deflect most of the questions about his past. A man didn't get too many opportunities to completely reinvent himself. Blake's own had come at a great personal, emotional and physical cost. Like Avon, he wasn't about to let that count for nothing.

'A former teacher, as it happens.'

Jenna frowned. 'All the way out here?'

'Raisa wasn't just my teacher, Jenna. She was one of the people who introduced me to the Freedom Party. Her family was originally from Kartvel. I'm fairly certain I remember that when things began to get difficult for us on Earth, Raisa transferred to a post at the University of Kartvel. Because of her family connections, it was the only way for her to get off-world without too much trouble.'

'She ran out on you?'

Blake found himself smiling at the implied criticism. 'I wouldn't call it that. It was all planned. We tried to place as many of our more senior party members out of harm's way.'

'I thought the Federation took you by surprise.'

'They did,' Blake said, curtly. 'It happened months after Raisa left. We'd allowed ourselves to relax.'

'Big mistake, when you're on the run.'

'I imagine that smugglers find it easy to remember that. But believe it or not, our first thought usually wasn't the danger from the Federation. That's the problem with politicals.'

'An operation like that needs to be run like an armed conflict.'

'I'm sure you're right,' Blake admitted, ruefully. 'Sadly, the Freedom Party was rather short on members who shared that mentality.'

Gan asked, 'Even if Raisa is on Kartvel, Blake, how is a university teacher going to help us with this?'

Blake shrugged. 'She's the only person on this planet with whom I have any link.'

'Do you trust her?'

'The Raisa Beridze I knew on Earth? Oh, I should say so.'

Vila couldn't seem to stop himself from visibly fretting. He paced back and forth in front of Gan until Gan resorted to restraining him to maintain a line of sight with Blake. Irritated, Vila blurted out, 'What if she's changed?'

'Everyone does, Vila. It's called growing up.'

Zen's resonant tones sounded across the deck. 'INFORMATION. PROFESSOR RAISA BERIDZE ORBELI IS LISTED ON THE FACULTY OF ELECTRONIC ENGINEERING AT THE UNIVERSITY OF KARTVEL.'

Blake grinned at Jenna, then Vila. 'Bingo!' He headed for the corridor. As he walked, he called behind him. 'Come along, Vila! Who knows what doors you may need to open for us.'

At what Blake calculated was thirty minutes before the start of morning classes, Jenna teleported him and Vila into a car park on the edge of the Kartvel City campus. A freezing mist hovered above the ground. Both men were glad of the insulated jackets they'd chosen, which not only kept out the deep chill but also concealed their hand guns.

The university was built like a grid, with two long horizontal blocks connected by a series of vertical ones. In between each vertical block was a garden. As Blake and Vila strolled between carefully manicured lawns and shrubberies, Blake noticed that the campus was patrolled by a discreet security presence. By the time a third uniformed guard had fixed him with a curious stare, Blake was beginning to wonder how safe this place could be.

Within five minutes they'd found a metal board, that displayed a map of the faculty buildings, and located the engineering block.

Raisa's office was on the second floor. The faculty itself was open but access to the administration section was via a card scan. Vila took a look for a few minutes and asked Blake to wait. Before Blake could agree, Vila had disappeared towards the vending machines, around which a handful of students in their twenties were chatting. He returned and flashed a grin at Blake.

'Let's go.' Vila opened his right hand to reveal a plastic card that he then scanned beside the door. 'Best way to open any door is to swipe someone else's key.'

'Ah. I take it you couldn't have cracked it.'

'I could have cracked it,' Vila said, sounding a touch offended. 'But I'm a professional. The simplest solution is always the most elegant.'

Professor Raisa Beridze Orbeli wasn't at her desk, but Blake found her in the faculty lounge, from where the smell of fresh-baked bread had penetrated into the nearby corridor. The staff were lined up next to the window, taking their turn to choose a pastry and to make hot drinks. Blake stood quietly, just to Raisa's left. When she turned, it took her a few seconds of gazing into Blake's gently amused features before she reacted with a small cry that stuck in her throat. Within a second, any joy she'd expressed had vanished. The colour seemed to drain from her face. Blake noticed that despite Raisa's efforts to control her response, several of her colleagues were glancing in their direction.

Carefully, she took his arm. 'My dear Roj...'

'Shall we go to your room?'

Raisa gave a quick nod. She led Blake and Vila back to her office, which was a few doors along. She closed the door behind them and snapped shut the vertical blinds in front of the glass. Then wordlessly, she embraced Blake.

'I'd heard the rumours... So it's true?'

Vila clicked his tongue, watching them hug. 'Oh yeah. All true. Everything you've heard. And a fair bit more.'

Raisa pulled away from the embrace. With one hand she smoothed back the lock of dark brown hair that had fallen across her face. She had a tired-looking face that showed her almost-sixty years, her lips thinned and concealing a row of slightly greying teeth. But her neatly bobbed haircut and bright, lively, almond-shaped eyes lent her a sudden youth, mischievous and spritely. She gazed up at her former student and reached out a hand to touch, quite gently, his face.

'Roj Blake. How strange to see you here. You might be walking into one of my classes, you've changed so little.'

Blake laughed. 'I hope I've changed a good deal since then.'

'What are you doing here?'

'This election, Raisa. What do you make of it?'

She glanced at Blake and Vila in turn. 'That rather depends on why you're here.'

'Shevard asked me to be an election monitor. Instead, I sent him two of my crew. My *friends*, Raisa. Now Shevard tells me they've been kidnapped by a man named Zviad Khurdia.'

Raisa shook her head and sighed. 'It wouldn't surprise me.'

'It's the kind of thing he'd do?'

In a noticeably lower voice, Raisa told them, 'Yes.'

'Shevard thinks they're going to ask for a ransom.'

She looked momentarily surprised. 'I... would wait and see.'

'You don't think that's likely?'

Silently, Raisa disconnected a wire from what looked like a communication device. In a voice barely above a whisper she said, 'Lately on Kartvel, things are never what they seem.'

Blake frowned. 'Are you saying that Shevard's misleading me?'

'I'm saying that you need to leave, as soon as possible. Shevard has his people everywhere.'

Immediately, Blake understood. 'I'm sorry Raisa, I didn't mean to implicate you in anything.'

She inclined her head, very slightly. 'Your people are missing.'

'What should we do? Shevard doesn't want us to attempt a rescue.'

'Naturally. He needs to see the card that Khurdia will play.'

'Why *my* people though, Raisa?'

'Shevard wants his election endorsed, most especially by someone connected to the famous Roj Blake.'

'If Khurdia is aware of that, might he try to kill them?'

She hesitated. 'Khurdia has no interest in having the election declared null and void. That would only bring the Federation back.'

'So what can he want with my people?'

Raisa fixed him with her gaze. 'Perhaps... he simply wishes to tell the truth.'

TEN

They were taken directly to the First Ministerial Palace. Shevard himself was waiting on the pavement, standing next to his own limousine. He greeted Avon and Cally, his tone all concern as they were transferred seamlessly from one car to the second, and he got in beside them.

'Thank God those gangsters did not harm you! Now we can tell your ship that you are safe. And that the ransom will not be necessary. Avon, my friend, how did you escape?'

Shevard claimed that Khurdia's followers had sent word out that Cally and Avon had been captured and were being held hostage, that they would be released only if Shevard conceded his position as Acting First Minister and allowed Khurdia to campaign openly for the top job. Neither Avon nor Cally moved to contradict him, it seemed plausible that Khurdia had told his opponent such a story to hide the fact that that he had tried to convert them to his cause. As it happened, they were not required to invent any truths because he was curiously uninterested in anything they had to say about the experience.

The limousine stopped in front of another opulent, marbled building, this time on the edge of the lake. From the lobby to the water stretched a colonnaded promenade. Street vendors were wandering along its periphery, offering roasted nuts, flowers and sweets.

Shevard escorted Avon and Cally down the promenade until they could lean on the enamel-painted, metal fence that bordered the water's edge. The lake was a silver mirror, mist-covered from about halfway across, a gauze of white vapour through which the sunlight scattered, a white curtain.

'What do you think of Kartvel?'

'It's stunning,' Avon admitted, flatly. He had never seen mountains as craggy or high, snow as thick and powdery, a lake of such natural beauty in both form and context. The city itself was an architectural wonder. It was obvious to Avon how the citizens might feel a pride about their planet that would lend itself to the desire for independence.

When Shevard spoke, a fine mist appeared before his mouth. 'I tell you truly, my friends, there are few places in the Federation – or outside of it – like Kartvel. The love and respect we have for our history is unique.'

Avon doubted that was true, but he didn't contradict him.

'I'm glad you admire our world, Avon,' Shevard said. 'Because Kartvel could be your home, too. Apart from the *Liberator*, I mean. A guaranteed safe base for you, for Blake and your other crewmates. I could arrange for a suite of rooms in our best hotel to be on stand-by for you. Or a house. It could be here in Kartvel City, so that you could enjoy the city life: arts, music. Or perhaps you have developed a taste for the mountains? You could have your own ski lodge. Waiting for you both here, whenever you need to recuperate. I'd let you vet your own security detail. Or, if you prefer, no-one would know. I'd handle everything personally. Total discretion.'

Avon listened carefully as Shevard spoke. A couple of times his eyes met Cally's. It was impossible not to visualise the picture that Shevard was painting: the scent of warm wood, the blinding white of snowlight streaming through windows, mornings of clear blue mountain air, the smell of freshly brewed coffee. On the *Liberator*, it was impossible ever to relax, he realised. Enveloped in a protective shell of technology, he was never at rest. Always on edge, always mistrusting. Technology was a barrier as well as a shell. On a planet like Kartvel, he might find another way to relate.

'I've wondered if perhaps we might have a base,' Avon conceded. He noticed that Cally seemed rather taken aback at this, but she said nothing.

'A base, exactly. Blake should think about it.'

'The problem is – knowing who to trust.'

'Friends know they can trust each other.'

Avon smiled, cynically. 'Blake doesn't have friends.'

'I think he does. You, Cally.'

'That's different. We're... colleagues.'

'I don't think so. When Blake believed you might be ransomed, he was desperate to send other colleagues to find and free you.'

'Yet he didn't.'

'I managed to persuade him to stay away. It wouldn't have been in your interest. You see, Avon, I'm trying to be *your* friend.'

*

They were shown to their accommodation: separate rooms, each with an armed guard. 'Takha and Georg will protect you against Khurdia's men, should they dare to try to kidnap you again,' was the explanation given.

It was clear that Takha and Georg did not intend to leave them unattended even for one minute, so there was no possibility of talking with Avon. Cally had felt his growing despondency since their night in the mountain lodge. She'd been close to saying something at breakfast the next morning, when Avon's normal manner had tipped almost imperceptibly into hostility. For all Avon's apparent coldness, she'd caught occasional glimpses of a brittle fragility within. Something had happened there, either in his childhood, or possibly more recently. It was enough to make it easy for Cally to keep her distance. She sensed that any woman would trifle with Avon at considerable risk.

But Cally sensed that Avon's mood was darker than could be explained by something as trivial as a shared moment of awkwardness. It had to be that, like her, he was anxious. They needed a chance to discuss what was happening on Kartvel. It seemed clear that Shevard wasn't going to make that easy.

The morning of the election began loudly, with the almost deafening clamour of the bells of St Mark's Basilica. Cally stared blearily out of the window as she heard a knock at her door. It was Avon.

'You slept well?' It seemed that he might want to say more, but as was often his way, Avon kept it brief.

Cally glanced around, quickly. The guards didn't seem to be in the vicinity. 'I must admit, I spent quite some time trying to work out just what is going on here.'

'I think we've avoided making any crucial mistakes so far,' was his careful reply.

On an impulse, she touched his hand. 'That's good to know.'

For a second, Avon glanced at her hand. 'The guards went to fetch coffee,' he said. 'And I, I keep wondering about Shevard. It worries me a great deal that we weren't allowed to keep our teleport bracelets.'

'Or offered a chance to talk to the *Liberator*.'

'Indeed.'

The voices of Takha and his colleague alerted Avon and Cally to their approach. They handed them each a cup of coffee.

'And now my friends,' beamed Takha, 'To the labours of democracy!'

ELEVEN

In the rear car park of the university, Blake and Vila waited with Raisa Beridze. In the hour since they'd arrived, the mist had given way to stark clarity. Beyond the car park to the south, a fringe of white-topped mountains that bordered the city appeared so close that you might reach out and touch them.

After a few minutes, a small, rather boxy car appeared. It was identical to about a quarter of the vehicles around them. Vila glanced about him, trying to conceal how impressed he was. On Kartvel, university workers owned cars. Unheard of, on Earth. The more Vila saw of Kartvel, the more he could imagine the people fighting for their independence. This was no poky Federation colony, packed with addled soma-heads. There was a sense of culture, of civic pride and magnificence in the city he'd seen so far. Not the kind of world the Federation would simply allow to secede.

It made all kinds of sense to Vila that Blake had fallen for a ruse. Unlike Avon, however, he couldn't find it in his heart to despise Blake for the occasional mistake. Eventually, everyone made them – even Avon. Vila preferred the kind of mistakes that didn't lead to his own death. The longer they lingered on Kartvel, the more dangerous things would get. So when inside the car Vila heard Blake's instructions to the driver, he boggled.

'We'd like to see the sphinx.'

The driver didn't bother to turn around. Instead, rather mechanically, she answered, 'And yet the sphinx inspires horror.'

'We dream the sphinx to explain the horror,' Blake replied.

The car began to move. Raisa had already gone, disappeared behind rows of cars on the way back to her office.

Blake asked, 'Will this take long?'

The driver didn't answer his question. Instead she said, 'There are blindfolds in the folder behind my seat. Please fasten them in place and sit well back.'

Vila jabbed a finger into Blake's arm. 'What the hell is going on? Are they taking us to Cally and Avon?'

Calmly, Blake tied a blindfold around Vila's head. 'Raisa assured me that Cally and Avon have been released. They're at the Palace.'

'Nice of Shevard to let us know,' said Vila. 'Or has he contacted the *Liberator*?'

'He hasn't,' Blake said. 'Which is one of the many reasons why I think it's time we met this... sphinx.'

'What *is* a sphinx?' Vila said, exasperated.

'I've no idea. Raisa told me to say it.'

'My name is Borena,' the driver said. 'Raisa Beridze has vouched for you. And I have already met your other friends.'

'My *good* friends,' Blake said, a steely note in his voice. 'I'm anxious to talk to them, as a matter of fact.'

'Your friends had a private audience with Zviad Khurdia, yesterday. They returned safely to the city. They are back with other monitors, under supervision of Shevard's men.'

'In that case, it's good to meet you, Borena,' Blake said. Vila recognised the reappearance of Blake's comradely charm. 'You're taking us to meet... Mr Khurdia?'

'Better that we mention no names.'

'You think we're being observed?'

'Tiny devices can be used to monitor conversations. Who is to say you don't have such a device planted on you?'

'Did my friends have such a device?'

'We didn't risk taking them anywhere secure.'

'Well, you can set your mind at ease. We haven't been anywhere but the university. Shevard's people don't even know we're here.'

'How do you know that? Perhaps you know the face of every one of Shevard's informers?'

'Ah,' Blake said. 'I see. In that case, I understand.'

Borena hesitated for a long time. Vila guessed that she was negotiating some tricky traffic. 'It is better we do not talk about your friends.'

'Borena, I need to know they're safe.'

'The election has begun. All monitors have reported for duty, including your friends.'

'So why haven't they contacted me?'

'The process requires sequestration of monitors for duration of the election.'

'Oh great,' Villa muttered. 'Makes me feel really safe.'

'Be at ease, Mr Restal. You will not be harmed.'

The drive was longer than Vila had anticipated. He could tell that they were ascending because occasionally there was pressure in his ears. After four hours they stopped and were allowed to remove their blindfolds.

Borena took their coats away to be searched for hidden transmitting devices. Vila rubbed his eyes, stared at the huddle of two- and three-storey buildings that comprised the tiny village. In a darkened, cosy room inside one completely timbered building, a lunch of hot, meaty stew with dumplings was brought to them, in deep ceramic bowls. A strong, clear liquid was served to them in small glasses.

'Drink,' Borena said. 'You have much further to go. From here, Iveri will drive. You should sleep.'

'You don't have air travel?' Vila grumbled.

'All air travel is monitored by government,' she replied in a level voice. 'If Shevard gets his way, soon enough all road vehicles will be controlled also.'

'That's how it is on Earth,' Vila acknowledged.

'Each of our freedoms has come at a price,' Borena said. Her voice was suddenly passionate. 'Do not imagine we give up so easy.'

Vila decided he might as well give in to the bottle. As they were about to leave, both coats were returned to them, apparently free of any transmitting devices.

He was awake just long enough to meet Iveri, a man about the same age as Blake. He was broad-shouldered and tall with a face that resembled, Vila thought, a granite wall. A scrub of immaculately neat black hair bordered the steely features: sharp cheekbones and eyes that were almost as dark as Iveri's hair.

Back in the car, Vila was asleep within ten minutes. When he woke, the sky had darkened. Blake, no longer blindfolded, was chatting in a low voice with Iveri, who drove.

'Ah, Mr Restal,' Iveri announced. He glanced at Vila through the rear-view mirror. 'You'll be glad to know we're almost there.'

'Where is *there*?'

'The home town of Zviad Khurdia.'

The village nestled on the lower slopes of a sheer mountain face and underneath a huge, tooth-shaped shadow.

Guided only by starlight and the light that leaked from tiny windows in the clustered wooden lodgings, Blake and Vila followed Iveri into one of the houses.

Vila said, 'Is this Khurdia's house?'

'It's my house,' Iveri replied. 'My wife, Gedia, made dinner. Mr Khurdia will be joining us.'

Blake nodded, gratefully. 'Please thank Gedia. We're very glad to have your hospitality.'

A slender, dusky woman stepped into the large hall. She was attractive, Vila noted, and despite her slim figure, not without curvaceous charms. He was careful not to look too hard, with Iveri standing right next to him. But he looked long enough to notice that Iveri's wife had been crying.

'Koba is dead,' she blurted.

Iveri seemed to reel. 'Koba?'

'They tortured him. They made us listen, Iveri. While they sliced him open and burned his guts in front of him.'

There was a blunt, horrified silence.

'Maybe it was faked?' Vila suggested timidly. It sounded too incredible to be true. Punishments like that on a former Federation world?

'You think I don't know my brother's voice?' said Iveri's wife, suddenly vicious.

'My friend is just trying to be hopeful,' Blake said. He spoke gently. 'I'm so sorry for your loss. Could you tell us why he died?'

Iveri was still adjusting to the paralysing news. 'Koba is – was – one of our best agents,' Iveri mumbled. He held both arms out to his wife, but she wiped her eyes, made a dismissive gesture and turned back towards the kitchen. 'Koba infiltrated Shevard's camp. He was one of his closest guards.' Iveri seemed to retreat into dazed contemplation of the news.

Vila glanced from Blake to Iveri. 'Khurdia had a mole inside Shevard's lot?'

Gedia returned. She seemed calmer. She ushered them into a room where a large dining table had been set with five places. As they took their seats, she started bringing in large pots of steaming food. It smelled delicious. Vila found himself reaching for the cutlery.

Iveri's wife sat next to her husband, opposite Blake. 'Before he died, Koba sent us a visual recording – an incident at one of the polling stations.'

Blake nodded, very attentive. Vila could see the anxiety in his face.

'Your friends,' Gedia murmured, 'are in terrible danger.'

TWELVE

Democracy, it seemed to Cally, involved a fair amount of standing around in the cold. People queued patiently for hours outside the only three polling stations in the city. Together with the other election monitors, they were driven around all three stations and spent time in each one, back and forth from Shevard's campaign headquarters, watching the 'exemplary' process by which citizens who looked pale and drained, cast their votes.

There were few police in evidence but Cally noticed a sizeable contingent of sour-faced young men in shabby clothes, their hands thrust deep into their pockets as they loitered around the polling booths. She noticed how people looked at them with expressions of loathing and even something resembling fear. As the day progressed, a palpable tension seeped into the freezing air.

Late in the afternoon, one of the voters spat at one of these young men. He turned to the party officials, shaking a fist. '*Apparatchiks*! *Nomenklatura*!' he shouted, before a small crowd of the dishevelled young men surrounded him. They dragged him away, still protesting.

Cally turned to Takha. 'What does he mean?'

'It is nothing. He is a cousin of Zviad Khurdia, he hates Shevard. Probably drunk, too. They will give him a shaking down and send him on his way.'

Avon and Cally exchanged glances, something that did not escape the attention of Takha, who gave them a long, thoughtful look. It was around this time that an elderly woman wearing the distinctive armband of the election officials came to them. Smiling, she asked, 'Are you ready to vote?'

There could be no doubt she was addressing Avon and Cally.

'We aren't citizens,' Cally told her, perplexed.

Takha brushed the woman aside. 'All the world wants to vote for Mr Shevard. This old mother is simply carried away by her enthusiasm.'

Cally began to watch the proceedings more closely. Few of the voters appeared to carry any identification. After a while she became certain that she'd seen several of the people previously, either earlier in the day or else at another station. From the corner of her eye, Cally could see that they were attracting the discreet attention of Takha and his older colleague. She slid her arms around Avon's waist and pressed herself to him, noticing that Takha immediately glanced away.

Don't be alarmed.

'Alarm... would never be my reaction to this,' Avon murmured.

Avon, what shall we do about the election?

One of Avon's hands dropped to her waist, held her at the hip. With the other, he stroked Cally's hair. It was her turn to be surprised. Fleetingly, Cally wondered if she'd made a mistake with her chosen method of distraction. It seemed to have worked – Takha had stopped looking at them. But Avon might be getting the wrong idea. If only he was easier to read.

Against her ear, Avon whispered, 'It is rather obvious to a close observer that the election has been rigged. The same people appear wherever you look. The system of registration that they told us about seems to be non-existent. And these thugs are clearly around to intimidate the voters. We'll report it.'

'And what of Shevard's promises to us?'

As Avon started to answer, a loud fanfare on the radio silenced everyone in the station. The silence lasted just long enough for the announcer to shout something, after which the majority of the assembled crowd as well as the officials, police and even the usually dour companion of Takha, burst into cheers and applause.

Avon and Cally released each other immediately.

'Would you care to let us in on the good news?' Avon asked Takha, who gave Cally a gentle smile.

'It is over, my friends. Mr Shevard has been elected.'

Cally said nothing. They were still in the process of stuffing the ballot box in their station. The election monitors had been instructed that not a single station was supposed to declare before all were closed. But before they had time to comment to each other, Takha gripped hold of Cally's elbow.

'And now, my friends, time for your report. Let us go and make a vidcast.'

Takha and three other armed men seized Avon and Cally. Blasters pressed into their backs, they were marched to another car. They were escorted to a low-rise building on the outskirts of the city and hurried into a small, well-lit studio. Takha played with cameras for a few moments. He turned to face them.

'Ready Cally?' he asked, expectantly.

He didn't wait for her answer. Instead, he thrust his boot swiftly into her ribs. It wasn't a very hard kick, she'd had harder. Yet it was totally unexpected. Cally had misread his body language completely – he'd concealed his intention rather well. She'd left herself open to being completely winded. She leaned against the wall, trying to recover her breath. Takha stood beside her, supporting her, encouraging her to put her head between her knees. Avon was kept to one side, restrained by two hefty-looking men.

Takha stared into Cally's eyes. 'Ready for another?'

The second kick was substantially more forceful. Cally staggered backwards in pain.

Avon pushed forward. 'Leave her,' he growled.

Without taking his eyes off Cally, Takha whipped Avon across the jaw with the barrel of his blaster. With Takha blocking her view, Cally couldn't see Avon's face. But she heard his sharp gasps of pain. Still Takha gazed at Cally, in a way that had begun to unnerve her.

'We haven't too much time, Cally,' he said. 'We need the reports from all the election monitors within the next three hours. First Minister Shevard is expecting a meeting of the neighbouring non-Federation worlds. They are going to want to see the reports before they endorse him as the leader of their local league of non-aligned worlds. So you see, we need your co-operation we need it *now*.'

He grabbed her roughly by the collar, threw her violently against the wall. This time she couldn't stop herself from crying out. Without warning, he brought his elbow up above her waist and slammed it hard into her belly. Cally managed to partly block him, but the blow still winded her. For a couple of seconds, she struggled for breath. She could just see Avon watching, his eyes dark with anger.

'Why did you bother to try to persuade us?' Avon asked, abruptly, the fury in his voice under tight control. 'Why didn't you just do this when we arrived and then let us get on our way?'

'If Khurdia's people hadn't got to you, you would have been none the wiser. Blame him, if you like, when you hear your woman scream.'

'I'm not his *woman*,' Cally spat. 'And he's given his word to tell the truth about this election. He's no good to either of us. Put the camera on me, I don't care what I say about your planet.'

'Maybe so, but who the hell are you, woman?' Takha replied. 'Some renegade guerrilla from a pathetic, irrelevant world? He's the famous one. Not as good as having Blake, of course. At least Kerr Avon is known as Blake's right-hand man. You're just another wanted rebel. If the thought of a little rough-housing scares you then I suggest you start begging – to him.'

He slapped her face, hard. He grabbed both Cally's hands, pinned them above her head until both wrists were in the grip of one of his hands.

'Take your hands off her. I'll make the report you want.'

Takha continued to leer at Cally. She stood, rigid, forcing herself not to shudder. He asked Avon, 'Are you sure it's worth breaking your word for? I'm going to be so disappointed.'

Cally's lips were trembling, her teeth clenched. 'Release me.'

'The report.' Avon's voice was like a cold, steel blade. 'Now!'

THIRTEEN

There was no longer any need for Shevard to keep up the pretence of being a good host. Avon was mildly surprised therefore when, after recording and re-recording a statement to Takha's satisfaction, he and Cally were taken with little more than a firm-handed escort to another hotel suite. The door was locked, two armed guards stationed outside. Nevertheless, Avon and Cally made a careful check of the room for any potential escape route. There was nothing obvious.

'Are you badly hurt?' Avon's eyes were on Cally, searching as discreetly as he could for any sign of trauma.

She shook her head but a hand went to her ribs where she'd sustained a painful blow. Avon could feel his own face bruising. When she reached out tentatively to touch his jaw with her fingertips, he flinched. Their eyes met for a moment, before he had to look away. She'd be worse hurt than he was, but her bruises were hidden.

'I'm all right,' he said, so quietly it was almost a whisper.

Cally took a step back. 'I'd have done the same thing,' she said. 'If it was you they'd threatened. Any of us would.'

'It was a mistake to trust Shevard.'

'Blake's mistake.'

A smile crept into his voice. 'That goes without saying.'

'You're awfully hard on Blake.'

'Someone needs to be. Or we'll all end up dead.'

'Do you really believe that?'

He paused for a moment, reflecting. To his surprise, he realised that he absolutely did. It could only be a matter of time. Amazing that they'd survived this long, with an ideological maniac as their leader.

'No,' he lied. There was something hopeful, perversely so, about the light in Cally's eyes. Despite himself, Avon didn't want to see that light dimmed. 'I think we're in a great deal of danger, most of the time. But at least Blake understands that.'

'We did what they wanted. They should be willing to let us go.'

'I'd feel more confident about that if Shevard would return our teleport bracelets.'

'He's taking no chances.'

'So what do we do?'

Avon glanced around the room. A bottle of vodka stood with two glasses on a round wooden table, with two deep, upholstered chairs nearby. There was a plasma screen hanging opposite the bed, which he supposed could be used to access news and possibly entertainment. A single shelf held three books. On closer inspection he saw that all three were based on the ancient religion practised on Kartvel.

'You should put some ice on your bruises. Get some rest. Take the bed.'

'You should rest, too.'

Avon nodded, absently. 'And try a drink. It'll help with the pain.'

Half an hour later, Cally was asleep. Avon dropped into the chair facing away from the bed, put his boots up on the second chair and poured himself a generous measure of vodka. When he tasted the spirit, he winced. Rough and acrid, with an oily residue, it wasn't anything like as good as the bottle that Khurdia had left for them in the mountain lodge. If the people of Kartvel could be judged by the true quality of their hospitality, it was clear to Avon which of their hosts had been the more sincere.

He'd allowed himself to be used as a pawn in Shevard's scheme. Avon thought of the drawn faces of all those Kartveli people who'd turned out to vote. They should have been enough to tell him that the election was a farce. Avon had never seen a world gain its liberty, but he imagined that such a population would celebrate with genuine enthusiasm.

Would Shevard even honour the promise to return them to the *Liberator*? Avon could well imagine what was being said to Blake. Khurdia would be blamed. The 'warlord' was the obvious scapegoat. Just how much ill-will did Shevard plan to stir up against his rival?

Avon grew colder as he realised that no amount would be enough. If Khurdia was the genuine people's choice, well on his way to becoming First Minister of Kartvel even before Shevard had 'escaped' from the Federation, then he was an enemy that had to be defeated in the media before anything else. The bigger his defeat, the more likely Khurdia was to remain alive.

The death of Avon and Cally under mysterious circumstances,

probably while they were leaving the planet, could easily be used to orchestrate propaganda against Khurdia.

Avon stopped drinking. He rolled the glass in his right hand.

It would happen on the way back to the *Liberator*. It wouldn't happen anywhere that might risk a connection to the custody or responsibility of Shevard.

Being Blake's so-called right-hand man was going to put him in situations like this, all the time. If he lived through this, Avon thought grimly, he would have to reconsider the logic of their alliance.

FOURTEEN

Khurdia arrived with a single bodyguard, who remained outside the lodge. Watching Iveri and his wife, he leaned for a moment at the threshold of the dining room. They were struggling to engage in conversation, pushing lumps of meat around their plates. Iveri couldn't look his wife in the eye.

Blake didn't much feel like talking either, after he'd seen the secret recording of Cally's beating. In Cally's case, Blake doubted the attack would alter her stance – she was an experienced guerrilla, after all. Such manner of violence as a tool of oppression was doubtless well known to her. Avon's stunned reaction was another matter. It looked like a watershed moment for him, one that Blake had quietly known was inevitable. Perhaps Avon's eyes hadn't yet been properly open to the price insurrection might exact. Now, they had to be. Avon was such an unknown quantity. Sometimes Blake wondered if he would ever adapt to the life Blake was carving out for the crew of the *Liberator*.

Zviad Khurdia seemed much older than in images Blake had seen. One eyelid and part of the left side of his face drooped slightly, an old injury, perhaps, or a current neurological affliction. It gave him a worn appearance, grey and fading. Hard to believe that the term 'warlord' had been applied to such a man – until Blake saw how Iveri and Koba's sister, Gedia responded to their leader. Any grief they might have been experiencing was swept aside as they stood and welcomed him with a mixture of relief and respect. Iveri himself served Khurdia with generous portions of thick, dark stew and soft, doughy dumplings. He poured him a large glass of pale green vodka.

'What can I do for you, Blake?'

'My friends. Shevard is holding them.'

'Yes, now that he has their statement of support, Shevard is about to give them up to the Federation for the reward. In fact, I have it on good authority that they're on a transport shuttle as we speak. Regrettable. Especially given their acquiescence.'

'He didn't give them much choice.'

Khurdia gazed at him from beneath heavy eyelids. 'It's a good thing you have the *Liberator*,' he said, eventually. 'Only such a stupendous technological advantage would allow you to operate any kind of resistance with such an easily discouraged team.' He hesitated, one eye on Iveri. 'You know, Iveri told us that Koba endured several broken fingers without talking. He only gave in once they pulled his guts out and started roasting them.'

Vila gasped, but Blake said nothing.

'It's not your fight,' Khurdia sighed. 'This much I understand. But I wonder if you – or your people – understand this: as you see Kartvel, so will you see all the Federation worlds. Where independence or secession threatens, even the Federation's own regulations will be subverted. Freedom, even for an outlying colony such as ours, will become impossible.'

'Surely Kartvel is a special case? Your nationalism, your religion...'

'Edu Shevard comes from a mould,' Khurdia growled. 'There will be others like him. Federation on the inside, but with a palatable coating.'

'What can we do?'

''I asked your friends to help me, to ensure the polls were fair – they didn't.'

'I am sure they tried. Maybe you should have warned them what was likely to happen to them.'

Khurdia paused, catching the edge in Blake's voice. 'Maybe.'

'Shevard has been trying to contact me on the *Liberator*. Jenna has stalled him, but...'

'He'll soon become suspicious. Use your communicator to reply.'

'I could,' Blake said. 'But if he traces the signal back here...?'

'We can let you use our relay. We have a satellite for bouncing signals from other locations.'

'Could you make it look as though it's coming from our ship?'

'If you can supply co-ordinates.'

'Thank you,' said Blake.

Khurdia took a piece of bread and dipped it in gravy. He took a bite and chewed, with thoughtful glances at Vila and then Blake. 'I know that your ship has a teleport device.'

'If I had one, wouldn't I be using it to rescue my friends right now?' said Blake, staring directly at Khurdia.

'Shevard will have removed the communication devices from your friends to stop you bringing them back,' said Khurdia with a shrug. 'Of course, you could teleport to the shuttle yourself to get them...'

'Yes,' said Vila, quickly.

Blake winced.

'... but Shevard would report it to the Federation as election tampering. Then you alone would be responsible for the return of Federation control to Kartvel. I'm sure you are aware that their response is likely to be... brutal. And I'm not sure you could live with that.'

Blake took a sip of vodka while he examined Khurdia's guarded expression. To anyone else, he would have denied having a teleport facility. But Khurdia's network of contacts seemed to be widespread.

'Shevard knows you have a teleport,' Khurdia said, gently. 'You must be aware of that by now. He was a senior officer in Federation Security until last year. Not, after all, in one of their prisons, as you may have been led to believe.'

Blake didn't reply right away. Instead, he wondered which of his other assumptions about Shevard had been as dangerously mistaken. The treachery involved was starting to look labyrinthine. And its architect, Blake realised with a sinking heart, was probably none other than Servalan herself. Servalan had probably calculated that Blake or his crew would serve as credible verifiers of a genuine victory by Shevard, convincing even those least likely to side with the Federation. If the election rigging were to fail, the election might be called into suspicion for precisely the same reason: the electorate had somehow been 'influenced' by Blake's dissidents. Either way, the Federation kept their influence, either through their secret puppet, Shevard, or directly as a Federation-governed world.

But she hadn't anticipated everything. Servalan probably had Edu Shevard in her pocket. Blake could well imagine the kind of bargain she'd struck with a former Federation security chief. He'd think he had autonomy, but his natural loyalty to a long-time leader who'd facilitated his transition to power would be a valuable bargaining chip.

Yet she didn't seem to have any grip on Khurdia. He was the

real wild card here. A genuine, verified victory at the poll by Zviad Khurdia was the one outcome that whichever Federation schemer had planned this would wish to avoid.

Avon and Cally would be safe only as long as their lives were the direct responsibility of Shevard. Once they left Kartvel, the clock was ticking. With a shudder, Blake reminded himself that the plan had probably been formulated with the idea that he himself would serve as one of the monitors. Under the protection of law. Until the very last minute.

Urgently he said, 'I need to find Avon and Cally. You say they're on a transport shuttle?'

'Yes, within the last hour. They won't come to harm on Kartveli territory. It would invalidate the election. Shevard thinks he's won – he won't want that.'

'But once they've left Kartveli space? He might allow the Federation to take them.'

Khurdia set down his own glass. He gazed back at Blake. 'First help me defeat Shevard. Defeated, his orders to that shuttle mean nothing. Then you can rescue your friends.'

'I'm listening,' said Blake.

'I want you to teleport me and a small team to the central broadcasting studios. The visual media are crucial here. We have very few outlets for information. If can get inside, I can broadcast a message to the population that Shevard's victory is a fraud.'

Iveri seemed to be hearing this plan for the first time. 'They'll shut down the transmission the minute you begin!'

Blake considered. 'Not if we re-route the transmission via the *Liberator*.'

Khurdia smiled. 'Then we have an agreement?'

Vila interrupted. 'What about Cally? And, you know, Avon?'

Blake said, grimly, 'I rather fear that Shevard plans to have them handed over to the Federation.'

Vila was no calmer. 'Won't we be provoking Shevard? Do you think he'd actually kill them?'

'Shevard will give the order to kill your friends as soon as Khurdia starts transmitting,' Gedia said, firmly.

Khurdia nodded. 'Then we must prevent that order from being received.'

'That's possible?'

'The Federation own the infrastructure for interstellar communication. But we own the Kartveli communications satellite. We could use it to send a scrambling signal to the transport shuttle containing your friends. That would stop any communication from Shevard getting through.'

'That should be possible,' Blake agreed.

Khurdia looked longingly at his unfinished plate of food before nudging it away. 'We should leave immediately.'

Blake reached into his pocket for the spare teleport bracelets he'd brought for Avon and Cally. He handed two to Khurdia. 'Let's start with you and Iveri. He can come back for the rest of your team. I'll come with you, Vila will do the doors, and we'll bring another of my people.' Then he stood, and lifted the bracelet to his mouth. 'Four to bring up, Jenna, Ask Gan to stand by. Ready.'

FIFTEEN

As Zen predicted, by early evening a freezing fog had enveloped the eastern flank of Lake Paravan, where the state broadcasting facilities were clustered. Blake and Vila waited with around twenty of Khurdia's fighters, including Iveri and his wife. All had been teleported into a warehouse used to store studio equipment. They'd been brought across, returning their teleport bracelets to Blake. He'd noticed a certain reluctance to hand them back, which made him even more determined to personally supervise the transfer to the warehouse.

Blake had declined Khurdia's request to let them use the teleport bracelets from the *Liberator* as communication devices. There was too much of a risk that they'd fall into the wrong hands, he explained, an answer that Khurdia didn't appear to find convincing. Once Blake had refused this favour, he noticed that Khurdia's interest in talking to Blake practically vanished.

Vila noticed it too. Darkly, he said, 'These Kartvel people are all very charming when you're giving them what they want. But they're not a lot of fun when you turn them down. I wouldn't want to be in Avon and Cally's shoes.'

He had a point. Helping Kartvel choose its 'rightful' leader was one thing. But it wasn't worth losing two of Blake's crew in the process.

Vila had jacked into the security cameras almost as easily as if he'd been Avon. Now it was simply a matter of waiting for the evening broadcast to begin. Almost everyone in Kartvel watched first evening news and then the exotic mixture of romance and high drama that followed in the world's most popular serialised entertainment. They'd be a captive audience.

Khurdia gave the signal for silence. With all radio signals monitored by the Federation's successors on Kartvel, Khurdia had taught his team a system of elaborate hand signals that could be used over short distances and a line of sight. It was far from ideal, but in a close-range raid, could work well.

Blake handed Khurdia two teleport bracelets. 'You'll need these to get inside the studio. Gan will meet you there. He'll help you to get the rest of your people through. You can hand the bracelets back to him.' Blake offered his right hand. 'Good luck.'

Khurdia seemed somewhat taken aback. 'Don't you want to see our victory?'

'I've helped you. Now I need to help my friends.'

'There's time for that. With that jamming signal there's no possibility they'll receive orders from Kartvel. They left yesterday – it'll be days before they arrive at the nearest planet.'

'Even so,' Blake said, with an air of finality. The two men looked at each other uncomfortably. 'So, your courts will deal with Shevard?' he asked finally.

Khurdia didn't look at him, but Blake could see the edge of his mouth curling into a wry smile. 'There's no precedent for his crime. What do we charge him with – selling us into slavery? The traditional punishment for treason was hanging. But I rather think I'll drag him through the streets by his ankles and then shoot his brains out through the roof of his mouth.'

Blake gazed in silence at Khurdia. He thought of the rather effete yet world-weary Sarkoff, restored President of Lindor. It wasn't hard, after all, to imagine how the man had been hoodwinked by Shevard. Avon had warned him once that Sarkoff was a nostalgic fool. With a trace of bitterness, Blake realised that he was probably right.

At least they'd been able to leave that world feeling a measure of assurance that they'd helped to restore order. On Kartvel, Blake wasn't sure what would happen. But he was very sure that it wasn't worth the lives of Avon or Cally.

'At least not to me,' he muttered, two fingers on his bracelet. 'Gan – are you there?'

'Standing by. I'm inside the studios.'

'Did anyone see you?'

'No – I found a cupboard. It's a squeeze but I just about fit.'

'Good work, Gan,' Blake smiled. 'What about Khurdia's team?'

'Have Jenna teleport them over to the same room. Once Khurdia gets here with the security codes, he can open the back door to let the rest inside. Tell them to come across with their weapons drawn. Best to be prepared.'

'Will do. Blake out.'

Vila was staring up at him, blowing on his fingers and shuffling. 'Can we go now? I'm turning to ice here!'

Blake shook his head, slowly. 'Change of plan. I'm not sure it's a good idea to leave Gan without any support.'

Vila's face fell. 'Really? But I can go, right? If it's muscle you need, I'm no help at all…'

Blake gripped Vila's shoulder and turned him around. Khurdia's men were already streaming out of the warehouse, headed for the broadcast studios. No-one was looking at him and Vila any more.

'You might not be the muscle of the team, Vila. But right now, you're the next best thing.'

They arrived in the studios, cautious, trailing well behind the last of Khurdia's men. Vila glanced around the rather shabby, poorly-lit facility. Narrow corridors with unpainted walls, light fittings that buzzed, as if the electricity supply was erratic. It felt makeshift, even temporary. Apart from the pounding of boots on the plastic-coated floor, there was no sound.

'Not a lot going on in here,' Vila observed. 'Where is everyone?'

Blake stopped walking. 'Good question.' A finger hovered above the communicator button on his bracelet.

From behind the both came a familiar voice. 'Not one word.'

Blake stood still as Iveri's wife came into view. In one hand she held a teleport bracelet, broken in two. In the other, a blaster.

From further down the corridor came sounds of gunfire. Two screams.

'Zviad Khurdia is a murderous gangster,' Gedia said.

Vila said, 'I thought you were the best of pals?'

Gedia's face screwed up, twisted with hatred. 'You think you know us? After only a few hours? Just because Roj Blake's friend Raisa sides with Zviad Khurdia, it doesn't matter that he is a known murderer? This is civil war, where uprisings begun by people like *you* lead. Brother against sister. Husband against wife.' She lifted the gun. 'I should kill you for interfering.'

'I'm not the one who tortured your brother to death, Gedia,' said Blake calmly. 'Your fight is not with me.'

There was a sharp bark of laughter. 'Koba is alive, you fool. We needed Khurdia here – what better way to bring the man running than to "torture" one his favourites?'

'He wasn't tortured?' Vila sounded confused.

Scornfully, Gedia said, 'I knew that Khurdia would believe a story like that. It is the way he deals with dissent himself.'

Blake paused. 'I see.'

Vila frowned. 'I don't.'

'It's a trap, Vila.'

'Oh.' Vila stalled for a moment, confused. Then, 'Oh. They're going to...' he drew a finger across his throat. 'You know? Khurdia? And all the rest?'

Gedia seemed eager to press her point. 'Koba and I used to believe in Khurdia. Until we saw what he's capable of.'

'So you both switched allegiance to Shevard?' asked Vila. 'You're his spies?'

'Khurdia wants to take this world back to the dark ages,' Gedia replied, defensively.

'The Federation are so much more humane?' Blake said, acidly.

'The Federation know how to keep order without resorting to tearing their citizens apart limb from limb.'

'Oh, I wouldn't have any illusions about the Federation if I were you,' Blake said, his voice suddenly brittle. 'They'll use any method that gets results.'

For a fraction of a second Vila's eyes lifted. If Gedia had noticed him looking sooner, she'd have turned to see the solid, heavy hand of Gan swooping in to land at the base of her neck. Her eyes flickered, rolled in her head for a second before she toppled to the ground.

Blake held his own bracelet to his mouth. 'Jenna, three to teleport. Centred on me. Now, Jenna!'

The moment they'd fully materialised on the *Liberator*, Blake handed Jenna a gun. 'Bring up the rest of Khurdia's men,' he said urgently. Jenna activated the teleport, and Gan, Vila and Blake waited, weapons ready.

But no-one arrived.

'They've taken off the bracelets,' Blake said.

'That's a lot of teleport bracelets to lose,' Vila said. 'Avon's going to be ticked off.'

'Vila! He's going to be *dead* if we don't get to him soon,' exploded Blake. 'Zen, locate nearest Federation ships.'

'INFORMATION,' droned Zen. 'FEDERATION SHIP.

STARBURST CLASS. APPROACHING THE KARTVEL SYSTEM. ARRIVAL ESTIMATED IN TWO HOURS.'

Blake's tone became urgent. 'Zen, give the location of any Federation shuttle craft that left Kartvel in the past twelve hours.'

'ONE SHUTTLE FROM KARTVEL ON COURSE TO RENDEZVOUS WITH THE STARBURST SHIP.'

'Can we reach the shuttle before it reaches the Federation ship?'

'NEGATIVE,' Zen said. '*LIBERATOR* WILL ARRIVE ONE MINUTE FOUR SECONDS AFTER THE SHUTTLE DOCKS IF WE TRAVEL AT THE CURRENT SPEED.'

'Then I suggest we move a bit faster!' Blake snapped.

SIXTEEN

Avon had lost track of how long they'd been aboard. Like Cally, he'd fought sleep off as long as possible. Eventually he'd felt her relaxing against him and moved to the seat opposite so that she could lie down. Then exhaustion had engulfed him, too. The speed of it convinced Avon that there'd been something in the air. When he awoke, he still felt groggy.

'Avon.' Cally's eyes were above his, soft and green, gazing at him. For a moment he remembered his dream and that she'd been in it. Shouting at him, some kind of instruction. Determined. *You need to fight it.*

'Fight what?'

The sedative. It's in the air.

He tried to sit up. He felt the firm grip of her arm underneath his, supporting him.

'Why you and not me?'

'Must have worn off,' she said, with a hint of a smile. 'My physiology. Not exactly like yours.'

'Tired,' he managed to say. When he closed his eyes, in his mind she was there again. Her voice. No ambiguity. *Fight.*

'They'll be watching,' she whispered. 'When they see us both up, they'll check. The doors will open and there will be clean air.'

He stared at Cally, trying to follow her logic.

Avon, focus on my voice. In your head. But let them think you're sleepy.

He nodded. The sound in his head was becoming more sharply defined. 'Won't be difficult to pretend.'

Avon was dimly aware of Cally standing up, pacing around the small passenger cabin. She rummaged inside a storage cupboard and came up with an umbrella, which she promptly hid under the nearest seat.

The shuttle craft was adapted for small freight loads, with only a tiny capsule intended for a passenger load of six. The capsule must have been well insulated because Avon didn't hear any sound from the corridor outside. The first he knew about the crew was when one of them started to open the pressure lock to their cabin.

Cally placed sat with her feet apart, hands loosely folded on her lap, directly above where she'd left the umbrella. Avon glanced around. It really was the only thing close to a weapon that was at hand.

Sleepy. Avon closed his eyes but let just enough light in so that he could see the door.

Neither of them moved until the first guard was fully inside the cabin. He seemed fairly relaxed to see Cally gazing at him with a groggy expression. Then she sprang to her feet. In one swift movement she'd swept a high kick to the man's chest, sending his gun flying backwards. She kicked the umbrella across the floor to Avon. He was immediately on his own feet. Cally followed up her first attack with a spinning heel-kick. This one caught the guard on his face, the satisfying crack of a broken jaw. Avon was there a second later, using the umbrella as a club to crush the man's windpipe.

In the outside corridor Cally picked up the discarded gun.

There was barely time to draw breath before two more guards burst into the corridor. Cally shot one in the gun arm. His blaster clattered to the floor, out of reach. Another two shots and the guard collapsed. Reeling slightly, Avon propped himself up in the doorway. From down the corridor, a third guard fired blasts into the panel that controlled the door. The door began to slide into the lock position. Avon and Cally leapt into the corridor, she behind him, providing covering fire until both were pressed flat against the wall. The gunfire stopped.

A voice called out, 'Drop the weapon.'

Silently, Avon took the blaster from Cally and prepared to make use of his better firing position.

'Kerr Avon, drop the weapon.'

The voice came not from the armed guard further down the corridor, but from a speaker in the wall.

'There are more of us, Avon. Too many more. You can't win. In a few minutes we'll be docking with a Federation ship. Every extra life you take will be on your record.'

He's lying. There are only two left – I remember how many boarded with us. We have to do this Avon.

Avon prepared to fire. But before he could, a gasp from Cally stopped him. He turned back to find Cally sinking to her knees. Her eyes were wide open, filled with pain. Behind her stood another guard, surprisingly young. He seemed to be supporting Cally at the back of her neck as she crumpled slowly to the floor. A trickle of blood suddenly circled from the back of her neck and ran down her throat. She seemed to be struggling to breathe.

'If I push the blade in any deeper, it will sever her spinal cord,' murmured the guard. The corners of his mouth turned upwards, into a slow grin. 'Better not make any sudden movements. Drop the gun.'

Avon tore his eyes away from Cally, on her knees. He peered at her captor, who stood behind her, one hand at her throat, the other holding the blade. The face was familiar. Angular cheekbones, handsome. They'd seen this one at the reception for the election monitors, on the first day. The man who had warned Cally about Khurdia.

'Ideally, I'd prefer not to,' breathed the guard. His teeth were set in a tight line. 'Because then she won't feel what's coming next. We told Khurdia's men that Shevard had me disembowelled. I'm Koba.' He looked at Avon to see if there was any recognition of his name, but there was none. 'Now – the guts being drawn. I've always wanted to see that done.'

Cally's eyes locked with Avon's.

Shoot him.

Avon swallowed. His fingers felt slippery against the trigger. The boy looked barely old enough to serve as a Federation trooper. Was he really a sadistic, expert killer? On a world as controlled as Kartvel, Avon couldn't see how he'd have gained the experience. The Federation didn't bother teaching inventive methods with blades. It had to be a bluff. He gave the young guard a long, hard stare.

Koba's eyes flashed with a spark of riot. 'Just the slightest extra pressure, Avon. That's all it'll take. And she'll never feel anything again. She'll never feel *you*.'

Kill him.

'Last chance, Avon.'

In the small of his back, Avon felt the hard nose of the other guard's blaster. The voice behind him echoed, 'Last chance.'

SEVENTEEN

Avon tilted his head so that he could just see the guard who stood behind him. He logged the man's height – slightly shorter than his own – and weight. He looked back at the boy who was about to skewer Cally's neck with his knife. Avon nodded. He began, slowly, to lower his weapon. As he did, he ducked low and tipped his weight backwards. The muzzle of the blaster behind slid across Avon's back. It fired a shot. Avon felt a hot, tearing sensation as the laser seared a line across his flesh. His weight toppled the guard behind. When Avon stood there was a blast of heat in his back as the first waves of agony began to hit.

Cally dragged herself slowly from underneath Koba's dead body. The laser blast had taken off the left side of his head. The stench of his singed hair filled the air.

Avon watched Cally stand. He winced. There didn't seem to be a position in which the fiery wound didn't burn. 'That worked rather better than I'd hoped.'

Cally placed a hand on Avon's waist. Very gently, she turned him so that she could examine his wound. 'Well, luckily for me, you deflected his aim somewhat.' Cally turned him back so that they were facing. 'That's a nasty burn.'

Avon licked his lips. The pain was as loud as a klaxon. 'I almost killed you.'

'It would have been preferable to being paralysed – or disembowelled.' She risked a smile.

'That... boy. He wouldn't have done it.'

Cally raised an eyebrow. In a cool voice she said, 'Never underestimate the brutality of youth.'

For a moment they didn't speak. Avon didn't enjoy the way she was looking at him. It wasn't pity but a detached curiosity. Maybe she sensed his sudden vulnerability. Maybe she was trying to find a way in.

'Do you think they were telling the truth about the Federation being on their way?'

'It felt like they believed it.'

'We'd better find some way to turn this shuttle round.'

The whole craft suddenly shook, enough that they had to hold on to each other to stay on their feet.

Cally turned to him. 'Something's just docked with us.'

Avon nodded. Her fingers were gripping his shoulders. For one dazed moment, he realised that he didn't want her to let go.

Close by, the air crackled with a familiar sound – the electrical discharge that accompanied teleportation. From behind him, Avon heard Blake's voice.

'Hullo you two, nice to see you getting along so well.'

Avon's hands dropped. He turned, blinking, to face Blake.

Cally said, 'Avon's hurt.' She seemed to have forgotten about the narrow line of blood that still flowed from the cut in her neck, soaking into the neckline of her blouse.

Blake handed them each a bracelet. 'Then I suggest we leave. There's a Federation Starburst class ship hanging off the end of this shuttle. I don't imagine we've got a lot of time to stand around chatting.'

On the *Liberator*, Vila was standing by with two glasses of adrenaline and soma and a medical kit. Avon downed his glass within seconds. After a brief hesitation, he accepted the glass that Cally offered, too. Blake peered closely at the long stripe of burned flesh on Avon's back. The laser blast had mostly missed him. But the edge of its flare had seared through the thick layer of his jacket. A direct wound could have been far more serious, Blake realised.

He watched as Cally injected Avon with a local anaesthetic.

Avon sighed with relief as the fiery sensation began to cool. 'So – did you get what you came for, Blake?'

'I'm not sure I understand what you mean.'

'Shevard in charge of a free Kartvel,' Avon said, grimly.

'I rather suspect that Shevard's planning to rule the planet on behalf of the Federation.'

Avon said, 'I'm certain you're right.'

'Then it was all a waste of time!' Vila whined.

Avon's eyes didn't leave Blake's. 'Isn't everything?'

'Meaning what?'

'Meaning that Cally and I almost...' Avon faltered. What had been the worst of it – the fact that they'd almost fallen into the hands of the Federation? That they'd been used as pawns in the politics of people in whom, even by his own low standards, Avon had zero interest?

'You and Cally showed tremendous loyalty to each other,' Blake said, softly. 'That's what it means to fight, shoulder-to-shoulder. Cally knows it, and you, Avon, if you didn't know it before, you do now.'

In a warm voice Cally said, 'He knew it before.'

Blake smiled, looking from Avon to Cally. 'I know, Cally. I know he did.'

Avon stared back at Blake, his eyes growing cold. If that's what Blake took from this then he was badly mistaken. Cally was smiling now, entirely at ease with Blake. Avon turned to let the two of them remove his jacket. His heart was pounding. He wouldn't easily forget what had almost happened to Cally, on the planet and now on the shuttle. To Blake, even to Cally, it seemed like nothing. Watching them now, they seemed in their element. Whereas Avon felt as though he'd been dragged back from the brink, a place redolent with memories that he'd worked hard to bury.

For a moment, Avon envied Vila his natural, unashamed cowardice. How much easier to avoid all potential confrontation, all potential to lose his control and lapse into feelings that weakened him.

'You're going to be fine, Avon,' Blake said, cheerily.

'There's a bloodbath going on in that studio, right now,' Avon said. 'And if Khurdia and his men get out alive, the violence is going to spill out onto the streets.'

'Have we started a civil war?' asked Vila, wonderingly.

Blake's expression immediately hardened. 'No.'

'We wasted our time,' said Avon.

'We tried to help,' said Blake.

'You trust too easily,' said Avon.

'Possibly,' Blake frowned. 'On this occasion, definitely. And I apologise for what happened to you.'

'You take responsibility?'

'I do.'

For a second or two, Avon was speechless. Then: 'It's so very easy for you, Blake, isn't it?'

Blake shook his head, slowly. 'You're wrong.'

'It *is* easy for you,' Avon thought. 'And impossible for me, unless I cease to care. Someone's going to die. First, anyone that matters. Eventually, me.'

But he didn't say anything. The habits of control took swift command of his saturnine features. Avon merely leaned against the edge of the teleport console and closed his eyes as Cally applied a salve.

ALSO AVAILABLE FROM BIG FINISH:

Available as CD and download..

THE LIBERATOR CHRONICLES: Vol 1
The Turing Test by Simon Guerrier
Starring Paul Darrow and Michael Keating
Solitary by Nigel Fairs
Starring Michael Keating and Anthony Howell
Counterfeit by Peter Anghelides
Starring Gareth Thomas and Paul Darrow

THE LIBERATOR CHRONICLES: Vol 2
The Magnificent Four by Simon Guerrier
Starring Jan Chapell and Paul Darrow
False Positive by Eddie Robson
Starring Gareth Thomas and Beth Chalmers
Wolf by Nigel Fairs
Starring Jacqueline Pearce, Jan Chappell and Anthony Howell

THE LIBERATOR CHRONICLES: Vol 3
The Armageddon Storm – Parts One, Two and Three
by Cavan Scott and Mark Wright
Starring Paul Darrow, Michael Keating, Jan Chappell and Tom Chadbon

THE LIBERATOR CHRONICLES: Vol 4
Promises by Nigel Fairs
Starring Jan Chappell and Stephen Greif
Epitaph by Scott Harrison
Starring Sally Knyvette and Michael Keating
Kerr by Nick Wallace
Starring Jacqueline Pearce and Paul Darrow

THE LIBERATOR CHRONICLES: Vol 5
Logic by Simon Guerrier
Starring Louise Jameson, Paul Darrow, Sally Knyvette and Jacqueline Pearce
Risk Management by Una McCormack
Starring Gareth Thomas and Sally Knyvette
Three by James Goss
Starring Jacqueline Pearce and Joseph Kloska

THE LIBERATOR CHRONICLES: Vol 6
Incentive by Peter Anghelides
Starring Paul Darrow, Steven Pacey and Adrian Lukis
Jenna's Story by Steve Lyons
Starring Sally Knyvette and John Banks
Blake's Story by Mark Wright and Cavan Scott
Starring Gareth Thomas and Paul Darrow

Available as hardback and ebook………………………………
The Forgotten by Mark Wright and Cavan Scott
Archangel by Scott Harrison

Available as hardback, ebook and audiobook…………………
Lucifer by Paul Darrow

Available as CD, download and ebook……………………..……
Warship by Peter Anghelides

www.bigfinish.com

COMING SOON...

Terry Nation's BLAKES 7

LUCIFER:
REVELATION

BY PAUL DARROW

Many years have passed since the death of his companions on Gauda Prime, but Avon is still very much on the minds – and a thorn in the sides – of those in power.

On the run in a stolen spaceship, Avon has world leaders, warlords, aliens, bandits and hitmen on his trail, all hoping to seize control of the super computer Orac, and to be rid of Avon once and for all.

But those who underestimate Avon do so at their own peril...